A Novel

TIMELESS
WALTZ

A Novel

TIMELESS WALTZ

Anita Stansfield

Covenant Communications, Inc.

In gratitude, for those gone before me.

Cover image photographed by Amy Bennion of Picture This . . . by Sara Staker
Special thanks to the model Angela Devine and to Linda and Lee Wakefield of the BYU Ballroom
Dance Company for their assistance with the photo shoot.

Cover design copyrighted 2005 by Covenant Communications, Inc.

Published by Covenant Communications, Inc.
American Fork, Utah

Printed in Canada
First Printing: September 2005

11 10 09 08 07 06 05   10 9 8 7 6 5 4 3 2 1

ISBN 1-59811-003-9

— 1 —

Alexander Keane left the busy dining room of the fine restaurant where he was waiting tables and entered the employee lounge. A fifteen-minute break was all he would get on the brink of the Saturday evening rush, and he was determined to enjoy it. He sat on the tacky sofa and leaned his head back, closing his eyes. Stretching out his longs legs and pushing both hands through his thick, dark hair, he wondered how long it had been since he'd had any real sleep. Tomorrow was actually going to be a real day off—from everything. As soon as this shift was over, he could sleep for sixteen hours straight, and no one would care. It sounded so luxurious that he sighed out loud, then he reminded himself that it wasn't a luxury. If he *didn't* get some serious sleep he'd never get through the next hazardous stretch of his life.

Forcing all thoughts out of his mind, Alex took advantage of the silence surrounding him and inhaled several deep breaths in order to rejuvenate himself. It was a technique someone had taught him years ago just as he'd been embarking on his journey through medical school. Working to survive, and determined to ace his classes, he'd accepted long ago that this was not a profession that allowed for great amounts of sleep. But he was eternally grateful to the fellow student who had befriended him with advice on relaxation and rejuvenation techniques. He could make a fifteen-minute break really count if he could breathe deeply, clear his mind, and allow the stress to drain out of every muscle of his body.

He was just starting to feel completely relaxed when someone entered the room. Alex looked up to see Brent—the only other person working here who could remotely be called a friend. But at the moment, Alex didn't want to see anybody—friend or foe.

"If you don't let me relax for a minute here," Alex said, "you're going to wish I'd never gotten you this job."

"Fine, relax," Brent said, sitting down. "Just listen to me talk while you do."

Alex glared at him. "That entirely defeats the purpose."

"Well, this is important."

Alex sighed and closed his eyes again. "Fine. Talk. But not too loud. And make it quick."

"I'll get straight to the point. We have a hole in the team and Coach Abernathy sent me to beg you to fill it."

Alex opened his eyes again, glaring even more fiercely. Brent hurried to add, "We have a competition in a little over a month, and one of our key people broke his leg. The backups are all indisposed for one reason or another. It's the weirdest thing. Abernathy said she's never had anything like this happen before. I mean . . . she is up a creek without a paddle, if you know what I mean."

Alex shook his head and groaned. He stated what he thought should have been obvious to Brent long before he came in the room. "I don't have *time* to do a dance competition. And in case you—or coach Abernathy—haven't noticed, I don't even go to school at this college anymore. How can I be on their dance team?"

"But you have previously danced on the dance team; you're Abernathy's best fill-in."

"I had time then; I needed a hobby. Right now I need sleep."

"Oh, come on, Alex. We really need you. You're a good Mormon boy from Utah, right? Aren't you supposed to be charitable and giving and—"

This time Alex's glare was so ugly that Brent immediately quit talking. Once Alex knew he had Brent's full attention, he spoke firmly. "I didn't move a thousand miles from Salt Lake City to live in some pathetic college town to have it widely known that I'm a Mormon. And you're forgetting that I am not necessarily a *good* Mormon boy. If you ever bring that up again, to me or anyone else, you'll not only lose a friend, you'll end up with a broken nose."

"Boy, are you in a lousy mood," Brent said.

"You bet I am." Alex resumed his relaxed position, wishing he felt even close to relaxed. "I'm exhausted and regretting the fact that I agreed to fill in *here* tonight."

"Okay," Brent said humbly, "my timing is lousy. And I'm sorry if I said anything to upset you. But hey, we're desperate. You're our last hope."

"Then that would make you hopeless," Alex growled, hoping his tone of voice alone would prompt Brent to drop the subject.

"No, that would make me determined to hound you to the ends of the earth until you agree to do this. If you don't I will make sure that you *never* get any sleep. If you do it, I will become your personal slave. I'll . . . I'll . . ." He snapped his fingers while he was clearly attempting to come up with some form of bribery.

"You'll what?" Alex countered. "You can't take my shifts here because this is the last one as far as I know at the moment, and you certainly can't take my shifts at the hospital."

Brent's eyes lit up. "No, but I *can* do your laundry and grocery shopping; I can run errands for you. If you don't have to do that kind of stuff, then you'd have time to dance. Eh? Eh?" He laughed.

Alex shook his head and made a disgusted noise. He had to admit that Brent was right. And truthfully, he loved to dance. He missed dancing. Dancing would be a heck of a lot more relaxing to him than doing laundry and running the errands that were necessary for survival. But Brent's plan still had some flaws.

"My shifts at the hospital are long and rarely negotiable. What if rehearsals don't fit in with that?"

"Abernathy said she'd schedule some private time with you and your partner, and it's more or less the same stuff you learned before."

"Boy, she *is* desperate."

"She said she knows you can handle minimal rehearsal with the group."

"And what about my partner?"

"Well, Coach said she can rearrange things so that you're with a girl who started with the team earlier this semester, but she won awards with some other school before she came here. She's been dancing her whole life; Coach says she's one of the best. If she puts the two of you together, she's sure we can pull it off." Alex sighed loudly and Brent added, "Come on, buddy. Say you'll do it, and I'll leave you in peace."

Alex groaned. "Fine," he said, "I'll do it. But you *will* be my slave until this is over."

Brent laughed and slapped him on the shoulder. "Oh, I knew you'd do it! Thanks, bud. You're a true friend."

"Hey," Alex said as Brent headed toward the door, "what's in it for you?"

"What do you mean?"

"Why would you come here on bended knee to do Abernathy's bidding—and be willing to be my personal slave to make it work?"

Brent smiled. "Well, first of all, Abernathy said she'd partner me with Sue."

"Sue the shrew?" Alex laughed.

"That's the one."

"You've still got the hots for her?"

"I do," Brent said proudly, and Alex made a noise of disgust. Sue was gorgeous, but she had a nasty temper.

"What else?" Alex said. "I don't buy that dancing with Sue is worth all this trouble."

"Coach will give me a guaranteed A if I get you to do it."

Alex laughed. "With the way you dance, that *is* a bargain."

"You know I'm a better dancer than you," Brent said with mock smugness.

"That's debatable. You just never turn in the actual assignments to get through the class."

Brent smirked and left the room, saying, "Enjoy your break."

Alex heard the door close as he turned toward the clock. He sighed, then groaned. "Yeah," he said to the empty room, "I'll enjoy the next two minutes of it." He was glad to know that Brent was working in a completely different section the remainder of the evening, which would keep him from wanting to give the guy a bloody nose.

Soon after Alex started back to work, a couple was seated in his section, and he quickly went to the table to explain tonight's specials and take orders for drinks. He couldn't help noticing the woman, who was sitting with her back to the gas fireplace. Her blonde, curly hair hung around her shoulders, and she had a visible innocence that almost glowed from her countenance. Such a quality was rare in women around here, especially the college-aged girls who were obviously only living in this town to go to school. On the rare occasions that Alex had seen girls who appeared sweet and innocent, he'd also noticed that they also seemed scared or shy—as if they were victims just waiting to be taken advantage of. And he knew well enough that most college guys in the twenty-first century were only too willing to do just that. But this woman had an aura of confidence that seemed to say she was completely in control of her life. Her date did most of the talking—with an arrogant edge, Alex noted. He ordered a margarita, which apparently made this woman mildly uncomfortable. She just asked for water with lemon in it. Walking away from the table, he could well imagine her demanding that her date give her the keys to the car once they left the restaurant. She didn't look like the type to ever get into a car with a man behind the wheel who'd had even a little bit to drink. Two minutes and Alex was already impressed.

While Alex stayed ridiculously busy, he reminded himself that he had no business being intrigued with somebody else's date. A few minutes after he'd served them their meal, it was standard for him to check back and see if the food was all right and if they had everything they needed. As he approached the table, he realized they were quietly arguing. It would have been appropriate to quickly make his presence known and say what he needed to say, or to discreetly move away and come back in a few minutes. But he just stood there, wondering why he felt the urge to knock this guy across the head and take this woman into some kind of protective custody. He really wasn't paying as much attention to what they were saying as he was to the body language and tone of voice. She was dignified, calm, and gracious. He sounded like a snotty playground bully.

After standing there for thirty seconds and not being noticed, Alex couldn't keep himself from tuning in to what was being said. "Face it," this guy said, "men and women are not created equally."

"No they are not," she concurred.

"There are so many things men can do that women could *never* do."

"And the other way around," she pointed out, but he gave a sardonic chuckle as if he were humoring her.

"Some people might say I'm chauvinistic, but I think the biggest problem with today's world is that women have forgotten their place. They should be at home raising children the way they were meant to."

Like an onlooker at a tennis match, Alex looked to this woman, expectantly waiting for her comeback. And she didn't disappoint him. "I won't dispute that no one can affect society for good more than a woman who is at home with her children to nurture them and raise them properly, but if you think that a woman's capabilities and potential end there, then you *are* a chauvinist." She calmly took a bite of her dinner and smiled at him as if to say touché.

Alex took advantage of the pause in the conversation to say, "Is everything all right here?" They both looked up at him, apparently believing he'd just approached the table. "With the meal, I mean," he hurried to say when the man's eyes appeared defensive.

"It's fine," he said without asking his date, and Alex silently agreed with her. This guy *was* a chauvinist.

Alex looked directly at her and asked, "And *your* meal?"

"It's wonderful." She smiled at him and his heart actually quickened. "Thank you."

Alex left the table and wondered what was happening to him. He felt emotionally involved with a woman he didn't know, hadn't met, and likely never would. He had no trouble keeping busy and was pleased to find that the tips for the evening were good; he really needed the money. While he couldn't keep his thoughts from straying to this woman and her jerk of a date, he was vaguely aware that their conversation over dinner had remained a debate. And she remained calm while he looked visibly agitated. When they had finished eating, she asked for her leftovers to be boxed up; he had cleaned his plate. They didn't ask for dessert, but the guy did have two more margaritas. The check sat on the table for a long time while they continued to talk. The guy finally put the credit card out so that Alex could process it and return the receipt to the table to be signed. The place had nearly emptied out while these two sat and continued to argue quietly. He wondered how long they'd been dating. Was this a serious relationship? Why should he care? He told himself to mind his own business, then he heard her say as he passed by, "Give me the keys. I'm driving."

Alex smiled, proud of himself for predicting her nature. Then he had no trouble hearing her date respond loudly enough to make it clear that he'd had more than one drink too many. "I'm not letting you drive my car. I'm just fine."

What few people were in the room all turned to look at them just as she countered in a voice that was not loud, but not quiet either, "Any drinking at all is too much to be driving. Now give me the keys."

"Oh lighten up," the guy said, and Alex felt no hesitation to intervene. He wasn't about to hear on tomorrow's news how this girl had been killed because her drunk boyfriend had driven her home.

"Excuse me," Alex said to the man, "but I believe the lady asked for the keys to your car."

The woman looked up at Alex with pleasant surprise in her eyes. The man said with a rudeness that was startling, "And what's it to you? This is none of your business."

Alex stated calmly, "In our lobby there is a sign posted, stating that the consumption of alcoholic beverages should not be mixed with driving. The lady simply wants to see that the two of you arrive home safely."

"Okay then." The guy quickly signed the receipt, putting a large zero on the line where the tip should have been filled in. He grabbed his credit card and stood, looking Alex in the eye. "Since you're so helpful, you can see that the lady gets home safely. I've had it with her. She's way too mouthy for my taste."

He walked away, and Alex swallowed carefully, counting to ten as he did. He turned to the woman, still seated, and hoped that she wouldn't be angry with him. "Forgive me," he said. "I hope that my intervening did not make the situation worse." She just shook her head, and he realized that she was trying not to cry. Did she love the jerk? The man who had just humiliated and degraded her in front of a perfect stranger? Alex quickly added, "Would you like me to call you a cab?"

She looked up at him, her eyes showing fresh surprise. When she hesitated, he added, "If you don't have any money with you, we can take care of it."

He saw her fight for her composure before she said, "I'm certain you can't afford to be paying cab fares for stranded women."

"Actually, this isn't the first time such a thing has happened. The restaurant will cover the fee if there is no other option. We want to be sure our customers get home safely."

She smiled—a warm, sincere smile that lit up her eyes. "Thank you," she said. "You've been very kind, but that won't be necessary. I can afford the fare, but . . . actually . . . if I could use a phone, I'll just call a friend who doesn't live far away. She owes me a favor."

Alex resisted the urge to offer to take her home himself when he got off work in another twenty minutes, but he knew it wouldn't be appropriate. "The phone is right this way," he said, and she stood and followed him. As he showed her where the phone was, he said, "You're welcome to wait here in the lobby. I'll check back and see if you need anything else."

"Thank you," she said.

As Alex walked away, it occurred to him that he might never see her again. Was there any possible way to give her a phone number—or to get hers? Not without making a fool of himself, he concluded. Then he realized that she knew he worked here. But not very often; he only filled in on very rare occasions. Technically, he wasn't supposed to be working a second job, but he only filled in a night here and there, and he really needed the money. Still, even if he were here regularly, it was ludicrous to think that she would ever try to find him. Besides, he was too busy to be dating anyway. He just didn't have time for a woman in his life.

Going back past the table where she'd been sitting, he noticed her boxed food still there. He took care of the tipless ticket in order not to appear too eager, then he impulsively prepared a piece of their best chocolate dessert to go, put both boxes into a bag and took it to the lobby.

"Thank you," she said, taking the bag, "I don't want to leave that behind. I was looking forward to eating it for breakfast."

"You earned it," he said, and she smiled.

"Thank you again," she said, then took him off guard when she stuffed a ten-dollar bill into his hand.

"No, no," he said, trying to give it back. "I don't need this."

"I'm sure you could use it," she said. "You're a good waiter. You worked hard to see that our every need was met. And that cheap . . .

jerk . . ." She said it as if she would have liked to use a stronger word, but profanity had probably never passed through her lips. "I know he didn't leave you a tip. Please take it."

"I really don't want this," he insisted. "If you—"

"Hey," he heard, and turned to see the manager motioning toward him.

"Thank you again," the woman said and moved abruptly toward the doors as a car pulled up just outside. He watched her walk away, then turned to face his manager.

"What is it?" he asked.

"Some guy told me before he left a while ago that you were a horrible waiter, that you were rude and out of line."

Alex sighed. "He'd been drinking. His date was trying to get the car keys from him so she wouldn't get killed on the way home. I kindly intervened. He left her here. It's my job to meet our customers' needs. I met hers."

He looked toward the glass doors just in time to see her get into the car. The manager's eyes followed, and he said, "Case closed. Let's get this place cleaned up and go home. I appreciate your filling in."

"Not a problem," Alex said more to himself, grateful that he'd been here.

Alex drove home in a car that was barely running, but he reminded himself that it had gotten him through many years of school, and he was grateful. Coming into the tiny attic apartment where he lived alone, he thought as he did every time he entered that the place was a dump and that he hated it. But like the car, it was only temporary. Undressing for bed, he paused as he often did to look at the pictures he had taped next to the mirror. Magazine pictures of the home and car he had always dreamed of stared back at him, reminding him that living this way wasn't going to last forever, that his hard work would bring about a better way of life—for himself and for the people he could help through his chosen profession. He wished it was possible to put up a picture of the woman he'd met tonight. He didn't even know her name, but for some reason he believed that just looking at such a woman every day could give him marvelous incentive to keep pressing forward in the difficult moments. She was the kind of woman who made him want to be a better man; the kind of woman that a man with any kind of brains would want to settle down with and live happily ever after.

Thoroughly exhausted, Alex crawled into bed and imagined this woman standing in the house he would own one day. He also imagined her taking the keys from him to drive him home in his black Ferrari because he'd been drinking. Not an ideal picture perhaps, but it made him smile. He wondered if he'd ever see her again.

Alex turned off the phone and inserted his earplugs, then slept until early Sunday afternoon. He got something to eat then went back to bed for another few hours. He'd determined a long time ago that if he didn't take a day once in a while just to sleep, he'd never survive. Once he came around, feeling well rested but relaxed enough that he knew he could go back to sleep in a few hours, he did a load of laundry, ate again, then he indulged in the highlight of his week.

"Hi Mom," he said into the phone when he heard Ruth Keane's voice.

"Oh," she said, "I always love to hear the evidence that you're alive and breathing."

"Vice versa," he said. He couldn't afford the time or money to go home—as if his car could make it. But he carefully worked this biweekly phone call into his budget. His mother paid for every other week. It was a relationship he treasured and needed. She was truly his best friend. They exchanged the usual trivial chatter to catch up on a week that was all too similar to every other week—for both of them.

"No news?" she asked.

He told her about Brent coercing him back onto the dance team, and as they talked he had to admit that he was actually looking forward to it. His mother declared that he needed some variety in his life, and he needed time to do something he enjoyed. He couldn't dispute that. She insisted it was a blessing.

"Maybe," was all he said. She knew that religion—including any reference to deity—didn't often come into his vocabulary, or his life. And she respected that, even though she didn't agree with it. But it didn't keep her from telling him about things that happened at church, or the trivial details of her visiting teaching. And that was fine. He loved to hear about everything in her life. And she loved to hear about everything in his. They didn't live the same lifestyle, but she loved him anyway. And he was grateful to have the most amazing mother in the world.

Alex told her all about the incident at the restaurant, and without intending to, he told her how impressed he'd been with this woman. He knew his mother had obviously picked up on his intrigue when she said, "You can't stop thinking about her, can you." It was not a question.

"No," he chuckled sheepishly, "I can't. But I'll probably never see her again."

"I'd bet otherwise," she said. "I believe our thoughts and feelings have much more meaning than we give them credit for. If you feel that way . . . if you keep thinking about her . . . then there's a reason. You'll cross paths again. And when you do, I want to be the first to know." She laughed softly. "Maybe it's destiny."

"You believe in destiny?" he asked.

"In a way, yes. But we can't talk about that without talking about God, and I don't believe you want to do that."

"Not really, no."

"So . . . just call it destiny. But when it happens, you'll have to know, somewhere deep inside, that God's hand is in your life. One of these days you'll see her again, and you'll have the opportunity to know whether or not she's the right woman for you. And even if she's not, she may still have an impact on your life for good—or you may bring something good into her life. In fact, you already did."

"How's that?" he asked dubiously.

"You were a hero to her last night. It may have been a simple thing, but you stood up for her and helped her. Women who have any character would never overlook an act of chivalry."

"Is that what it was?"

"Yes, indeed," she said, then declared the need to get off the phone. "We've passed our time limit. Next week I'll call you."

Lying in bed that night, Alex pondered his mother's words— probably far too much. Destiny? As attracted as he felt to this woman, he'd like to think that such a thing was possible. But highly improbable. If he did believe in destiny, did that mean he was putting some credit in God's hands for guiding his life? He *did* believe in God. There was no question about that. There were certain beliefs that he held to without question. But he didn't necessarily like the way God had arranged certain aspects of life and this world, and he had no interest in dealing with Him too closely, or putting any trust in Him whatsoever.

The alarm woke Alex out of a deep sleep filled with bizarre dreams that he couldn't remember. In the darkness of early morning, he hurried to get to the hospital to begin his shift. Brent showed up at the hospital at lunchtime with a sandwich, a soda, and a typed schedule for the week. He'd called earlier to get Alex's hospital shifts, and he had coordinated dance rehearsals with the coach. Some were with the group, others private. Alex had to admit that the schedule would work out fine—at least for this week. And Brent had added notes on when he would be picking up dirty laundry and a grocery list, and when Alex could plan on having Brent supply him with a quick meal.

When his twelve-hour shift ended, Alex drove straight to the building on campus where the dance rehearsals took place. Brent met him with food, and clothes to change into, since Alex had given him a key to his apartment. He took bites of his hamburger between changing out of his scrubs and into the jeans and T-shirt that were his most comfortable, and a stark contrast to the shiny black dancing shoes that had been dragged out from under his bed where they'd been stored in a box for months. With his meal barely chewed he took a quick detour into the men's room, then hurried down the hall. He met Coach Abernathy on the way. She was a middle-aged woman with a great figure, big hair, and too much makeup. But she was a sweetheart and he'd loved working with her on the dance team through his years of medical school in this town. She laughed when she saw him and gave him a quick, tight hug. "You are my hero," she said.

"Brent should be your hero," Alex said. "He's my personal slave until this competition's over."

"Well, I'll hug him too."

"Maybe you'd better hold back until you see if I've still got what it takes. I haven't had these shoes on for months."

"It's just like riding a bicycle," she laughed. "You'll do great. I'll see you in there in five minutes. Go warm up."

"Yes, Ma'am," he said and went into the studio. The room was huge with mirrors along one wall, warm-up bars along another—and a beautiful, polished-wood floor. He breathed in the aura of the room, feeling suddenly grateful for this opportunity. He just hoped his partner was as good as Brent had claimed. And with any luck she wouldn't have a personality like Sue the shrew.

* * * * *

Jane Layton sat on a bench at the edge of the dance studio and buckled her dance shoes around her ankles. Alicia sat down beside her to do the same and asked quietly, "So have you met your new mysterious partner yet?"

"No," Jane said in a tone that clearly expressed her dread. She'd heard nothing but praise about this guy's dancing ability from the coach and others on the team who had been here long enough to have worked with him many months ago. But she knew from experience there was one trait that commonly coincided with being a great dancer—arrogance. She knew well enough that to make a great ballroom dance pair, there would need to be a lot of eye contact, and even a fair amount of acting. They would have to dance as if they were in love with each other. She'd been doing this for years, and some experiences hadn't been so bad; others had been a disaster. When the coach had told her she was pairing her up with some guy they were bringing in to fill the hole, she'd felt both dismayed and flattered. Abernathy had chosen her because she could handle the limited preparation time and still do a great job. But to be under the pressure of a big competition with a partner she'd never even seen before was something that put her stomach in knots every time she thought about it.

"Oh, come on," Alicia said, "he can't be too bad. I hear he's a friend of Brent's. Brent isn't such a bad guy."

"That is completely irrelevant."

Feeling irritated, Jane reminded herself that she was grateful for Alicia's friendship. They'd both transferred here from other schools at the beginning of the spring semester and had both been given a spot on the dance team. They had a lot in common, and it was nice to have a friend, but at the moment Jane just wanted to be alone with her thoughts.

"So, I'll take your mind off it," Alicia said, and Jane told herself to be patient. "Tell me again about the guy at the restaurant."

"I told you that story on the ride home Saturday night; there's no need to repeat it."

"But . . . it's so . . . chivalrous."

"He's a waiter, okay? He was being a nice guy. I'll probably never see him again."

"But you admitted that you kept thinking about him," Alicia said.

"Yeah, so?" She hoped her feigned indifference would motivate Alicia to drop the subject. She wished that she'd never told Alicia she'd been thinking about this guy—and she'd not admitted to the half of it. She'd hardly been able to sleep Saturday night as she'd pondered how it had felt when he'd looked momentarily into her eyes in the lobby of the restaurant. Something inside of her had changed almost immediately, and she was still trying to figure it out. And if that weren't bad enough, the next day when she'd opened the sack of leftovers she'd stuck in the fridge, there was an extra box containing a delectable chocolate dessert. On it was written, *Thought you could use some chocolate to recover from a bad date. Enjoy the rest of your weekend.* But there was no signature. She knew absolutely nothing about him, not even his name. The amount of time she'd spent thinking about this man and their encounter—and the way it had made her feel—was something she'd simply never experienced before. And she wasn't sure how to deal with it.

"You know where he works," Alicia said, breaking into her thoughts.

"And the point would be?"

"And you know his name, right?"

"Actually, no."

"Didn't he have a name tag, or something?" Alicia asked, and Jane stood up to stretch and warm up a bit.

"If he did, I don't remember what it said. And I am not going to go in that restaurant and ask for the guy's phone number."

"But . . . you think he's cute and—"

"Alicia," she interrupted, "I'm not going to do it. If I . . . ever see him again then . . . maybe it's destiny. Otherwise . . . whatever. But let's drop it, okay? Right now I just need to get through this rehearsal."

"Fair enough," Alicia said, then the door across the room opened. "Oh, my gosh. I think that's him."

"Who?" Jane asked, rummaging through her purse for a breath mint. She wasn't about to be put face-to-face with a stranger and have bad breath.

— 2 —

"I think your dance partner just walked through the door," Alicia said. "He's cute."

Jane purposely kept looking in her purse, even though she'd found the mints and had one in her mouth. She refused to appear even slightly curious. Everyone on the team knew she was being paired up with the new guy. Or was he considered the old guy? He'd been on this team long before she'd ever transferred here. Either way, she was determined to be completely nonchalant.

"Oh, he's really cute," Alicia added. "Tall, dark, broad shoulders. Doesn't look like the dancing type, to be truthful."

"That could be a good thing," Jane said without looking up.

"He's warming up; he's talking to Brent. It's got to be him."

"Is he looking this way?" Jane asked.

"Nope," she said, and Jane stole a quick glance. She had to look again, then she took such a sharp breath that her mint slid down her throat, and she started to cough.

"Are you okay?" Alicia asked as Jane turned to face the wall, and Alicia started slapping her on the back.

"I'm fine," Jane managed to say but couldn't stop coughing. She could almost feel the attention of everyone in the room, but worst of all she could be sure that the new guy had to be looking in her direction while her coughing reverberated through a room that had magnificent acoustics and no furniture or carpet to absorb the sound.

Jane was relieved when Coach Abernathy came into the room in her typical way—like a poppy bursting through a patch of crabgrass. She never entered a room unnoticed, which put all of the attention immediately on her. "Okay," she hollered, "let's get started. We have a lot of work to do." Jane was relieved that her coughing eased off. "Pair up," Coach added. "We're starting with the waltz for a slow warm-up."

Abernathy then said directly behind Jane. "You okay?"

"Uh . . . yeah," Jane said and coughed. "I just . . . swallowed my mint. I'm fine."

"Good." She took Jane's arm. "It's time to meet your new partner. I have a feeling the two of you are going to sweep each other right to the top of this competition."

Jane shook off the coach's arm and walked beside her across the room, attempting to appear indifferent while her heart threatened to jump right out of her throat.

* * * * *

While Alex was warming up, he heard someone coughing and glanced across the room to where some of the girls were gathered. His heart quickened when he saw a woman with blonde, curly hair that reminded him of the woman he'd met at the restaurant. While his thoughts wandered back to their encounter—again—Abernathy came into the room and gave orders. Everybody paired off except for the blonde. Was that her? His new partner? The coach approached her, and together they walked toward him. It had to be the woman he was supposed to dance with. His heart quickened further before she actually looked up. Then his knees went weak, and his mouth turned dry while he heard his mother's voice in his head, *Just call it destiny . . . One of these days you'll see her again, and you'll have the opportunity to know whether or not she's the right woman for you.* He couldn't believe it! He actually squeezed his eyes closed and opened them again to make sure he wasn't hallucinating. Maybe it was her sister or her cousin. It just couldn't be the same woman. But it was! He could see it in the way she smiled mischievously as their eyes met.

Jane felt suddenly calm when she made eye contact with him. Maybe it was the way his countenance lit up when he saw her. Maybe it was the way something warm and tingling filled her entire being. Maybe it was the way she recalled telling Alicia that if she ever saw him again it might be destiny. And maybe it was that somewhere deep inside, for reasons she could never put into words, she knew that it was.

Coach Abernathy stopped right in front of Alex while he willed himself to remain calm and casual. "Jane Layton," she said, "meet Alex Keane. A match made in heaven."

Alex couldn't keep from smiling, especially when Jane—*her name was Jane*—glanced away and blushed slightly. He felt relatively certain that she might actually be as intrigued with him as he was with her, and the possibility quickened his blood.

"What makes you so sure?" he asked the coach without taking his eyes off Jane.

"Instinct," she said and walked away, saying over her shoulder. "I don't think I need to tell either of you what to do from here."

Jane summoned the courage to look at him again, fearing he would read her entire life in her eyes. "Wow," she said, needing to say *something*. "I must say I didn't expect this."

"Nor did I," he said. "Quite a coincidence."

"I don't believe in coincidence," she said, and he lifted his brows.

She wondered if that sounded too forward, too coy. But he quickly replied, "Then it must be destiny."

The music began to play, and she was spared from having to respond. He held up a hand, saying quietly, "Shall we?"

Jane put her hand into his and positioned her other hand against his shoulder as he put a hand to her back. His touch produced a tangible warmth throughout her. She was grateful beyond words that dancing came so naturally to her, especially when she felt so thoroughly flustered that she feared she'd trip over her own feet, if not his. But he led her easily into a simple waltz, and she followed his lead as naturally as breathing. They maintained eye contact while gliding gracefully across the floor, and Jane felt oblivious to anything in the room except this man and the way he seemed to be waltzing her on thin air. He guided her into a slow, graceful dip, then back into an effortless waltz. It would have been possible to share some simple conversation, but she felt completely speechless and sensed that he was the same. Looking into his eyes, Jane wondered how she could almost believe he would be the most important man in her life. She didn't know him. She knew nothing about him—except that he was decent and kind and a marvelous dancer. But she chose not to analyze or speculate, only to enjoy the moment. She'd always found a certain thrill in dancing, but never had it affected her like this. As the music ended, they came to a unified, elegant halt.

"Very nice," he said with a smile. Oh, what a smile!

"Indeed," she said just before the music changed, and Abernathy hollered to be heard above it.

"Now the quickstep," Abernathy said.

Jane focused more on her feet now since faster footwork took more thought. They managed rather well together, only fumbling a couple of times, which made them both laugh. Jane knew that some private time with the coach was being arranged in order to accommodate this man's busy schedule and to bring him up to speed with the rest of the team. She wondered what he did besides wait tables that took so much of his time. She was considering asking him and wished she'd thought about it while they were waltzing. Now they were moving far too fast to share any conversation.

Alex attempted to grasp the reality that he was actually dancing with the woman who had consumed his thoughts since he'd met her two days ago. He couldn't believe it. And even more profound was the look in her eyes that seemed to be a reflection of his own feelings. He felt dazzled, enchanted, and completely awestruck, while something sparkled in her expression that seemed to innocently portray that she was as thrilled to be with him as he was with her. She really was a great dancer, a true natural. But he'd done a lot of dancing—and dating—in his life. And it had never felt like this. *Never!*

Jane found it difficult to believe the enchantment she saw in this man's eyes. Each time she looked at him, she expected to see some evidence that it was only her imagination. But the longer they danced, the more enchanted he seemed to become. She felt as if she were the most beautiful thing he'd ever seen—and this while she was sweating and wearing her hair pulled back in a haphazard ponytail.

For more than an hour they danced hard, with an intensity that was both invigorating and exhausting. When it came time for a break he simply said, "I'll see you in a few minutes," before he left, likely to go to the men's room. Jane took a quick trip to the ladies' room, then sat next to Alicia while she drank from a bottle of water.

"His name is Alex," Jane said.

"Who?"

"The waiter—the guy at the restaurant. His name is Alex."

"You remembered?"

"No, I met him again."

"No way!" Alicia laughed. "And you didn't tell me?"

"I'm telling you now."

"I knew it would happen," Alicia said. "It's destiny."

"You know what?" Jane laughed softly and saw Alex come back into the room. He tossed her a discreet smile before he turned to talk with Brent. "You might be right."

"So where did you meet him?"

"On the dance floor." She nodded toward Alex across the room. "He's my new partner."

"No way!" Alicia said again, more loudly.

"Hush," Jane said.

"That's him?" Alicia gave an incredulous laugh. "That's the waiter who saved you from that jerk?"

"That's him."

"Oh, my gosh!" Alicia said. "He is adorable. And gallant too."

"Stop staring," Jane said, noting how Alicia couldn't take her eyes off the topic of their conversation.

Jane wanted to burst out with giddy words of how thoroughly smitten she felt. She wanted to tell Alicia that she'd never felt this way before in her life, that she felt certain life would never be the same again. But she chose to keep her thoughts to herself. Perhaps to hold them close and savor them more fully, or perhaps due to some level of fear. If she expressed her feelings completely, would she somehow jinx the possibility of something good coming from the way she felt?

The second half of practice was even more exhausting, and the only conversation that passed between her and Alex was the simple communications necessary between dance partners in order to improve their performance. When they were going through the rumba number, Jane couldn't keep from laughing. While Alex led her through the dance with astonishing skill, his expressions became comically dramatic in the spirit of the dance, as if he were purposely trying to provoke her laughter. She couldn't recall ever having so much fun dancing, although she felt certain the greatest source of exhilaration was the way Alex Keane made her heart skip. For all the hundreds of hours she'd spent dancing, she had never before considered that a dance itself could be so emotionally intimate. While the moves they shared were never remotely inappropriate, the eye contact they exchanged provoked butterflies in her stomach. The way he held her hands, and touched her shoulders, her waist, and her upper back felt completely sensual without being remotely improper. She'd never felt so light on her feet, so agile, so perfectly in tune with a dancing partner. And she longed to feel this way for the rest of her life. But she reminded herself that this was dancing, not real life, not some romantic fantasy. She nearly laughed aloud at the thought. Until she'd met Alex Keane, she'd never indulged in a romantic fantasy in her entire life. She was the least romantic person she knew.

Jane felt severely disappointed when rehearsal came to an end, her only relief being that she knew there were many more rehearsals to come. This was far from her last opportunity to dance this way— although dancing wasn't necessarily conducive to getting to know each other better. She hoped that an opportunity for *that* would present itself, without putting either of them into an awkward situation. She was just wondering how to thank him and make a graceful exit when the coach appeared next to them, saying, "You two look great, but there are some details you need catching up on." She nodded at Alex. "Would the two of you be able to stay another hour? Or do you have somewhere you need to be?"

"I can do it," Alex said, then turned to Jane. "But if you can't, I can make other arrangements to—"

"No, that's fine," Jane said, thinking that her studying could certainly be put off. "I was going to ride home with Alicia, but maybe she can study or something while she waits and—"

"I can give you a ride home," Alex said, hoping that didn't sound too bold. He quickly added, "unless . . . you're not comfortable with that or—"

"No, that would be fine," Jane said, smiling at him. He felt like a giddy school boy at the prospect of actually spending a few private minutes with her. "I'll tell Alicia to go," she added.

"Okay then," Coach said. "Take a ten-minute break and meet me back here."

Jane walked toward Alicia, and Alex forced himself not to stare after her. Ten minutes later they were going step-by-step through the unique aspects of the rumba number they would be performing. He was surprised to hear Coach say that she was considering having them do the number solo, and she was counting on them to represent the team well. Then Coach turned on the music and watched closely as they went through their dance number. Alex felt his exhilaration over the experience rise as they became more comfortable in moving together. With the absence of other dancers on the floor, he could easily believe that the whole world revolved around them.

Alex knew the practice was nearing an end when the coach said, "I want you to run through the waltz number one more time. I'm going to make a quick phone call and I'll be back."

She started the music and left the room while they repeated the first number they'd danced together. Only now it was more fluid, more cultivated; it was perfect. They kept complete eye contact, except for the brief moments when he lowered her into a dip, or guided her through a twirl. Jane became distracted by the details of his face, and she found herself wondering what it might be like to kiss him. She'd been kissed a few times through her years of dating, but it had always been quick and meaningless. Of course that was fine, considering that she'd never dated any guy seriously enough to warrant more than a quick peck on the lips. The difference was that she realized now she'd never *wanted* to be kissed before. In truth, she'd never understood why the girls she knew made such a big deal out of it. But now she was beginning to understand. Just the thought made her insides turn to jelly. She reminded herself that she hardly knew this man, but that was difficult to accept when she felt as if she had known him forever. There was no denying the way that everything inside of her had been thoroughly awakened to a new level since she'd met him about forty-eight hours ago.

Alex loved the way he could look directly at this beautiful woman without feeling conspicuous or out of line. He was *supposed* to look at her; he was supposed to waltz her as if she were the love of his life. That's the way Abernathy had taught him to waltz, and it had been drilled into him over and over. For the first time in his life, that was not a problem. He wondered if he were crazy to believe that she was the love of his life. The innocence he'd noticed about her when he'd first seen her at the restaurant now radiated brilliantly from her. He had no trouble guessing what she might be feeling. He simply had trouble accepting that it might be true. She felt the same way he did; he knew it beyond any doubt. He just wasn't sure what to do about it. For the moment, he just wished this waltz could last forever. It didn't seem to matter that they were both wearing jeans. It was easy to imagine that he was decked out in a classic black tux with tails, and that she was wearing white—satiny and billowing around her as if she were a part of the ethereal atmosphere where they danced.

When the music ended, their dance came to a graceful halt, but Alex remained as he was, one hand holding hers, the other against her back. He felt thoroughly entranced and somehow hypnotized by the absolute silence in the room. Could she hear his heart beating? Could she hear him breathing? He saw her lips part subtly as if to draw a deep breath, and without any thought or premeditation, he lowered his lips and touched them to hers. In the same moment that he felt the electricity of their kiss, he told himself he was likely an idiot to be so bold when he hardly knew her. He was careful to keep his kiss meek and unassuming, even though he kept his lips against hers as long as he could get away with before he had to draw breath. Afraid that he might have blown it by being too intrepid by kissing her when he hardly knew her, he opened his eyes to check her expression. He couldn't help smiling to see such overt yearning. Her eyes came dreamily open, and she looked at him as if she were looking at her first sunrise. It took no effort whatsoever to kiss her again.

Jane felt as if her spirit might fly out of her body and let out a shout of joy that could penetrate the universe. When Alex's lips first met hers, she couldn't help wondering if he had read her mind—or perhaps her eyes. When he kissed her again, she wondered at what point she had completely lost her senses—and her sensibility. She felt like an absolute hypocrite as she recalled all the self-righteous speeches she'd given to girlfriends over the years about the silliness of going ga-ga over a simple kiss, and the importance of never kissing a man unless you'd spent enough time with him to know who you were kissing. *A kiss should be sacred,* she heard herself say in her mind, words she had said to others a hundred times, words her mother had taught her. And then she realized that this one was. Never had she imagined that a kiss could be so completely spiritual and at the same time penetrate her every nerve. When she felt his arms come around her, she found herself praying that this moment would be the beginning of forever, and not something that would end up breaking her heart. As she put her arms around him, returning his embrace and the lingering kiss, she couldn't help hoping that she would never have to let him go.

While time seemed to stand still, Jane pondered a hundred thoughts in the breadth of one long moment. When it finally occurred to her that she was kissing a complete stranger in a way she'd never kissed anyone before, something of her practical nature intruded, demanding a logical explanation for this. She withdrew her lips and felt herself go tense. Immediately she saw regret in his eyes, and he stepped back, abruptly letting go of her. His expression made it evident that he was as surprised by his own behavior as she was by hers.

Alex knew he had really blown it when he felt resistance, however subtle, creep into her embrace. He'd been careful to keep their kiss suitable and unassuming, but simply kissing her at all when he hardly knew her was foolish at best. The last thing he wanted was to make her feel like he didn't respect her, but he was afraid he'd just put himself into the same category as most of the jerks around here who wanted only one thing out of dating. He was searching for the words to defend himself when the coach came back into the room. He and Jane each took another step back, as if adding some distance between them might make them appear innocent. Coach was apparently oblivious to the tension in the room as she complimented them on their performance and congratulated herself for putting them together. As she concluded their session and sent them home, Alex was pleasantly startled to recall that he was giving Jane a ride. Perhaps he would have a chance to explain, after all. They both gathered their things and walked together into the hall without uttering a word. He was wondering how to break the silence when she said, "What I heard about you is true."

"And what's that?" he asked with a self-conscious chuckle, prepared to hear her say that he was some kind of philandering jerk, although he couldn't imagine himself getting any such reputation. He'd hardly dated at all in the years he'd lived in this town.

"You really are a great dancer," Jane said and resisted the urge to tell him that he was a great kisser as well. She felt almost wicked to think of how much she'd enjoyed it, then she reminded herself that she'd done nothing wrong. She just needed to be careful and make certain that she kept her logic intact enough to balance this overwhelming attraction. Again she felt like a hypocrite for all the years she'd assumed that remaining moral should be easy. She'd simply never taken into account the power of physical attraction; she'd simply never been attracted to anyone this way in her life. She wondered then if *she had done something wrong.* Had she become so consumed with her attraction to Alex that she had led him to believe she was the kind of girl to give in easily to such affection? What if he were simply a smooth talker, a man sensitive to when an innocent woman found him attractive? What if he were accustomed to saying and doing the things that made a girl swoon? She felt suddenly terrified that she'd been a fool, and she was about to get in a car with him.

"Well, I was told the same about you," Alex said, intruding on her thoughts. "And truthfully, you're likely the best I've ever danced with."

"You're very sweet," she said, praying that this experience would not turn out to be the kind of disaster she'd heard about from girls she'd talked to over the years.

"Just being honest," he said, and she prayed that he truly was an honest man—with his words as well as with his affection.

Silence fell as they stepped outside and moved toward the parking lot, while Alex wondered if he'd ever felt so tongue-tied in his life. Realizing this tension would never go away until he did something about it, he put a hand on her arm and stopped her. "Hey," he said, turning to face her, "there's something I have to say; it can't wait."

"Okay," she said, her heart quickening as their eyes met.

While Alex felt tempted to just ignore what had happened, he knew it was impossible to disregard something so profound and overpowering. He forced himself to just be honest with her and say what needed to be said. "I . . . I'm sorry about what happened in there."

Jane felt a little baffled until he added, "We are practically strangers, and I had no business kissing you like that. I . . . I . . . don't know why I did it. I just . . ."

Jane watched his eyes closely in the glow of a nearby streetlight. She had no doubt about his sincerity, while his nervous stammering only added validity to what he was saying.

"I don't know, Jane, I just . . ." His voice softened. "I just . . . lost myself somewhere back there during that waltz. I . . . don't know what to say. The last thing I want is for you to think that I'm like so many of the guys around here who would do or say just about anything to get what they want out of a girl. There's no reason for you to believe that I'm telling you the truth, because you hardly know me, but I'm begging you to believe me when I tell you that . . . that's not me. That's not why I did it."

Jane knew he was telling the truth; she could feel it radiating from him. She felt her respect for him deepen as she witnessed his concern over her perception of his motives. And she appreciated his willingness to make a fool of himself rather than have her believe something that wasn't true. Inspired by his candor, she couldn't resist asking, "Why *did* you do it?"

Alex smiled, relieved to see that she wasn't upset or uncomfortable with this conversation. "I don't know," he admitted. "It might take me a little time to figure that out. In the meantime, if we could just . . . start over, and . . . pretend it never happened, I think that might be wise, and . . . prudent."

"Starting over might be good," she said. "And I think it would be good to be wise . . . and prudent, but . . ."

"But what?" he asked when she hesitated.

"You can't ask me to pretend it never happened when . . ." Jane hesitated, wondering if she should be so thoroughly honest. Trying to trust her instincts, she felt no reason to hold back.

"When what?" he pressed again.

"When . . . I'll never be the same."

Alex heard her words and felt them clearly glowing from her countenance. It took every ounce of his willpower to resist kissing her again, knowing it would make the speech he'd just given her sound hypocritical and pathetic.

"Come on," he said, moving toward the car, "I'll take you home."

He was relieved when she asked, "So, what made you start dancing?"

He laughed softly. "My mother loved to dance. She signed my sisters up for ballet, but that didn't fly with me. When I was fourteen she signed me up for a ballroom dance class. She told me to give it three months and if I hated it, she'd never bring it up again. Lucky for her, I loved it, even though I made sure none of the kids at school knew what I was doing. Once I got in high school I didn't care what anyone thought."

"So, they had ballroom dance at your high school?" she asked, knowing it wasn't necessarily common.

"They did once my mother joined the PTA and made it happen."

As they approached the car, Alex said, "I'm afraid my car leaves much to be desired. I call it the caterpillar."

"Why is that?" she asked as he opened the door for her. She hesitated to get in until he explained.

"Like everything else in my life, it's in a state of metamorphosis. Someday it will come out of its cocoon."

"And then what will it be?" she asked with a little laugh.

"A black Ferrari," he stated, and her laugh deepened.

Jane got in, and he closed the door. She noted that the car was clean and well kept. She couldn't deny being impressed. It was apparent that he wasn't being given a free ride through college. And obviously his education was more important to him than driving a car that might impress women. Once in the driver's seat he turned the key in the ignition and asked, "Where to?" She told him the area, and he added, "I didn't know there were any college apartments up that way."

"There aren't," she said. "I went to school elsewhere for quite a while, but my parents thought it would be good for me to get out into the world. But not *too* much out in the world." She smiled. "I'm living with my aunt and uncle."

"You get along well with them, I assume."

"I do," she said, "although I'm not home much."

"I can relate to that."

She told him that beyond her classes and the dance team, she worked at a clothing store. Alex was about to ask where she was from and a few other trivial questions that were typical of getting to know someone, when she said, "I hope I'm not being presumptuous, Alex, but . . . given the conversation we had in the parking lot, I assume it's okay to be candid here and . . . there's something I really need to say."

"Okay," he said.

"Is it all right if I call you Alex? I mean . . . we are dance partners, but . . ."

"Of course it's all right . . . Jane. That's a very pretty name, Jane."

"Is it?" she asked, surprised. "I always thought it was . . . dull. You know, plain Jane."

"Oh no! Never plain." He looked at her for a long moment as if to imply something deeper, and her heart quickened. "You were saying?" he urged.

"Oh yes," she said, trying to find her train of thought again. "Well . . . some people accuse me of being too straightforward, and maybe I am, but . . . so forgive me if I am, but . . ." She hesitated, thinking how strange it sounded considering the kiss they had shared. Ignoring thoughts of that, she pressed on with her point. "I just really wanted to say how glad I am it worked out this way . . . that I saw you again. I mean, I never dreamed when I met you Saturday night that we'd end up paired together this way. It's just so weird." She laughed softly. "But . . . I guess I'm trying to say that I'm glad I saw you again because I really wanted to tell you how much your kindness meant to me."

Alex glanced at her again and then back to the road. The mounting evidence that he had left an impression on her—as she had on him—deepened something inside of him that he had yet to define. But it was warm and comforting and real. "I didn't do that much," he said. "I just . . . didn't like the way he was talking to you."

"Well, I didn't like it either. And . . . what you did may not have technically been much, but many people wouldn't have bothered. I just wanted to say thank you . . . formally."

"Okay. You're welcome . . . formally." He debated whether or not to tell her the truth, and figured it couldn't hurt. "You want to know why I did it?"

"Why?" she asked, tossing him a sharp glance, as if she feared he'd confess to something that might lower her opinion of him. He hoped that it wouldn't.

"You caught my eye when I first approached your table. I might not have even noticed there was a problem if I hadn't been paying such close attention. There was just . . . something about you that made it impossible for me to ignore you."

Jane felt suddenly flustered and close to tears. When she said nothing, he added, "Did I say something wrong? I mean . . . the last thing I want to do is make you uncomfortable or—"

"No," she said, sounding more composed than she felt. "You're just so . . . sweet. I don't think anyone has ever been so sweet to me." She laughed softly. "Except maybe my dad, but that doesn't count, does it?"

Thinking of his own father, Alex said firmly, "Oh, I'd say that counts for a great deal."

Jane told him where to turn now that they were in the right neighborhood.

"So, are you majoring in dance?" he asked.

"No," she laughed softly, "it's more just a . . . hobby. Not a very practical profession."

"Not for most people, no," Alex said.

"I'm going to be a teacher."

"That's great," he said. "Do you have a particular field in mind?"

"Children," she said, and he laughed. "No, I mean . . . I want to teach young children. Kindergarten would be ideal."

"Wow," he said, "you must have a gift."

"Maybe. I've just always felt drawn to young children."

"That's great."

"What about you?" she asked. "What's your gift?"

He gave a dubious chuckle. "I don't know that I have a gift. But I guess you could say that I too have felt drawn to certain things."

"Wouldn't you think that's some indication of a gift? Just being drawn to something?"

"Perhaps."

"So what is it that you're drawn to, Alex Keane?"

"Blood," he said and chuckled when he got the desired reaction, and her eyes widened with shock. "Actually, I'm fascinated with medicine."

"You're going to be a doctor?" she asked, sounding impressed.

"Well . . . technically I already am. I graduated from med school here last year."

"Really?" She gave the soft laugh that he was growing to love. "That's amazing. So, you're *Dr.* Alex Keane."

"Yeah, I guess I am, although I have a way to go yet. I'm doing my internship now. I was really lucky to get an opening at the hospital right here in town, which meant I didn't have to move."

"You must really like it here."

"Truthfully, not really. I just . . ." Alex hesitated as the words he was about to say suddenly took on new meaning with the events that had led up to getting to know this incredible woman.

"You what?" she pressed.

"I just . . . felt like staying here was the right thing to do."

"Maybe it was so Coach Abernathy could have you on the team."

"Maybe," he said, giving her a sly smile.

Jane guided him to her home, and he pulled the car into the driveway.

"Here we are then," Alex said with dread at the thought of being away from her.

"Yes, this is it. Now you know where to find me."

Alex hoped that was intended as an open invitation.

Jane glanced at Alex and found him looking at her. She felt hesitant to get out of the car but didn't want to monopolize him or seem overbearing. But perhaps she could drag it out just a few more minutes. "I have a question," she said.

"Shoot."

"You get paid for your internship, don't you?"

"I do, but not much."

"I was just wondering why you're waiting tables, too."

"I only do it now and then to fill in when they're shorthanded. I worked there a long time before I graduated, so I can take over easily. I don't have a lot of time, but any extra income helps. I'm just trying to get my student loans paid off as quickly as possible."

Jane couldn't help being more impressed with him by the minute. She wanted to know everything about him and never wanted to be away from him. "So, how long is your internship?" she asked, hoping that his work would keep him in town at least until she got her own degree.

"I'll be done with it in about two months," he said.

"Oh." She looked down. "And then you'll be able to start practicing on your own and—"

"Not yet," he chuckled. "Then I have three years of residency, and I could be all over the place. I'm starting at a hospital in Michigan. It's all arranged. For what I'm doing it's ideal, really."

"I see," she said without looking at him.

Alex scrutinized her countenance and checked his instincts before he said, "I could almost guess that you're disappointed to find out I'll be leaving."

Jane looked up abruptly, startled at having her mind read. She considered skirting around the issue, but she felt compelled to just admit to the truth. "Actually, I am. But since we hardly know each other, perhaps we should continue *that* conversation another time."

Alex wanted to remind her of the breathtaking, unforgettable kisses they'd shared just a short while ago, but he was the one who had said they should forget about that and start over. He was wondering what else to say when she asked, "Why is it ideal?"

"What?"

"Why is the hospital in Michigan ideal?"

"It's in an area with a lot of action. High crime rate, stuff like that."

Jane's expression turned skeptical. "And this is ideal because . . ." She motioned with her hand for him to explain.

He chuckled. "Because I'm specializing in emergency medicine. It will give me a lot of great experience. Of course I'll be doing rotations all over the place through the next three years, but if I can master working at this hospital, I can work just about anywhere."

"Wow," she said. "Emergency medicine. That's quite an undertaking."

"Well, it's been a big investment—in many ways. But it's what I've always wanted."

"Why emergency as opposed to . . . delivering babies, or prescribing creams for rashes?"

He chuckled again. "It's hard to explain, but . . . the thought of being holed up in a clinic just makes me stir-crazy. I learned a long time ago that I work very well under pressure. I guess the unpredictability gives me an adrenaline rush or something. Even though an ER gets a lot of broken bones, stitches, babies with earaches, and stuff like that, there's still the big stuff, and . . . well . . . I've just learned that I'm better at that than prescribing creams for rashes."

The following silence indicated that they'd run out of things to say. Alex finally said, "I should probably let you go, even though it's tempting to sit here and talk all night."

"Yeah," she said, "it is. But I'll see you tomorrow?"

"That's right. I'll be looking forward to it." Alex hurried around the car to open her door, but she already had it opened.

"You don't have to do that," she said, standing beside him as he closed the door.

"My mother taught me to open doors for ladies."

Jane smiled. "My knight in shining armor."

He gave a dubious chuckle and added, "Not really, but I am going to walk you to the door and make sure you get inside safely."

"You really are sweet, Alex," she said.

"I think you inspire me to be on my best behavior," he countered, and then they were standing at the door.

"Thank you so much. I appreciate the ride, and I enjoyed the conversation."

"Me too," he said. "I'll see you tomorrow then."

Jane went reluctantly inside, and Alex went back to his car. He got in and turned the ignition. As he drove, he unconsciously reached a hand over to the passenger seat and touched it, barely able to believe that the woman he'd been thinking about all weekend had been sitting there, showing an overt interest in him and his life. He could hardly believe that he'd kissed her, and the way it had affected him. The prospect of seeing her again tomorrow—and the possibility of getting to know her better—made him feel happier than he had felt in years, perhaps ever.

* * * * *

Through the next few days, Jane found herself on cloud nine—a place she had only heard about, and had completely believed to be mythical. But there was no other way to describe the way she felt in Alex Keane's presence—and her memories of him when she wasn't. Alicia took great pleasure in teasing her about her present state of mind. But Jane quickly realized there was no point in trying to hide her feelings for Alex, and she couldn't deny some pleasure in Alicia's common reminders that Alex really had become a part of her life. Their time together at rehearsals was absolutely divine, but their busy schedules coming and going made it impossible to see each other outside of the studio—even though he had asked more than once if she needed a ride home, or if she'd like to get something to eat. Simply sensing his interest in her was enough to provoke butterflies in her stomach. But she felt a growing frustration in wanting to get to know him better. They could dance together as if they'd been doing it for a decade, but beyond their conversation when he'd driven her home after that first rehearsal, she knew absolutely nothing about him. During their break Thursday evening, she was naturally relieved when he said, "So tell me, Miss Layton, are you trying to avoid me off of the dance floor, or do we genuinely have a severe clashing of schedules?"

"Now why on earth would I want to avoid you?" she asked.

"That's what I'm asking," he said, but he smiled as he said it.

With no more rehearsals until Monday, she didn't know how she could go so many days without seeing him. "You tell me when you're free, and I will do my best not to avoid you."

"Okay, Friday—anytime. I don't have a hospital shift until Sunday, and I'm doing a shift at the restaurant Saturday evening."

Jane groaned. "Sorry. Friday is booked from dawn until midnight. Classes, work, family thing."

"Okay," Alex drawled, wondering why fate seemed to be keeping them from spending any time together when destiny had brought them together. "How about Saturday morning?"

Jane felt immensely relieved to be able to say, "That would be perfect. Do you have something in mind?"

"Yes, I do, actually. How about if I pick you up in that dreadful little car of mine and we can go out to breakfast, and then do something thoroughly boring and cheap."

"What's that?"

"Go for a very long walk." Jane smiled, and he added, "You see . . . if I take you to a movie or something, then it would be impossible to ask you all the questions I've been dying to ask you."

She felt her smile widen. "It sounds delightful. I'll be looking forward to it."

"Yeah, me too," he said, then they split for a quick break before going back to the dance regime.

— 3 —

By the time Saturday morning came, Jane was so full of jittery excitement she could hardly sit still. "What's going on, girl?" her uncle Jeff asked, looking at her over the top of the newspaper he was reading.

"Just nervous, I guess," she said, pacing the floor and glancing at the clock.

Jeff chuckled. "Is that good or bad?" She only felt confused by the question, and he clarified, "Are you nervous because you're dreading this breakfast date, or because you're excited?"

"Oh, I'm definitely not dreading it," she said. "He's the most amazing man I've ever met."

"Well, that's good then," Jeff said. "I don't think I've ever seen you this enthused about a date before."

"I've never been this enthused about a date before."

Jeff chuckled as if he found the situation highly amusing. "Well, I hope it goes well." He put his paper back in place and muttered, "I assume he's a member."

Jane felt her heart drop like a rock. She'd certainly gone out with guys who weren't members of the Church, but never more than once or twice. She'd met and dated guys through church and other related activities, but none of them had piqued her interest or kept it more than an hour or two. Even though she had strong convictions about marrying within her religion, she hadn't given the matter much thought for months. She hadn't been looking for a husband. She hadn't been asking to fall in love. It had just happened. As she considered this amazing thought, her stomach tightened in the same moment that her heart quickened. Was that what she felt? *Love?* Surely it was far too soon to assess such feelings, but there was no denying the profound effect Alex Keane was having on her—and her heart. But if she was honest with herself, she couldn't deny that no matter how she felt about him, she could not set aside her most important convictions and get serious with a guy who didn't share her religious beliefs.

Suddenly the appeal of seeing Alex was coupled with some anxiety. He'd told her they were going to talk and get to know each other. She simply had to address it. But it wasn't going to be easy. The doorbell rang and startled her. It saved her from having to respond to her uncle's comment, and she forced the problem out of her mind for the moment. She knew it had to be addressed, but she uttered a quick prayer that the right opportunity would present itself, and in the meantime she was determined to enjoy herself.

"Hi," she said, pulling the door open. Just seeing him provoked a giddy lurch somewhere inside her.

"Hi," he replied, his countenance brightening visibly when he saw her. "You ready?"

"Yes," she said and stepped outside.

He opened the car door for her, then got in himself and backed out of the driveway. "Wow," he said, looking over at her.

"What?"

"I think we finally did it; we're on a date."

"So we are," she said and smiled. They talked about dancing and the weather until they were seated in the restaurant and had ordered their breakfast.

Alex took a long look at this woman sitting across from him and wondered how to deal with his feelings. Ever since he'd made an official date with her, his mind had been spinning with the things he wanted to say, and how to go about saying them. He'd survived medical school, graduating with honors, but he'd never felt so nervous and flustered as he did at the thought of trying to steer his way through the way she affected him. Early this morning he'd concluded that he just needed to be honest—tactful of course, but honest. With the enormity of his feelings, he couldn't go on beating around the bush and living on assumptions and implications. Now she was here, and the silence was begging him to just say what needed to be said and get it over with.

"Jane," he began and took a deep breath. As if some physical contact might make this easier, he gingerly took her hand across the table. She seemed pleased by the gesture, and her expectant eyes urged him to go on. "I just . . . need to be honest with you. Maybe you can guess how I feel about you; I certainly haven't made any effort to hide it. And I can guess that you enjoy my company as much as I enjoy yours, but . . . I just really need to voice it. I need to let you know where I'm coming from, straight up, and . . . well . . . if you think I'm crazy then you can write me off now, and we'll be done with it. But . . . I guess I just have to know where I stand, and . . . I need to let you know where I—"

"You're stammering, Alex," she said gently, with a little wink. "You stammered when you were trying to tell me why you'd kissed me."

"So I did," he said, looking down.

"Actually, you never did tell me exactly *why*."

"I guess that's what I'm getting to," he said, still visibly tense.

"Why don't you just say it. Nervousness doesn't suit you."

Alex let out a sheepish chuckle, and Jane felt like a hypocrite for saying what she'd said. She'd never felt so nervous in her life as she waited for what he might say—knowing there were things she needed to say to him as well. She reminded herself that they had some time together. She didn't need to spill everything right now. But she prayed that whatever he might say might make her own issues easier to face.

"Well," he chuckled again, "you seem to have that effect on me."

"Is that good or bad?"

"That depends on whether or not you think I'm crazy."

"Just tell me what you want to tell me, Alex."

She gently squeezed his hand as if to offer encouragement. He looked into her eyes and suddenly it was easy. "I am head over heels in love with you, Jane. Something happened inside of me the minute I saw you, and the more time I spend with you the more I feel like there has to be some significant meaning to the way I feel. I just . . . don't know what it is or what to do about it."

Jane allowed his words to sink in, wondering how to respond. The vulnerability in his eyes made her glad that she could be completely honest and at ease at the same time. As the words came to her mind, she allowed them to escape her lips with little effort. "If you're crazy, Alex, then I'm crazy too. I feel exactly the same way."

Alex's relief came out with a brief surge of laughter, and she laughed with him. "I was hoping you'd say that," he said. They laughed again, then silence fell while they stared at each other as if to mutually accept the bridge they had just crossed together.

The hot chocolate and orange juice they had ordered were brought to the table. Jane figured that following his lead to be completely candid was the best way to break this lingering tension. "This is just so weird," she said and laughed.

"Well . . . I could agree with that." His voice expressed his relief at having the ice broken. "But . . . why don't you tell me why you think it's weird."

"And then you'll tell me why *you* think it's weird?" she asked.

"Fair enough."

Jane let out a long, dreamy sigh. "Okay, well . . . I'm going to follow your example and be completely honest here, and then maybe we can both stop guessing and feeling nervous."

"Good plan," he said and took a sip of his hot chocolate.

"You have to understand, Alex, that I am a realist. I have a stark reputation for being anything *but* romantic. Growing up, I was the only girl in my neighborhood who wasn't going ga-ga over boys all the time. I had boys who were friends, but never a boyfriend. I just didn't care. I started ballroom dance in high school, and I went to all the school dances with guys on the dance team. It was just treated as . . . an opportunity to show off our dancing and have some fun together as friends . . . teammates. When I got into college I finally started dating some, but it was all from a very pragmatic perspective. It was either a need for some socializing to balance out my life, or, from an even more practical standpoint, I would rationalize, 'Oh, he seems like someone I could have a great conversation with.' So I'd go out. But I don't think I've ever felt attracted to anyone. I've found certain men to be interesting perhaps, but never attractive. I just couldn't understand all the talk among my peers about how they felt about men, and the way their knees would go weak and they'd become ridiculously obsessed with someone."

Alex watched Jane wrap her hands around the warm cup on the table, and she sighed again, seeming nervous, as if she were spilling a deep confession. He was grateful not to be alone in that.

"I have a friend who told me she thought there was something wrong with me," Jane went on, "like I was missing a certain hormone or something." Alex chuckled, knowing that certainly wasn't the case. He motioned for her to go on. "I must admit there were moments when I wondered if she was right, but my instincts told me that I'm simply not a romantic. It's not a hormone; it's a character trait. A flaw, perhaps, but simply a part of my character. My parents are good people, and they have a good marriage, and I think I just always figured that someday I'd meet a guy who would have all the right qualities and I'd check them off of some kind of list, and we'd decide to get married."

"Very practical," Alex said.

"That's right." She tightened her gaze on him. "And there are advantages to that, you know. I've seen people go absolutely crazy over those . . . romantic hormones . . . or whatever you want to call them."

Alex chuckled. "I think for many people the hormones are far more carnal than romantic."

"Very likely." Jane looked away, appreciating his straightforward attitude even though it very nearly made her blush—one more thing to prove her point. She'd never really blushed in her entire life until she'd met Alex. She forced herself to finish her point.

"So you see, there I was, all practical and pragmatic, out on a date with some guy who offered to buy me dinner. I felt certain the evening could be stimulating, if not enjoyable. But it quickly became evident he was a chauvinistic jerk, and I was thinking that no free meal was worth taking these veiled insults to my gender. Enter knight in shining armor." She glanced at him and smiled to see his dubious gaze. Maintaining eye contact, she went on in a voice that was more tender. "I don't know what happened, Alex, but . . . sitting there in that lobby, after I'd called for a ride, I thought about what you'd just done for me and . . . well, my first thought was that chivalry still existed."

"All I did was tell the guy to—"

"I know what you said . . . what you did. It was the way that you did it. And truthfully, it was just something that happened inside of me when I looked into your eyes. I got into Alicia's car that night with weak knees, and my heart was beating fast. I remember thinking, 'So this is what it's like to feel attracted to someone.' And the next day when I couldn't stop thinking about you, I suddenly felt that I'd been very judgmental toward all the girls I'd known through my life who had been crazy and ga-ga over some guy they hardly knew. I felt certain that our meeting up again was highly unlikely unless I thought of some excuse to go back into that restaurant and find you."

"Would you have done that?"

"You know . . . I think I might have become just that desperate to see you again. I started trying to come up with all kinds of excuses to go in there, but . . ."

"But?" he pressed when she hesitated.

"My practical nature brought me to the conclusion that if I ever did such a bold, insane thing, I would simply have to be honest."

"I'm listening."

"I would have just had to say . . . 'I was very impressed by what you did. Can I buy you a burger or something? Here's my phone number.'"

Alex smiled. It was easy now to just spill the rest without feeling nervous at all. "Funny," he said. "I found myself wishing that you'd come back and say something just like that, because I couldn't fathom what I would do if I never saw you again, and I had no way of knowing who you were or where to find you. My only hope was that you would find me, even though I felt sure that such a thing was ludicrous . . . that you would have no interest in me whatsoever. And then, I'm not at the restaurant very often."

Jane laughed softly. "And now here we are. Instead of having to muster up the courage to come and find you, I ended up dancing with you—and it took no effort at all. And everything inside of me feels more alive and awakened and . . . right . . . than it's ever felt before." She looked down. "But at the same time it's frightening."

"Why is that?"

"First let me say that I'm really grateful you opened this conversation the way you did, because . . . I want to be open and honest with you. I don't like holding all of this inside and trying to figure it out on my own."

"There's one very practical thing that we have in common," he said, and she smiled.

"So it is," she said.

"Why is it frightening?" he asked, taking her back to her point.

"I told you I'm a practical person, Alex. I never expected something like this. I've never longed for some wildly romantic story to tell my grandchildren someday. And the reality is that we know absolutely nothing about each other. This . . . attraction we feel, as wonderful as it is . . . I know it's technically just . . . infatuation. It's incredible from an emotional perspective, but in the big picture of life, it's . . . just not the stuff lasting relationships are made of." She looked directly at him again. "But maybe . . ." She gave an embarrassed chuckle. "I can't believe I'm saying this."

"Maybe what? Just say it."

"Maybe this kind of attraction is God's way of getting two people to pay attention to each other long enough to see if they have what it takes to work out all of the practical stuff."

"Maybe," he said in a tender voice that made her insides quiver.

Alex hesitated as a thought occurred to him, and he attempted to express it. "And so . . . maybe that makes . . . such feelings more . . . instinct than infatuation." He leaned forward and spoke zealously as the idea took root. "Haven't you ever just . . . done something because you know it's right? You may not be able to explain how it's right, but you just know. Wouldn't that be . . . trusting your instincts?"

Jane smiled at him, feeling her heart quicken just to see such overt evidence of his feelings for her, and his desire to be able to make sense of them. It was easy for her to say, "Yes, I think it is—which works as long as a person knows how to listen to those instincts and trust them. And that takes some . . . practical experience."

"Yes," he agreed.

"So," she probed, hoping to perhaps get a feel for his beliefs, "what do you think instinct is, really?"

He shrugged his shoulders. "I don't suppose I've ever thought about it. Obviously you have."

"I have a theory, a belief."

Alex smiled. "I hope you're going to share it with me."

"If you're interested."

"Very much, of course."

"Well, I believe that it's God guiding our lives. If we live in a way that keeps Him close to us, He will guide us through our thoughts and feelings to the path He wants us to take."

Alex pondered her words for a long moment, realizing, much to his own surprise, that in the deepest part of himself he actually believed that. She'd changed something in him already, or at the very least she had brought something to the surface that he had long believed dead or nonexistent.

"Okay," he said when the silence grew too long, "which brings me to why this is all so weird for *me*."

"Okay," she said eagerly.

"First of all, I believe I *am* somewhat of a romantic. But through several brief infatuations I've come to find that when I got past all of that, there's never been any substance to hold onto." He smiled at her. "Maybe you could chalk that up to some trial and error." His expression became sober, his eyes intense. "What I have felt since I met you doesn't even come close to anything I've ever felt before; that alone tells me that this is not merely infatuation."

Jane felt her breath quicken as the implication settled in. She glanced down when she felt certain she couldn't bear the intensity of his gaze another second. She was relieved when he went on.

"I pretty much gave up on dating when it took all of my energy to keep up with school and pay my bills. But . . . I just have to say again that . . . I have *never* felt the way I've felt since I laid eyes on you. And the way this whole thing came together, it just sings of destiny. And I guess the problem with that would be . . . well, I didn't think I believed in destiny."

Alex saw Jane's brow furrow, and he looked down as he attempted to explain. "You see, my parents are not happily married. They appeared to be for a long time, and I remember my mother telling me and my sisters about how they had met and how in love they had been. But when I was thirteen, my father left us for another woman." While Alex felt tempted to delve deeper into that and how it had affected him, he felt more prone to just leave it alone for now.

Jane broke the grueling silence by saying, "So, are you really saying that in spite of what two people might feel when they fall in love, that it won't necessarily last?"

Alex was firm as he said, "I think my father could have made the choice to make it last. I just think that . . . somewhere through all of the grief he put us through, I stopped believing that God would have any hand in bringing good things into my life."

Jane smiled. "Did I prove you wrong?"

"Maybe," he said with a little chuckle, grateful for the first time in his life that the service was slow. Silence fell between them while Alex gave in to his urge to take her hand and kiss it.

Jane watched, as if in slow motion, the way Alex pressed her hand to his lips. She'd never imagined that such a simple gesture could communicate so much adoration.

Alex allowed his lips to linger against her hand for a long moment while he checked her eyes to gauge her response.

"So, what now?" she asked, almost looking as if she might cry.

Alex thought about that for a long moment. "Well, I could give in to my romantic side and get down on one knee right now and propose to you. We could get married right away, live in abject poverty while we both finish school and hope that we could actually make it work. But I have a feeling you probably wouldn't go for that." She smiled but said nothing so he continued. "*Or* we could take the practical approach—which is likely more suited to both our personalities, not to mention more likely to succeed."

"And how does the practical approach work?" she asked.

"We keep forging ahead through school, see each other every possible minute so that we can get to know each other as much as humanly possible without being married, and eventually, when we're still hopelessly attracted to each other *and* we know we can make a relationship work, we get married and spend the rest of our lives proving it."

"I think I like the practical approach," Jane said. There were other issues for her that still needed to be addressed, but she didn't believe now was the right time. Still, there was one point she felt needed to be clarified. And she felt that it couldn't wait. She cleared her throat gently and said, "At the risk of embarrassing myself, there's something I need to say . . . that needs to be very clear."

"Okay," Alex said, loving her straightforward approach. It was so refreshing in contrast to the game-playing he'd dealt with in the past. He recalled that one of the first things he'd admired about her was her self-confident aura, and the way she'd been telling her date exactly what she thought. He felt distinctly privileged to be the man sitting across from her now, being the recipient of her convictions.

Jane glanced down and realized this might not be so difficult to say if she didn't feel so thoroughly attracted to him. She thought of how it had felt to have his arms around her, to have him kiss her, and she was attacked by a swarm of internal butterflies. All the more reason she needed to say this and get it over with. Her parents had clearly taught her that ignorance of or dismissal of the challenges of the world would not protect her from them; it would only make her more vulnerable. Such teachings were now being put to the test.

"Alex," she said, looking directly at him, "if we're going to have any relationship at all, you need to know that I don't believe in sex outside of marriage—not to any degree."

Alex felt more stunned than surprised. He never doubted that she would hold such a conviction, but he was pleasantly astonished by her ability to say something like that and mean it. His respect and admiration deepened for her immensely, and he was grateful to be able to say with complete honesty, "Neither do I, Jane."

He watched her look deep into his eyes, as if to gauge his sincerity. "You really mean that," she said. "You're not just saying it to make me happy."

"I really mean it," he said firmly. "I just didn't know if there was anyone else in this town who felt the same way." Again he kissed her hand. "And for the record, I want to say how much I love the way you take such things head on. I hate having to guess. Do you know how many dates I've been on where I've been relatively certain the girl was hoping I'd invite her to stay the night, and then became angry because I didn't?"

"I'm afraid I've encountered the same thing . . . and that after only one or two dates," Jane had to admit. "I guess it's the way of the age we live in, but it's truly sad."

"Yes, it is," he agreed and briefly pondered how she became more attractive as her true character came to the surface. He found it an interesting contrast to realize that he'd never in his life wanted so desperately to take a woman in his arms and hold her close, but at the same time he'd never before had such a strong desire to protect and defend her—and her virtue—at all costs.

Their meals were brought to the table, and they ate while they recounted once again the circumstances of their meeting—twice in two days—and how it had affected them both. Alex felt completely comfortable and relaxed now that their feelings were in the open— and deeply relieved to know that he didn't feel this way alone.

When the check was brought to the table, she said, "You really don't have to buy my breakfast. I mean . . . I know it's the standard dating thing, but I can appreciate that you're struggling to pay for school, and I don't have a problem with going dutch."

"I asked you out," he said, "and I'm buying your breakfast. I'm using my tip money from Saturday night—which included a tip from you that you shouldn't have given me. So in a way, we are going dutch, which means I'll have to take you out to eat at least one more time in order to assuage my male ego."

Jane chuckled. "You don't seem like the type to be concerned about your male ego."

"That depends on how you look at it, I suppose. I certainly don't consider myself a chauvinist, but I do believe in traditional roles, for the most part. Which is the reason that I will pay for a date when I ask you out on a date. *Maybe* one of these days I'll let you take *me* on a date—when I run out of tip money."

"I'll count on it," she said, and they headed toward the cashier after he left a generous tip on the table.

Stepping outside, they were met by a cold breeze and heavy clouds. Alex groaned and looked skyward. "The weather is not cooperating with my plan for a long walk. It looks like we're in for a spring rain."

"How about the mall?" she asked. "Or a museum?"

Alex smiled as he opened the car door for her. "How about both?"

"What a marvelous idea," she said.

"It wasn't my idea; it was yours." He closed her door and hurried around to his side.

Alex drove to an art museum that he'd visited only once, but it had been a long time ago. They were disappointed to find that it wouldn't be open until eleven.

"Okay," he said, "we'll have to save that for later."

"Or another day," she said. Thinking of the issue she needed to address with him, she couldn't keep from adding, "That is if you want to go out with me again."

"No problem there," he said, but Jane knew something he didn't know. She forced thoughts of it out of her head for the moment as he drove toward the mall. He found a parking space not far from one of the main doors, since it was still fairly early. They hurried through the wind, holding hands, and into the mall corridor.

"Where to?" he asked.

"Nowhere. Let's just . . . walk."

Alex smiled and once again kissed her hand while he looked into her eyes. She sensed that he felt as tempted to kiss her as much as she felt tempted to kiss him. But he'd expressed regret over being so bold over that first thoughtless kiss. He'd told her they were going to start over in that regard, and she could clearly see his effort to maintain an appropriate boundary for a first date. Jane sighed and said, "If you keep doing things like that, you're going to have to carry me back to the car."

"Weak knees?" he asked, lifting his brows.

"Yes, actually."

"Yeah . . . well . . . me too. You might have to carry *me* back to the car."

Jane laughed softly and resisted the urge to touch his face. Oh, how she wanted to, if only to convince herself that he was real, that *this* was real. Instead she started walking, keeping his hand in hers. They ambled along slowly for a few minutes before she said, "You know, Alex, there's a big flaw in this plan of taking time to get to know each other and . . . how did you put it? To see each other every possible minute?"

"And what's that?" he asked, trying to remember what life was like *last* Saturday morning.

"You're moving to Michigan in a couple of months, and I have to stay here until I get my degree."

Alex glanced away abruptly, hating the way that something he'd greatly looked forward to had now become difficult. "Yes, I know. We'll just have to make the most of it. Maybe by then you'll have already decided that being in love with me really isn't practical."

"Don't count on it," she said, a distinct sadness in her voice.

Alex absorbed the reality that she truly wanted him in her life. He resisted the urge to pinch himself and said, "I'll just have to put some phone time into my budget; I will be making more money there than I am now. And there's always e-mail."

"Yes, of course."

"Well, it's easier than regular mail—not to mention much faster. And it's cheaper than the phone, although I will need to hear your voice on a somewhat regular basis."

"E-mail might be cheaper and easier, but isn't there something nice about handwritten cards and letters coming in your mailbox?"

Alex couldn't help appreciating her sentimentality; she reminded him of his mother that way. He couldn't resist saying, "And this from a woman who claims not to be a romantic."

"Oh, I'm reformed. I would say in the past week I've definitely become a bona fide romantic. You changed me."

"Not too much, I hope."

"Only for the better," she said. "And I changed you too. You admitted it."

"Remind me."

"I made you believe in destiny."

"So you did," he said earnestly.

"Except . . . it wasn't really me. I'm just the one who was maneuvered into your life to prove that God is really there."

Alex thought about that for a moment and felt freshly amazed to realize that something in him truly had changed in that regard. He'd never stopped believing in God, but it was a passive, indifferent kind of thing, coupled with a great deal of cynicism. But now he simply couldn't deny that God had brought them together. It was too bizarre for coincidence, and too emotionally consuming for happenstance.

Jane sensed that Alex was thinking deeply about something. She allowed him his silence as they strolled slowly on, taking advantage of the quiet to ponder her own thoughts. Knowing there was an important issue she needed to address with him, she wondered how to bring it up without sounding obnoxious. And she wondered what the possible outcomes might be. She couldn't expect Alex—or any man—to join the Church for her sake. And she wouldn't want him to. But the very fact that she'd fallen in love with someone who didn't share the same religion made all she was feeling seem completely ludicrous. They were talking about plans for maintaining a relationship months from now, but could she encourage such a relationship when she had no intention of marrying outside of the temple? She almost felt angry at the idea of being lured into a relationship with such profound feelings, only to have it go nowhere because of religious differences. The very idea of ending what had just begun made her feel even more sad than angry. Why would God allow her to feel this way about someone if there wasn't an answer? Then it occurred to her that there just had to be an answer. Surely God *wouldn't* put her in this position without providing a solution. On the other hand, she knew well enough from her own experiences, as well as those of many people she knew, that God's ways were often difficult to understand. Perhaps this was just a learning experience for her, some kind of test, and in the end she would have to make a choice between Alex and her convictions. She prayed that it would never come to that; she knew what the choice would have to be, but the thought of losing him felt unbearable.

While she longed to put off ever bringing it up, she knew that it would be better to just address it and get it over with. So far, addressing their thoughts and feelings head-on had worked out rather well, which gave her some degree of hope. She uttered a silent prayer and attempted to feel the guidance of the Spirit. She felt good about going forward and getting it over with, and prayed that it wouldn't ruin their time togther—or prevent him from ever wanting to see her again.

"Alex," she said and motioned toward a bench in a somewhat secluded corner, "could we sit down? There's something I want to talk to you about."

"Of course," he said, and they sat close together while he kept her hand tightly in his.

"What you said earlier about . . . being honest and up front . . . about voicing your feelings . . ."

"Yes?" he drawled when he realized she was nervous.

"There's something I need to say . . . but it's not easy. To put it simply, there's one very big issue that I need to talk to you about. An issue that no amount of weak knees or fluttering hearts will override."

"Okay," he said, now feeling nervous himself. If she told him something that made it impossible to pursue this relationship, would he be able to cope with that?

Jane took a deep breath and reminded herself of her convictions. She almost talked herself out of bringing it up, wondering if it would end the relationship here and now. But she knew that she had to do it.

"It's only fair to warn you, Alex." She forced herself to just say it. "I have very firm convictions on marrying within my religion. I have a personal policy not to go out with anyone more than once or twice unless they share those beliefs." She laughed softly and wrung her hands, certain she'd never see him again once she finished this discourse. "But then . . . so far I've never found anyone worth going out with more than once, anyway. So . . . it's never been a problem."

"And now?" he asked. "Would you consider me worth going out with more than once?"

"Absolutely," she said with no hesitance. "I think that's already been well established."

"Except that . . . you have a policy not to date outside of your religion."

Jane looked down. "That's right."

"So . . . do I need to join your church or something in order to go out with you?"

"Would you join a church for such a reason?"

"No," he said firmly, and she felt some relief.

"I'm glad to hear that."

"But what other solution is there?"

"I don't know the answer, Alex. I've never felt this way before, but . . . it doesn't change my convictions."

Alex sighed and thought for a long moment. Was it possible? Could it be possible? He felt relatively certain that his reasons for not being upset by this conversation were likely his strong suspicion that what she thought to be a problem simply wasn't. But he'd never know until he asked.

"So . . . what religion is it exactly that gives you such strong convictions?" He put up a hand. "No, wait. Don't tell me. You're Lutheran."

"No," she said, looking down. She obviously didn't know him well enough to catch the teasing tone in his voice.

"Catholic? Protestant?"

"No."

"Jehovah's Witness." She shook her head and he said, "I know. You're Buddhist."

She actually laughed, and by the sparkle in her eyes it was evident she'd figured out that he was kidding. "Okay," he said, "I give up. You must be a Mormon."

Her expression became somber, while her eyes betrayed something akin to fear. "That's right," she said.

Alex looked into her eyes and touched her face while reverberations of destiny touched his every nerve. "Jane," he said and kissed her cheek, "this is your lucky day."

"What do you mean?" She pulled back.

"Because I'm a Mormon, too."

Jane gave him a startled stare, unable to believe what she was hearing. Her voice quavered with emotion as she said, "Don't joke about something like this, Alex. If you're—"

"Jane," he said, turning more toward her, "with all we've talked about, we've never discussed where we're from. Go ahead. Ask me where I grew up."

"Where did you grow up?" she asked, as hopeful as she was afraid. It just couldn't be possible. Could it?

"Salt Lake City, Utah," he said proudly. "A ten-minute drive from Temple Square."

Jane drew a sharp breath and put a hand over her heart in an attempt to ease its pounding. "You're serious," she said breathlessly.

"Quite serious," he said, but still he saw disbelief in her eyes and hurried to add, "Do I need to prove it? Would you like me to tell you one of the stories I grew up with? Which one do you want to hear? Nephi? Moroni? How about Ammon cutting arms off?" Jane sucked in her breath, then clapped a hand over her mouth. "Or should I tell you what I know about Joseph Smith?"

Alex wasn't certain what he'd expected, but it wasn't for her to start sobbing quietly into her hand. He put his arms around her and drew her head to his shoulder, feeling tears sting his own eyes. He held her while she discreetly cried, wondering what he'd done to deserve such an opportunity as this. To have this amazing woman come into his life, under such circumstances, seemed nothing less than a miracle. He found himself silently thanking God, then he realized he couldn't remember the last time he'd made any effort to communicate with God—silently or otherwise. She *had* changed him. She'd softened something in him. Having her come into his life had made him believe in things that he thought he'd stopped believing in a long time ago.

When Jane finally calmed down, she gave a tentative chuckle and dug in her purse for a tissue. "Oh, I'm so embarrassed."

"Why?" he asked, helping dry her tears, allowing his fingers to hover against her face. "I consider it a singular honor to have you share your tears with me."

She smiled and touched his face in return. "I can't believe it." She laughed. "This is just so . . . weird. So bizarre. So *incredible*."

"Yes, it is," he agreed, laughing as well.

"How did I miss it?" she asked. "I mean . . . usually I can tell. There's no reason why I should have thought otherwise, except that—"

"Except that LDS people are such a vast minority here. The chances weren't real high, now were they? Is there anyone else at all on the dance team who's a member?"

"Not that I know of," she said and sniffled.

Through a long moment of silence, Alex realized he needed to tell her the whole truth. And no, it couldn't wait. He was struggling to find the words when she said, "Well, since that's settled we can finish that walk and—"

She started to stand up and he put a hand on her arm to stop her. "Not yet," he said seriously. "It's not entirely settled. Since we're making confessions and getting the issues out in the open, there's something you need to know." Alex let go of her hand and leaned his forearms on his thighs, pressing his fingers together. "I am LDS, Jane. I believe the Church is true, and I believe in God. Just being here with you and adding all this up is evidence that He's there. I can't question that. But I'm afraid I don't share your convictions." He sighed and looked away. "I haven't been to church since I was fifteen."

— 4 —

Jane felt her heart plummet. She couldn't deny that his confession definitely put a damper on her happiness. Still, he had been raised in the Church, and he was obviously such a good man. Surely this problem was solvable.

"I see," she said quietly when the silence became strained. "Is there a reason? I mean . . . there must be a reason. I guess you don't have to answer that right now if you don't want to. Look at us. We hardly know each other . . . really, and . . . there's no reason why you should be willing to answer such questions."

"That's what we're doing here, Jane. We're getting to know each other. You are welcome to ask me anything you like. If I don't want to answer a question, I'll tell you, but you're not going to offend me."

"Or at least if I did you'd tell me about it."

He laughed softly, but the tension in his laughter was evident. "Yes, I suppose I would. And I hope you would do the same."

"So . . . is there a reason? You don't strike me as the type to just . . . not go to church because it takes too much effort. And you certainly don't seem like a rebel, like you'd be trying to prove something by rebelling against beliefs you were raised with."

Alex blew out a long, slow breath. He glanced around to see that the mall was becoming more crowded, but their bench was out of the way, and no one was paying attention to them. "I don't have a problem with putting effort into something if I believe in it. Maybe I am trying to prove something; I don't know, but . . ."

"You just said you believe the Church is true, that you believe in God. Then you said you don't have a problem putting effort into something you believe in."

"Which means it's not about the effort, Jane. I suppose there is a bit of a rebellious streak in me, but not like there used to be."

"What do you mean?"

"Quite frankly, in high school I was smoking, getting drunk on weekends. I contemplated drugs, but I knew that was just a little too stupid, even for me. About the time I made a decision to never do drugs, I quit smoking and getting drunk."

"So . . . you were what? Out of the habit of going to church?"

"Yes, but . . . it's more complicated than that."

Alex sensed her frustration, and while he couldn't blame her, he felt it was important to make a point. "Jane, I know you have certain expectations, and if we're considering a serious relationship, then you have a right to those expectations. I can well understand how my attitudes could be disappointing for you, but . . . you need to hear me out. You asked if there was a reason, and I'm getting to that. I'm not inactive because I'm lazy or defiant. I have some issues; I know that. But until you've taken some time to seriously consider those issues and the reasons for them, you can't stand on the outside and judge a person for making the choice not to attend church meetings."

Jane realized that he was very kindly and appropriately telling her not to be judgmental. It only took her a moment to realize that she had been just exactly that. But she felt grateful that he was obviously not a man prone to get angry or defensive. She was quick to say, "Forgive me. You're right. I don't know enough about you to understand your choices." She met his eyes. "But I want to."

Alex let her words sink in, reinforcing the evidence of her humility and compassion. "I told you already that when I was thirteen, my father left us for another woman." She nodded and he continued. "My parents were married in the temple, Jane. We were the model family. I mean, we certainly weren't perfect, but we had a relatively happy home. We held family home evening, and prayed, and read the scriptures together. Certainly not every day without fail, but we did pretty well. My parents both had prominent callings in the ward. And then it hit. The woman he'd been sleeping with decided to come clean. She went to her bishop, confessed everything, and my father was caught with his hand in the cookie jar. He'd apparently had no desire to confess or make it right; he was angry that he'd been caught. I remember the arguments between my parents as he tried to justify his reasons for pretending that he was worthy to have a Church calling and take the sacrament. He was angry with her because she wouldn't forgive him and let him stay, when he apparently had no remorse and couldn't understand why everyone was so upset. He was excommunicated and moved in with the woman he'd been cheating with. Two broken families—in the same ward."

Jane took a sharp breath. She knew what that meant. He'd been cheating with someone that they knew and trusted. She took Alex's hand and gave it a compassionate squeeze as he continued. "Then the real grief began. Everything went right for my father, while everything went wrong for us. The software company he'd been working for suddenly took off. He was promoted and started raking in big bucks. Our financial security went down the toilet. We had one problem after another: sickness, accidents, you name it. Such things on top of long-term financial challenges became very wearing. But the worst of it, on top of everything else, was the way everything at church changed. The other family moved away, but we stayed because our home was there and we loved it. Some people were accepting and kind and supportive. But others just never looked at us the same after that. It was as if we'd been forever tainted by my father's sins. My mother cried every Sunday after church. I actually heard a lady once ask her what she'd done to drive him away." His voice picked up an edge of anger. "He *cheated* on her. He *betrayed* her. She was a good woman, and whatever problems there may have been between them that I might not have known about, *that* was not the solution. Worst of all, he was a hypocrite about it, putting on a perfect face to the world—and his family—while he was willfully breaking his most sacred covenants."

Alex sighed and looked away. "So when I was fifteen I just . . . quit going to church. I'd put up with it long enough. I stopped exposing myself to the judgments of others. As I told you, I went through a severely rebellious stage. Before I graduated from high school, I realized that if I was ever going to meet my goal of becoming a doctor, I needed to act like a man and be responsible. In spite of my substance abuse, I still managed to pull good grades. I wanted to be a doctor, and I knew I needed to get a scholarship to get me started, or I'd never make it." Alex debated whether or not to express his next thought, then he realized that she shouldn't have to wonder. He looked directly at her and added, "You need to know, Jane, that for all my stupidity, I was never promiscuous. I steered clear of girls altogether, for the most part. Maybe I didn't want to have any kind of behavior in common with my father; I don't know, but . . . morality issues were never among my problems. I want you to know that."

He saw tears come to her eyes, and she gave him a wan smile. "Thank you," she said. "It is nice not to have to wonder."

Alex took a deep breath and leaned back. "For the sake of clarification, I want you to know that I've put a fair amount of effort into solving this problem. I'm relatively certain of the reasoning you might use to counter my grounds for being inactive, so we'll just clear those out of the way. I am well aware that this is Christ's church, and whether or not I go should not be determined by the bad behavior of some of its members. I am also well aware that my father's poor choices and hypocrisy are no excuse for me to stay away. I know that this is my problem, not his. The truth is that I can't even walk into a church without having it all come back to me. I've had counseling, to be completely truthful. I've sorted it through, stewed over it, analyzed it until it nearly ruined me. Then one day I just . . . decided that I didn't have to go to church to be a good person. Since then, my only sin has been that I have an occasional drink—socially." He sighed. "But I think I could give that up . . . if you asked me to." She said nothing, and he added, "Of course, if you don't want anything to do with me now, I understand. Really, I do." He took both her hands and looked into her eyes. "Jane, I respect your convictions. I really do. And I would never ask you to marry me unless I was willing and worthy to go to the temple. But I'll be the first to admit that I have a hard time with it."

"Do you think it's possible?" she asked. "Do you think you'll ever come to terms with it . . . enough to turn it around? Because if the answer is no, then . . . well . . . we can be friends, but . . . I won't settle for less, Alex. I won't." Tears trickled down her face, and he wiped them away.

"And I wouldn't want you to," he said gently. "Truthfully, I don't know. I think a part of me has always wanted to go back, to have religion be a part of my life, but . . . you don't have to be religious to be spiritual."

"And you don't have to be spiritual to be religious," she countered. "But . . . I know that being both brings about great blessings in a person's life. You must know that God's hand is in your life, that He blesses and guides you."

"Until I met you, I wasn't so sure about that. But I must admit I've softened in that regard. It actually occurred to me while I was lying in bed last night that . . . maybe it happened this way because I needed irrefutable evidence that He brought us togther, that He is mindful of me. I feel very humbled that, in spite of my challenges, He would still bless me so indisputably." He touched her face as if they'd been close for months, not hours. "Be patient with me, Jane. Only time will tell if this relationship has what it takes to last forever."

He saw her smile and felt immeasurably grateful for her acceptance. He resisted the urge to kiss her, even though the moment would have been perfect. While their conversations and confessions had taken their relationship to an emotional level that he doubted many people reached through months of dating—if ever—he still had to concede that it was technically their first date, and he wasn't about to blow it by moving too quickly. He needed to hold to his word that they were starting over in that regard; he needed to earn her trust back after blowing it once before. Instead he indulged in a fantasy of what it might be like when he *did* kiss her again. Whenever and however it happened, he would make sure it was a kiss they would recall fondly for the rest of their lives.

"Of course," she said and laid her head on his shoulder.

Alex put his arm around her and hoped that somehow, someday, he could get beyond the inner demons that held him back. Jane Layton deserved to be happy, and he longed to be the man to make it happen.

"Should we walk?" he asked.

"Give me a few minutes," she said. "I think I'm exhausted."

"Yeah, me too," he chuckled.

"I like it right here," she said.

"It is a nice bench," he commented lightly.

She chuckled and snuggled a little closer, adjusting her head against his shoulder. "No, I mean . . . right here."

A few minutes later she reluctantly declared the need to stretch her legs. "And a ladies room wouldn't hurt."

After finding the restrooms, they walked the mall a while longer, talking as they aimlessly browsed through a number of stores. Alex stopped to buy some chocolate mints out of a machine and pulled the change out of his pocket to look for the correct amount. Jane noticed that in his hand, along with some coins, were a pair of nail clippers, and a ring.

"What is this?" she asked, picking it up. Alex saw her eyes sparkle with fascination as she added, "It must have a story behind it."

"It does," he said while Jane admired the ring. She felt thoroughly intrigued as she wondered what would make a man like Alex carry something like this in his pocket.

Once he'd gotten the mints out of the machine, he put one in Jane's mouth and then his own before they started walking again, and he said, "That ring belonged to my great-great-grandfather. Truthfully, I know very little about him. But he was somewhat of a hero to my mother. That ring was passed down and is the only possession my mother has from any of her ancestors. She gave it to me when I got my medical degree; she told me the man who owned it would be proud of me. But it's too small." He chuckled. "Not that I'd wear it anyway; it's really not my style, but . . . it has great meaning, so I carry it."

"That is so sweet," Jane said and tried it on. She found that it was too large for every finger except her thumb, and even then it was doubtful that she could keep it on. She held it up and admired it again. "It kind of reminds me of those mood rings from the seventies; my dad had one."

"That's exactly what I thought," he said with a little laugh. "I believe it's an opal, but the band is actually quite fascinating."

"Yes, it is," Jane agreed and handed it back to him. He slipped the ring into his pocket and took her hand.

As they walked, Jane asked him questions about his childhood and his family, which he answered eagerly. He talked about the close relationship he had with his mother, which made up for the way he felt barely acquainted with his sisters. They had both left home during his rebellious years, and were both now married and raising children.

"Are they active in the Church?" she asked.

"Becca is," he said, "but Charlotte isn't. She rebelled before I did; married outside the Church."

"So, you're not the only casualty of your father's sins," she said, hoping he wouldn't be offended by such a comment. Instead his eyes seemed to grasp some profound meaning from her words.

"No," he said, "I'm not the only casualty."

"How has your mother dealt with it?"

"Incredibly well overall. Those first few years were really tough on her, on all of us. But she never questioned God, never stopped going to church or being faithful. Once she found a way to support us comfortably and be at home, she gradually started coming back to life. She's amazing."

"I can't wait to meet her," Jane said, and Alex smiled. He loved every inference that they would be together for the rest of their lives—even though it still felt a little crazy.

"I'm looking forward to that, myself," he said. "Hey, are you getting hungry again? I am."

"I could stand to eat," she said, and they found the mall food court.

Once they were seated over a couple of deli sandwiches, he said, "Now, you've asked me questions about myself for about twelve hours."

She glanced at her watch, "No, two."

"Okay two, twelve. What's the difference? It's my turn. You haven't even told me where you're from. Not Utah, I'm betting."

"What makes you think so?"

"I don't know. Just a hunch."

"Well, I'm from California, Sacramento area." She went on to tell him about her family and her upbringing. She was the middle child of seven; four of her siblings had been married in the temple. One was serving a mission, and the youngest was in high school. She told him a great deal about each of them, but he figured it would take time to remember all their names. Her father was co-owner of a company that grew and sold plants, flowers, and trees. He had been a bishop more than once and had served on the stake high council, among other callings. Her mother taught third grade and was currently the Primary president. She said more than once that she couldn't wait for him to meet her family, but he wasn't so sure her family—especially her parents—would be pleased with the man their daughter had fallen in love with.

After they had eaten and browsed a bit more while they talked, Alex glanced at his watch and said, "I really hate to say this, but . . . I have to be at work in a little over an hour. I need to take you home."

She pushed her lip out with an exaggerated pout which made him laugh, then he put his arm around her shoulders and they walked to the car. While he was driving, she said, "Will I get to see you tomorrow?"

"Maybe," he said. "I have a shift at the hospital that starts early evening."

"And I get out of church at noon," she said.

He was relieved to hear that, since he wouldn't be getting to bed until very late, and he was accustomed to being able to catch up on some sleep. "Okay, well . . . call me, or I'll call you."

"We'd have to exchange phone numbers to do that," she said and pulled a pen out of her purse. She took his hand and wrote her number on it, then she wrote his on her own hand when he told it to her.

"Can I get this tattooed?" he asked, looking closely at the number.

"Don't do that. My number might change."

"Oh, good point. I should just get Jane tattooed on my shoulder."

"No, don't do that, either. I'd prefer that you just hold it in your heart."

"I think I just might do that," he said and took her hand.

"On the chance that you stick it out with me, I'd really prefer no tattoos."

"Well, I already have one that says Mother," he said, then laughed when her eyes widened. "Just kidding. Don't worry. My levels of stupidity and self-destruction only descend so deep."

At the risk of souring the mood between them, Jane said, "You mean like having a drink occasionally?"

He looked a little taken aback but simply said, "Yeah, like that."

"You told me you might be willing to give it up . . . if I asked you to. Did you mean it?"

"Are you asking?"

"You've only known me less than a week. Maybe it's ludicrous for me to expect you to do anything . . . just because I ask it."

"It only took about five minutes for me to be willing to do whatever you might ask of me."

"So, if I asked you to go to church with me . . ."

"That one might take some time," he said without looking at her.

"Okay," she said. "It's okay, really. I'm not here to try and change you, and I really can understand why it's difficult for you."

"Thank you," he said. Several minutes of silence passed before he added, "I'll give up the drinking—not that I was doing it that much anyway, but . . . consider it done."

"Thank you," she said and kissed his hand.

Jane found it difficult to say good-bye at the door, but it was evident that he felt the same way. They shared a hug that felt more like the embrace of dear friends than anything romantic.

"I'll talk to you tomorrow," he said, walking toward the car.

"Thanks for a wonderful day," she called.

"My pleasure," he called back, and she went into the house.

Jane found her Aunt Marla in the kitchen, perusing a recipe book. "Hi there," she said as Jane opened the fridge to pour herself a glass of juice. "How did it go?"

"Where do I start?" Jane asked with a little laugh. "He is the most . . . amazing man I have ever met."

Marla closed the recipe book and leaned her elbows on the table. "I want to hear everything," she said with a childish grin. "And then after you tell me, you'd better call and tell your mother."

"Yeah, I think I'd better," Jane said.

As easily as if she were talking to a best friend, Jane told her aunt the story from the beginning. Marla was amazed at what she called obvious miracles in their coming together and the way they felt. She expressed some concern over his reluctance to be active in the Church, but she echoed Jane's thoughts clearly when she said, "It sounds like he's got it in him somewhere. Maybe you're what he needs to bring about some good changes in his life, as long as you hold to your convictions."

"I hope so," she said. "But I don't want him to feel like I'm trying to change *him*."

"As long as your boundaries are clear and you stand by them, there's no reason you can't let him know that you care for him unconditionally."

"Yes, I'm sure you're right," Jane said, then her thoughts wandered to how it had felt to cry in Alex Keane's arms.

"So," Marla said, startling her, "do you think he's the one?"

"Well . . . obviously it's far too soon to know any such thing. But, truthfully, I've never felt this way before. And he feels the same way. I really don't think time will change those feelings."

"You're in love with him, then," Marla said with a smile.

"Does it sound immature and silly to say that I am, when I've known him so short a time?"

Marla reached a hand across the table and took Jane's. "It would sound immature and silly if you were telling me that you were getting married next month and you believed that you knew everything you needed to know in order to make a good marriage. But you're telling me you have strong feelings for someone, a good man with a good heart, and the two of you are communicating openly and are willing to give the relationship time to evolve. I think it's not so difficult to fall in love with someone. The trick is whether or not you can truly *love* them—forever, no matter what you might come up against. And to know if he can love you the way you deserve to be loved. You have the gift of the Holy Ghost, my dear. It speaks to you through your thoughts and feelings. As long as you keep paying attention, you'll know what to do."

Jane contemplated her aunt's wisdom, then she called her mother and had a nearly identical conversation. Jane was concerned with how her parents might feel about her getting serious with a man who wasn't active in the Church. But she felt a deep gratitude when her mother simply said, "It's so sad to see the innocent victims of such sin and hypocrisy. You certainly can't blame a man for struggling with that. His issues probably have a lot more to do with his father than with religion itself."

"I'm sure you're right."

"And I'm sure he'll come around; if he's the right man for you, he'll come around."

Jane could hardly sleep that night as she recounted all that had changed in her life since she'd gotten out of bed that morning. Alex Keane loved her. And she loved him. Now she was on the brink of a journey that would prove whether or not that love could stand the test of time.

* * * * *

While Alex worked his shift at the restaurant, he couldn't help being preoccupied with his encounter here one week ago—and all the magic that had happened in his life since. As he drove home, he pondered the conversations he had shared with Jane and the wonder of her feelings for him, her compassion, her kindness, her support. He felt completely overwhelmed and wondered how long it would take him to fully accept all that had been said, all that had changed. He finally slept and woke to the phone ringing.

"Hi," he heard Jane say, and he felt a deep relief to know that his time with her hadn't been some kind of dream.

"Hello, gorgeous," he said.

"Hey, my aunt and uncle want to meet you. Dinner's at two. What do you say?"

"Um . . ." Alex forced himself to come fully awake. "Um . . . are you sure you're ready to have me meet family? I mean . . . maybe they'll be disappointed in me and advise you not to date me."

"Sorry to burst your bubble, Alex, but they already know every-thing, and they still want to meet you."

"Everything?" he echoed.

"Well, not *everything*," she corrected. "But they know enough that they're not going to invite you to church or anything. They want to meet you."

"Well, okay," he said. "If you're not ashamed of me, then . . . I won't turn down a real dinner, especially if you're going to be there."

"Great," she said. "I'll see you at two. It's casual."

Alex felt distinctly nervous as he knocked at the front door, but once he'd met Jeff and Marla, he had to admit that he felt completely comfortable. They were warm and friendly, and he felt some relief in knowing that they knew he didn't necessarily measure up to the religious standards of a clearly religious family. He enjoyed their visit as much as he enjoyed the home-cooked meal of roast beef, potatoes and gravy, and cooked carrots. He loved the way Jane held his hand and kept looking at him as if he were the beginning and end of all life for her. Perhaps he appreciated the overt evidence of her feelings because he felt the same way about her. It was nice not to have to wonder where he stood.

After he insisted on helping wash the dishes, Marla called Jane's parents, and he officially met them over the phone. Walter and Louisa Layton were also very kind and seemed pleased with their daughter's association with him. He wondered why he had expected them to look down at him and be judgmental over his choices. Judging by the daughter they'd raised, however, he probably should have known better.

Alex hated having to leave to go and get ready for work. At home he made a quick call to his mother, certain he'd missed her attempt to call him. He apologized and gave her a three-minute explanation of what had happened concerning Jane. First she laughed and said it certainly was destiny, then she sounded like she might cry as she told him how happy she was that he'd found a wonderful girl. He promised to catch her up on more details later, then he went to the hospital; even there he felt happier than he ever had, and he couldn't deny a new sense of purpose in all that he was doing. Just past nine o'clock, he was leaning at the main desk of the ER, signing off a patient to be admitted to the cardiology unit when he heard one of the nurses say, "There's someone here to see you, Dr. Keane. Says her name is Jane. Should I let her in?"

"By all means," Alex said, and a minute later he looked up to see Jane standing there, a plate in her hands, a bright smile on her face.

"Hello," she said. "I hope it's okay that I came here."

"Of course it is," he said. "Just . . . give me a second."

Jane observed Alex in this setting where he was obviously very comfortable. He wore green hospital scrubs and a hospital badge that hung on a cord around his neck. It clearly read: Dr. Alex Keane. She watched him write some things on a paper, which he handed to a nurse as he said, "Mr. Billings is ready to go upstairs. I promised him a pretty nurse would take him up, so you'd better do it yourself."

"Yes, Doctor," she said with a little laugh.

"I'm taking a break. I'll be in the lounge if you need me."

"No problem," the nurse said, tossing a smile toward Jane.

"Hi," Alex said with a smile as he approached her.

"Hi," she said again and held out the plate which he could now see held frosted brownies beneath a layer of plastic wrap. "You weren't able to stay long enough for us to make dessert. Marla suggested some chocolate might help you get through your shift."

"Can't hurt," he chuckled. "Thank you." He took the plate in one hand and her arm in the other, urging her into a room nearby. She noted a fridge, a small counter with a microwave, a coffee maker, and a few odds and ends. There was a table with chairs around it, and a couple of couches. He sat down on one of the couches and urged her beside him before he pulled back the plastic wrap and took out a brownie. After taking a bite, he said, "This is marvelous. Don't tell me you're a fabulous cook as well as being gorgeous, sweet, sensitive, and a marvelous dancer."

"It's Marla's secret recipe, but I did make them myself."

"You're a genius," he said and took another bite. Then he put it in front of her mouth, and she took a bite of his brownie.

"I already had more than my fair share," she said and licked chocolate frosting from her lip.

When she didn't get it all, Alex resisted the urge to kiss it away. Instead he wiped it away with his finger, then put it in his own mouth. "It's even better that way," he said with a wink, and she laughed.

"So," she said, taking hold of his ID badge, "you really are a doctor."

"Sort of," he said. "I have a medical degree, but around here I'm very low on the totem pole. I take care of the simple stuff, do what I'm told, and mostly observe when the real scary stuff comes in."

"One step at a time, right?"

"That's right."

They talked for a few more minutes before a different nurse pushed the door open abruptly and said with urgency, "We've got three victims from a traffic accident coming in. They're two minutes out."

"I'm there," he said, coming to his feet as the nurse left the room.

"Guess I'd better go," Jane said as they both stood.

"I'm glad you came." He took both her hands into his. "You're timing was good. If you'd come ten minutes later I wouldn't have been able to see you." He pressed a quick kiss to her brow. "Drive home safely."

"I will, thank you. I'll see you tomorrow."

Jane watched him hurry out of the room. She stepped into the hall to see several medical personnel gathered together near a set of double doors. Alex joined them while a nurse helped him pull a plastic gown over his scrubs and tie it behind his back. He glanced over his shoulder at Jane, giving her a smile and a wink.

"There it is," she heard a voice say and realized an ambulance had just pulled up on the other side of those doors. Suddenly everyone rushed into a flurry of organized chaos as the first patient was brought in. She watched Alex moving alongside the gurney as it was rolled into a room with bright lights and vast amounts of medical equipment. A paramedic walked beside him, giving a report in words that Jane didn't understand, but she knew it was serious. Then they disappeared into the room, and the doors were closed.

Jane left the hospital and drove home, wondering what she had done to deserve having such an incredible man fall in love with her. She'd never really stopped to ponder the kind of man she might end up with, as far as what his profession might be. Perhaps she'd imagined he might also be a teacher, since it was something she related to. But it had never occurred to her that she might end up with a doctor. At this point, she could only hope that when all was said and done, she really would end up with him. He was truly amazing.

* * * * *

During the next couple of weeks, Alex saw Jane every possible minute. Some days that wasn't much, and others not at all. Coordinating their schedules, especially when his shifts at the hospital regularly changed, sometimes felt practically impossible. He managed to make it to some of the group dance rehearsals, and private rehearsals were scheduled for him and Jane. If they were really lucky, they would get a little time before or after to talk or get a quick bite to eat. He was grateful for the way Brent held to his promise and helped Alex with some things that would have taken even more time out of his life. Brent had quickly noticed Alex's intense interest in Jane and had insisted that Alex tell him the whole story. Brent was thrilled to see Alex actually dating for a change, but he regularly teased Alex about the fact that he owed Brent at least some of the credit for bringing him and Jane together. Alex couldn't deny that Brent was right.

In spite of Brent's help, Alex felt ridiculously busy, but then, he'd felt that way since the day he'd started medical school, which had made his previous years of college seem like a piece of cake. Still, he'd never felt happier. The more he got to know this incredible woman, the more he loved her. The only thing that created any concern between them at all was his issue about not going to church, and her firm convictions that he should. But even in that there was a fixed mutual respect. She made it clear that it was important to her and she would prefer that he embrace his beliefs completely, but she also made it clear that she couldn't possibly see inside of his heart and understand the pain and grief associated with the issue. And she loved him anyway. Jane's attitude persuaded him to look inside himself and consider the source of the issue more than he had in years. She certainly made him want to be a better man. But he always hit a brick wall. Somewhere inside it just reached a point where it didn't completely add up; he simply knew that the very idea of going to church made him highly uncomfortable. He concluded that he could be a righteous and spiritual man without actually attending church meetings. Jane agreed with that, but made the point that in order for him to get a temple recommend, he would have to resolve his issue and conform to the standards of the Church. And he had to agree with that, but at the present time it didn't give him the incentive to do anything about it. They weren't in a position to be seriously considering marriage anyway. Perhaps when that time came, he would be able to cross this difficult bridge. He simply asked her to be patient with him, and she made it clear that she had no intention of ever living without him—for any reason.

Jane looked back over the weeks since she'd met Alex, and she couldn't comprehend life before then. She was continually amazed at how much they had in common, how thoroughly they enjoyed each other's company, and how perfectly happy she felt to simply be sharing her life with him as far as it was possible under the circumstances. His reluctance to be fully active in the Church certainly concerned her, but she had a great deal of evidence that he was a good man, and in every other way he was the perfect man for her. She had prayerfully considered the circumstances, and in her heart she believed that eventually he would come around. She simply had to hold to her own convictions and love him unconditionally—which wasn't at all difficult. He was an easy man to love. And he was an easy man to talk to. Through many deep conversations, it was evident that his belief in God was firm, and that at some level he knew that the church he belonged to was true. She challenged him to pay his tithing—something he'd not done since his early youth. He said he'd think about it, and a few days later he told her that he'd asked his home teacher to get him some tithing envelopes and that from now on he would pay it. Until then, Jane hadn't realized that Alex received regular visits from home teachers, and while he kindly refused their persuasion to get him to go to church, he did enjoy their visits and the message they shared. Jane felt some peace to see the steps Alex was taking, and she felt certain that with time he would find his way to the temple. On that day her joy would be full.

In the meantime, Jane simply enjoyed this blossoming relationship. She was both disappointed and deeply impressed that with the passing of weeks he had never even attempted to kiss her lips. He'd certainly had many opportunities, and she would often catch his eye and imagine that he was seriously considering a kiss. But as of yet, it hadn't happened. He'd kissed her hands countless times, her brow, her cheeks, the top of her head—but beyond those first kisses at the conclusion of that memorable waltz, he had never kissed her lips.

On their one-month anniversary from the day they had first met in the restaurant, Alex insisted that he was taking Jane out for a nice dinner. He'd been putting a little money aside with this in mind. As they sat across from each other in a fine restaurant, Jane watched him closely while he talked about a particularly difficult trauma that had occurred in the emergency room that day. She felt such a deep respect for his gift of compassion that went so perfectly with his gift to offer medical aid quickly and efficiently. He talked of how it had made him feel to see a young woman die following a car accident, and of his helplessness over not being able to keep her here in spite of all of his training, not to mention that of the personnel working with him. Jane felt touched by his candid discussion of his own feelings, and she realized then that they shared an emotional intimacy that was no small thing. She'd spent years hearing her peers talk about their relationships, and she suspected that such intimacy was rare in dating—especially at this stage of their association.

As Alex completed sharing his day's events, Jane reached across the table and touched his face. "I love you, Alex Keane. I think you're an amazing man."

He chuckled softly. "I don't think I could ever be amazing enough to deserve the way you love me. But I'm grateful . . . because I love you too."

He took her hand into his, and in his typical way he pressed his lips into her palm while he kept his eyes intently focused on hers. She relished the expected tremor that reverberated up her arm and landed in her stomach with a distinct flutter. "I love it when you do that . . . the way you do that."

"Well then, I'll do it again." He took her other hand and did the same thing. "A kiss is a very profound thing, you know." He said it as if he'd contemplated the matter deeply—and perhaps he suspected that she had too. "I think that kissing is treated way too lightly in this world. It's my personal belief that if people took kissing more seriously, it would solve a vast amount of the world's problems."

He said it with a serious voice but a sparkle in his eyes. Jane laughed quietly and said, "I'm sure you're right."

The subject of kissing was dropped when their meal was brought to the table. They talked constantly through the meal and stayed a long while chatting even after they'd finished eating. Once outside, holding hands, Alex hesitated on the sidewalk some distance from the restaurant doors and looked upward at the star-filled sky. "What a beautiful night," he said.

"Yes, it is," she eagerly agreed.

"Let's dance," he said, urging her into a dramatic waltz step. She laughed as he lowered her back into a histrionic dip, holding her there for several seconds with her head nearly upside down. He lifted her back up and continued to dance as seriously as they would at a rehearsal.

"I hate to point out the obvious," she said as he urged her into a twirl and then back into a classic waltz. "But there's no music."

Alex urged her closer and put his lips close to her ear while they continued to dance. "We don't need any music," he said.

A warm shiver rushed down her spine. She relaxed her head against his shoulder as they danced to the silence of the night sky. With no warning he compelled her into a vibrant spin that made her dizzy and got her laughing. Then abruptly he stopped, holding her waist to keep the motion from pulling her away from him. She looked up at him and became immediately fixated on the intensity of his gaze. And then it happened. She held her breath as he lowered his lips to hers. The magic she'd felt from that first waltz, that first kiss, now magnified tenfold and encompassed her entire being the moment their lips met. In one swirling moment, she felt hot and cold, weak and strong, completely lost and forever found. His kiss was meek and unassuming, yet warm and lengthy, as if he was determined to savor the moment fully without being intrepid. When their lips finally parted, she slowly opened her eyes and forced herself to breathe.

"I have wanted to do that for so long," he murmured quietly.

"So why did you wait until now?" she asked, touching his face.

"I was waiting for the perfect moment," he said. "I wanted it to be a kiss so memorable that you would one day tell our grandchildren about it. I imagined you as a little old lady, with a sparkle in your eyes and a dreamy voice, telling them about this kiss."

"So much like our *first* kiss."

"Yes," he said. "After being such a fool over that, I wanted to wait long enough that . . . you wouldn't have to wonder about my motives.

As I said, kissing is taken far too lightly in this world."

"Who taught you that?"

"My mother, actually. You can't give me credit for anything I just said. It was a lecture I got from her several times."

"But you were listening . . . and you followed her advice. I can give you credit for that."

"I suppose you can," he said.

"Still . . . I really like your mother."

"So do I," Alex said and kissed her once more before he put his arm around her shoulders and guided her toward the car.

Once he was driving, Jane took his hand and said, "It worked."

"What?"

"It was the perfect moment . . . and very memorable."

"Yes, it was," he said and kissed her hand.

"And now I can stop wondering if it was just my bad breath that put you off."

Alex chuckled. "Not hardly. But even if you *did* have bad breath . . . I'd kiss you anyway. I'd just give you a mint first."

$$— 5 —$$

The next morning Alex was awakened by a knock at his door. He pulled on a bathrobe and stumbled to answer it, only to find himself facing Jane Layton. He was a little taken aback, since she'd never been to his apartment before.

"Good morning," he said, rubbing a hand over his face to help himself wake up.

"I just wanted to see you for a minute before my first class. After classes I have work, and by the time I get off, you'll—"

"Be at the hospital, I know," he said. He motioned her inside. "I'm glad you came. It's good to see you. Except now you'll know how I live." He flipped on a light since the blinds were closed. "It's really a dump, to be truthful. But I don't have to put up with room-mates, and the rent is cheap."

"It's not so bad," she said, looking around. Being a studio apart-ment, everything was pretty much altogether in one room, except for a little bathroom built into a corner. Beyond the bed being rumpled from recent use, the place was actually quite tidy and clean. She took notice of some framed pictures and recognized his mother and sisters from other photographs he'd shown her.

Alex leaned against the door and watched Jane take in his living quarters. He couldn't resist saying, "You did this on purpose, didn't you? You came here at a moment when my guard was down, and you were completely unexpected so that you could spy on me and see if I'm really a slob, or if I have any sick habits."

"Maybe," she said with a sly smile. "I wasn't really worried about any sick habits." She noticed some magazine pictures taped to the mirror and stepped closer to examine them. One was a home, simple but beautiful, not overly large or extravagant, Victorian style, with a wrap-around porch and white shutters. The other was a black Ferrari. "What are these?" she asked, and he moved to a chair to sit down.

"Goals," he said. "When I was quite young, I showed my mother a picture of a black Ferrari and told her one day that's what I was going to drive. A somewhat shallow goal, perhaps, but . . . she didn't tell me I was silly or impertinent. She just told me that in order to drive a car like that, I would need to work hard to make that much money. She also told me that the real pleasure in owning such a car would be in knowing that the car itself was only a thing; that such a possession should never represent pride or arrogance, but rather it should be a personal symbol of achieving something I'd worked hard for. This was near the same time I decided I wanted to be a doctor. So . . . it just kind of became a symbol to me. When I can make enough money to drive a car like that, then . . ."

"You'll know you've made it," she said with a smile. Alex knew well enough that she was not a woman to be impressed by a hot car. He hoped that she knew he meant it when he said that his desire for it was not something arrogant. As with everything, he sensed that she respected his feelings and opinions, and she would support him in anything he chose to do—well, almost anything. He doubted that she'd be very happy if he took up drinking again. But he had no intention of ever doing that. With her by his side, why would he ever want to?

"And the house?" she asked, pointing to the other picture.

"The same, in a way," he said. "I just . . . saw that picture one day, and thought, 'That's the kind of home I'd like to live in someday.' So . . . those pictures kind of keep me going when things get tough."

Jane smiled at him again, but her voice was earnest as she asked, "May I live there with you? It doesn't matter where it is, so long as I can be your wife and live there with you."

"I'm counting on it," he said, loving the way she wasn't afraid to say exactly what she felt for fear of being forward or presumptuous. Their eyes met with a time-stopping gaze that wasn't uncommon, and he added, "I love you, Jane Layton."

"I love you too, Alex Keane."

She glanced down and laughed softly. "You know the real reason I came here, don't you?"

"No, tell me. I mean . . . besides seeing my Ferrari picture."

"Well . . . you are the man who kissed me last night, aren't you?"

"I'd better be," he said and she laughed.

"Oh, there's no doubt about it," she said. "And I was hoping that maybe . . . I could get another one to get me through a long day."

"I could probably do that," he said with a crooked smile that made Jane laugh again. "Except I just woke up and I have morning breath. Until we're married I don't think you really want to deal with my morning breath."

"I really don't care," she said as Alex stood up and walked across the room to face her. He touched her face, then bent to give her a gentle kiss. Jane let out a long, dreamy sigh and said, "Okay, I think I can make it on that." She moved toward the door and added, "I've got to go. Call me on your break."

"I'll do that," he said and watched her leave, after which he perfectly echoed Jane's long, dreamy sigh.

A few days later, Jane's car was in for a minor repair. She got a ride to the hospital so that she could take Alex's car to do some errands while he worked. She picked him up when his shift was finished and drove to his apartment. When they went inside, she had the table set for two, candles ready to light, and dinner prepared.

"You sneaky little thing," he said, giving her a quick kiss.

"I think I'd like to cook supper for you every day of my life."

"How very traditional of you," he said. "But you're going to be teaching school when you're not raising kids, so maybe I should help with the cooking more than once in a while."

"Okay," she said. "And sometimes . . . we can go out, or order pizza, right? Because you'll be a doctor and we'll be able to afford it, right?"

"You bet we will," he said and kissed her again before they sat down together to eat, then he insisted on washing the dishes.

Later, after Alex had taken Jane home, he returned to his apartment and noticed a little picture of the Salt Lake Temple taped to his mirror along with the pictures of the car and the house that had been there since he'd moved in. He couldn't help smiling at the implication. *A goal,* he thought, and left it there.

* * * * *

With a day off, Alex forced himself to do a number of things that he was behind on—things that Brent couldn't do for him. Most specifically, he needed to pay his bills and balance his checking account. Going over his finances, he felt decidedly discouraged. He had no debt beyond the huge accumulation of student loans, and his bills were all current. But the move to Michigan was going to take most of what he had been putting away for that purpose, and his rent there would be more expensive. His salary would increase, but it was still going to take a long time to pay off the student loans and actually start making any profit from all he'd invested in his education. He was concerned about his car, fearing that a number of things were barely hanging on. His instincts told him he shouldn't be driving it to Michigan, that he should be getting something different. But even payments on a better used car would be difficult to manage at this point if he was going to keep up the payment schedule on the student loan. In reality, he'd had the option to wait until he'd completed his residency before making payments on the loan, but he was determined to get out of debt as quickly as possible. Now that the payment arrangements had been made, he couldn't back down on them.

Deciding he'd just have to hope the car lasted and do the best he could, he finished up and left the apartment to mail his bills and go to the bank. At the teller's window, he handed her his deposit and the payment for his student loan, then he became distracted by a young boy trying to blow up a balloon while his mother did her transaction at the next window. He wondered what it would be like to have children of his own; he thought of having them with Jane and couldn't help smiling.

He was startled when the teller said to him, "I'm afraid there's a problem."

Now what? he moaned inwardly. Had he messed up on his math in the checkbook? Was he overdrawn? Had something bounced?

"You don't need to make this payment," she said, sliding the check and loan coupon back toward him. "The loan has been paid in full."

"What?" Alex countered, then laughed. As wonderful as that sounded, he knew it had to be a mistake. "That can't be right."

"Well," she stated, "you're Alexander Keane, right?"

"Right."

"It says here that the balance was paid in full last week."

"But . . . that can't be. That's thousands of dollars. There must be somebody else with an account here who meant to pay off *their* loan, and it went into the wrong account. It just can't be right."

"Just a minute," she said and pushed some buttons on her computer to lock it while she stepped away. A few minutes later she came back and said, "No mistake. The loan has been paid in full."

"But . . . who . . . would do that?" Alex stammered.

"I don't know," she said, handing him a receipt for his deposit. "You might check with the student financial office that originally gave you the loan. Maybe they can tell you."

"Thank you," Alex said and left the bank. He sat in the car for nearly ten minutes just trying to make sense of such an incredible occurrence. For the life of him he couldn't think of anyone who would do such a thing for him—at least not anybody who would remotely have that much money. Deciding he'd get nowhere just sitting there, he drove to the campus and went to the office of financial aid where he had submitted all the paperwork for the government-funded loans that had helped him get through school. Once he'd had his degree for two semesters, a bank had taken over the loan that had accumulated through the years, and he'd had to start making payments. He explained the situation to the girl at the desk. She left and came back with a man following her. He looked vaguely familiar, and Alex felt certain he had worked with this man at some stage of the financial process.

"Alex," he said, extending a handshake, "I must say I expected to see you in here sooner or later."

"Why is that?" Alex asked, and the man guided him into his office and closed the door.

"Well," he said, sitting behind the desk and motioning Alex into a chair opposite, "I felt sure you'd be wondering why your loan had been paid in full."

"You got that right. So . . . are you telling me it *has* been paid in full? It's not a mistake?"

"No mistake."

"But . . . who . . . why?" Alex stammered, unable to believe it. There had to be a catch.

"The loan was paid by an anonymous donor; someone who simply wanted to help a potentially great doctor get a good start. Apparently you were chosen because your grade level and your performance record were especially excellent. That's all I can tell you."

"Unbelievable," Alex muttered, suddenly finding it difficult to breathe. He thought of the amounts that had accumulated through the years, all being blended together and deferred until he got his degree. In spite of earning some scholarships, he'd had to make a huge investment to get this far. He heard the man across the desk chuckle and recalled that he wasn't alone.

"I can understand your shock," he said. "But it must be nice to have a positive shock in life."

"Yes," Alex managed to say, "yes, it certainly is. I just . . . can't believe it. I don't know what to say." He met this man's eyes. "Are you sure there isn't a way of knowing who it is? Of knowing who I should be thanking?"

"Sorry. I don't even know who it is. I was told very plainly that the donor required strict anonymity. You want my opinion?"

"Sure," Alex said, a bit breathlessly.

"Just . . . pass it along. You've got the opportunity in your career to bless many lives. So, be grateful for this gift and let it influence your career for good."

Alex absorbed this man's words. "Thank you. That is excellent advice. I'll certainly do my best."

Again Alex sat in the car for several minutes, trying to accept the miracle that had just taken place. When he finally gathered his senses, he drove to the clothing store where Jane worked and was glad to find that it wasn't busy.

"Hi," she said, her face lighting up as it always did when she saw him. "What a nice surprise."

"Can you take a break?" he asked.

"If you'll give me five minutes," she said. "Is something wrong?" Her brow furrowed. "You look a little . . . ashen."

"No, I'm fine. I just need . . . to talk to you."

When she was able to leave, they walked next door to a deli where Alex bought a root beer freeze that they could share, since he didn't want much. "Okay, talk," she said, sitting across from him.

"Somebody paid off my student loan—all of it."

She let out a burst of surprised laughter. "Who?"

"I don't know. Anonymous donor."

"But that's . . ."

"A lot of money," he chuckled as the reality began to creep past the shock.

He went on to tell her in detail what had happened and what he'd been told.

"Wow," she said, "I've *never* seen a tithing blessing that was such an obvious miracle—and such a big one."

Alex felt a little stunned by the concept, and the idea hovered with him for days. When he'd started paying his tithing, he hadn't really expected anything to change. It had tightened up his budget, but he'd been determined to stick with it, if only to honor Jane's desire that he do it. He hadn't asked for any such miracle, and hadn't even entertained the thought of one. Maybe it was coincidence. Maybe it wasn't. Either way, he couldn't help feeling greatly blessed, and he was determined to take seriously the advice he'd been given. Through the course of his career, wherever it led him, he would do his best to help others and to bless their lives as his had been blessed.

* * * * *

Jane was surprised to get a phone call from one of her older sisters. Lana lived in California with her husband and three children, about an hour's drive from where their parents lived. Jane had a good relationship with each of her siblings, but didn't feel especially close to any of them. They all cared for and respected each other, and they could have a lot of fun when they got together. But personality and age differences had kept them from developing close friendships among themselves. Lana was the oldest and had always taken some-what of a parental role with her younger siblings—perhaps a bit too much at times, in Jane's opinion. But she loved her and it was nice to hear from her.

"I hear you're in a dance competition next week," Lana said.

"I am, yes."

"Well, I've been able to arrange babysitting for the kids so I can fly out with Mom and Dad to see it."

"That's great!" Jane said, genuinely pleased with the idea. It was always nice to have family in the audience, and to feel their love and support. And it would be great to see her. It would be even better to introduce her to Alex.

As if Lana had read her mind, she added, "I also hear you have a boyfriend. That's a first."

"Yeah, it's weird," Jane said with a chuckle, "but he's pretty amazing. And now you get to meet him."

"Mom said he's actually your partner in this thing."

"That's right. He's an amazing dancer."

"You know, sis," Lana said, and Jane could feel it coming. She was in for a maternal lecture from her big sister. "Just because you enjoy dancing with someone doesn't mean he's good husband material."

Jane took a deep breath and reminded herself to stay calm. "And what makes you think that my criteria for dating him would be based on the fact that I enjoy dancing with him? I've been dancing for years, and I've had a lot of good partners."

"I just don't want to see you hurt by getting caught up in some . . . romantic fantasy."

Jane actually laughed. "Me? Romantic fantasy? You're kidding, right?"

"No, I'm quite serious. I think the very fact that you're not a romantic makes you all the more vulnerable to romance when it comes along."

Jane had to admit, "Well, you may be right about that, but I can assure you that my relationship with Alex is very healthy—and practical, in spite of how I feel about him . . . romantically."

"Okay, but . . . I understand he's not active in the Church. Forgive me if I'm being intrusive, but—"

"You are being intrusive," Jane interjected.

"I care about you," Lana said. "I want you to be happy."

"And I am. I've made it very clear to him that I won't be getting married outside of the temple. Either he'll come around or I'll marry somebody else."

Lana was silent a long moment before she said, "Well, I must admit I'm surprised by this from you. I just don't think it's a good idea to spend so much time with someone who isn't living close to the Spirit."

"What makes you think he's not?"

"How can he be if he's not going to church?" Lana asked.

"I concur with the fact that his church attendance could make a positive difference, but I know a lot of people who go to church who don't necessarily live close to the Spirit." Jane could hear anger subtly creeping into her own voice and did her best to keep her tone even. "But you don't know Alex. He's a good man. He's honest and compassionate, and has a strong value system that he lives by without question. He's a Christian man who lives his religion in every way beyond actually attending meetings. I'll tell you what I'm surprised by. I'm surprised that you would be so judgmental. You have no idea what's going on in his heart. And you'd do well to remember that you are not my mother. My mother gives me advice appropriately without judging something she doesn't understand, and she treats me like an adult."

Again Lana was silent for several seconds before she said, "I'm sorry if I upset you. I think you're being awfully defensive. I'm just concerned for you."

"Okay," Jane said, more calm, "I appreciate your concern. I can assure you that I've already taken your concerns into consideration a long time ago. Now let's change the subject or hang up."

Lana forced the conversation to her children and gradually the tension between them eased up, but Jane still felt in a bad mood when she arrived at dance rehearsal later that day. This was the first of two dress rehearsals, and she had to get into full costume, including putting up her hair as it would be for the performance. The coach wanted everything to be as it would be then, so that any challenges could be ironed out. Jane was glad to be alone while she got into the red, flowing dress, scattered with sequins. Coach had asked her and Alex to begin half an hour before the others since they were performing a rumba number solo, and she wanted to go through it a few times in costume. Once in the dress, Jane twisted her hair up and pinned it into place. She would take more time with it for the actual performance; she just needed it up and out of the way, since that's how it would be worn then. Glad for the silence, she stewed over her thoughts. She still felt angry over her conversation with Lana and didn't want to talk to anybody. The problem was that in a few minutes she would be facing Alex, and she didn't want to tell him about this. But she had to. They didn't keep secrets from each other, and he was too perceptive not to notice that something was wrong.

Once she was ready, Jane uttered a quick prayer, took a deep breath, and headed to the studio. Entering the room, she found Alex already there, wearing black slacks and a loose-fitting, silky red shirt made from the same fabric as her dress. She was able to watch him for a minute before he realized she was in the room. Just seeing him dressed like that took her breath away. He was just way too handsome for her own good. She steeled herself to cover her sour mood and enjoy this.

Alex heard a sound across the room and turned to see Jane looking at him. He caught his breath to see her dressed in red for the rumba number, her hair put up. He'd seen the dress before, but he'd not been prepared for how stunning she would look in it. Since they were the only two people in the room, he didn't hesitate to say as they moved toward each other, "Wow, I think I'm in love."

She laughed softly. "I know I am."

As they came face-to-face, Alex noticed something dark in her countenance.

"You okay?" he asked, and Jane felt disconcerted to realize that in spite of her efforts to appear normal, he could still see the truth in her eyes.

Before she could answer, Coach Abernathy came into the room, saying loudly, "Oh, good. You're here. Let's get started."

"Later," Jane said to Alex.

"You both look stupendous," Coach said with a little laugh before she started the music. Jane quickly turned her back to Alex and felt him standing close behind her for the starting position. In time to a lively Cuban drum beat, they began with intricate footwork that was perfectly synchronized.

Coach hollered to be heard above the music, "This is the real thing. Dance like you love each other with a love that is forbidden."

"Like we've never heard that before," Jane said and heard Alex chuckle behind her ear. Coach Abernathy had been aware of their dating almost from the start, and she thought it was wonderful. She also enjoyed teasing them about it in relation to their dancing.

"Dance like you love me, babe," Alex muttered lightly.

Through the first several bars, Jane remained with her back to him, and he kept his hands behind him, then in an abrupt move she turned toward him and he put a hand to her back. The delicate footwork continued while they mirrored each other's steps meticulously. It was so quick and their feet were so close together that if either of them missed a step by even a split second they would likely tread on each other's toes or stumble.

"Look into her eyes, Alex," Coach shouted. "Let your eyes betray that she is the only woman you will ever love."

"That shouldn't be too difficult," Alex said to Jane and smirked while they danced face-to-face, his hand pressed to her back.

"Yes, but think how embarrassing this would be if you hated me."

"And vice versa," he said.

Through a series of abrupt movements that coincided with the music, Alex took both her hands, pulled her close to him, then pushed her away. He lowered her abruptly into a dip that looked like she would fall flat on her back. After holding her there, seemingly suspended a few inches off the floor, he pulled her up abruptly and sent her into a series of elaborate spins while he held one of her hands above her head. He pulled her back against his chest by holding to her waist, while she lifted both hands high above her head and rolled her head forward. With a clear view of Jane's bare neck, Alex couldn't resist pressing a kiss there while her head was down. She laughed softly as if it had tickled, then he lifted his arms to take both her hands into his. Holding her hands suspended, the intricate footwork continued until the dance ended with another elaborate spin, an unexpected dip, and the last note left her leaning against his chest with one foot poised behind her.

"Magnificent!" Coach said and applauded as the music ended. "And I like that kiss on the neck, Alex. That's a nice touch. Keep it in."

Alex and Jane exchanged an amused glance as Alex said, "Now the whole world will think we're in love."

"That's the idea," Coach said, overhearing him. "Let's do it again."

They went through the number again, then Coach told them to take a quick break and they'd run through it once more before the others arrived. Alex took Jane's hand and urged her to a bench at the side of the room.

"Okay," he said. "What's wrong?"

Jane sighed loudly; she didn't want to tell him. But she knew she had to. Lana was coming to town, and she wasn't going to leave him unprepared for any possible tension that might be in the air between them.

"My sister called," she said.

"Which one?" he asked, his brow furrowing.

"Lana."

"The oldest."

"That's right. The one who thinks she's my mother."

Alex began to see where this was headed and asked, "What did she say?" When Jane hesitated he said, "It was about me, wasn't it."

"I'm afraid it was. She thinks I shouldn't be dating someone who isn't going to church; she thinks I'm infatuated with you because we're dancing together."

Alex sighed. "Well, to be truthful, I'm surprised that it hasn't come up before now. I expected Jeff and Marla—or your parents—to have a problem with it. I'm glad they didn't but . . . face it . . . this is an important issue in your family, and I don't fit the bill."

"I love you, Alex," Jane said, touching his face. "It doesn't matter."

Alex gave a tense chuckle. "Now, that's not true." He looked down. "I know you love me, Jane. And I love you. But it certainly *does* matter. Not because it's important to your sister, or your parents, or anybody else, but because it's important to you." He paused and asked, "What did you tell her?"

"I told her you were amazing and she should mind her own business. I told her what I told you, that I'm not going to change my convictions."

"Okay, so . . . there's no problem, right?"

"Not for me, there's not, but . . . Lana is coming with my parents to the competition. I just wanted you to know what she'd said, because . . . you're going to meet her in a few days."

"Oh, I see," he said. "Well, I'll do my best to be my most charming self."

"Just be yourself, and there will be no problem," Jane said. "I don't care what my sister or anybody else thinks, I know you're the man for me."

Alex smiled and kissed her quickly. He touched her face and said earnestly, "I pray that I don't end up disappointing you, Jane."

"You just keep praying, and everything will be fine."

They went through the rumba number once more, while most of the team filtered into the room. When they were finished they got a hearty round of applause, then they went to change into the same costumes as everyone else for the group waltz number. The women wore white dresses trimmed in a shimmery gold. The men wore classic black tuxedos with coattails.

Just before the waltz began, Jane took note of the way Alex looked and again felt breathless. Perhaps most intoxicating of all was the look in his eyes as he took her in with overt adoration. She'd never felt so beautiful in all her life as she did when Alex looked at her that way. As they began to dance, she looked into his eyes and uttered a silent prayer that she could spend the rest of her life with this incredible man, and more importantly, that she could spend eternity with him.

* * * * *

The dance competition turned out to be a huge success. Jane felt as if she were literally floating on cloud nine while she and Alex danced several numbers together in front of judges and an audience. The team won two awards, and she and Alex each received an individual trophy for the rumba number they'd done on their own.

Once the competition was over, Alex couldn't deny feeling decidedly nervous. He knew that Jane's parents and her skeptical sister had been in the audience, and once he changed his clothes he would be officially meeting them. He'd never actually been confronted with meeting a woman's family before; he'd never dated anyone long enough for it to be an issue. Alex met Jane at a designated spot near one of the main doors and was relieved to hear that they would be driving separately and meeting the family at a nearby restaurant.

"You're nervous," she said with a little laugh as she observed him driving.

"Yes, I am," he admitted with no argument.

"There's no need, truly."

"Well, your parents have been very kind long distance, but . . . I know your sister already doesn't like me and—"

"I never said she didn't like you; she doesn't even know you. How can she not like you?"

"Okay, she doesn't like things about me," he said with mild irony.

"It's going to be fine, Alex. I promise. If it's not, we'll leave, but that won't be necessary because they're very nice people."

"Well, they're related to you," he said, "so I would assume that's the case." He said more severely, "I simply fear that they'll think I'm not good enough for you, that I'm not worthy of you." He looked at her hard, then glanced back to the road. "And maybe they'd be right."

"Alex," she sighed, "I love you."

"I love you too, but that doesn't mean I'm good enough for you."

"You're a good man, Alex. Don't go distorting the facts over one issue that in no way diminishes everything else about you that is so amazing . . . at least it is to me."

Alex looked at her again, marveling at how she could assuage the doubts that crept into his mind. He was relieved to arrive at the restaurant and find that Jeff and Marla were there as well. Jeff shook Alex's hand, and Marla gave him a hug before he was introduced to Jane's parents, Walter and Louisa, and her sister Lana. He felt complete acceptance from her parents, and they seemed genuinely pleased to meet him. Lana appeared a bit wary, but she was kind and polite. As they were seated, the conversation remained strictly on the dance competition for several minutes, which helped break the tension. They were all clearly impressed, and Louisa said more than once, "I've never seen Jane dance more beautifully." The second time she added, with a wink toward Alex, "You must bring out the best in her."

"It's the other way around," Alex said, smiling at Jane.

Alex truly liked Jane's parents, and so far he couldn't deny that the evidence kept stacking up in favor of him and Jane remaining together. He truly believed they would share their lives completely, that they would raise a family. The only problem was a deep uneasiness that crept up occasionally. He pondered their conversation in the car. Jane wanted to be married in the temple, to have living the gospel an active part of raising a family. And Alex carried something deep and painful inside of him that made such a prospect feel tantamount to climbing Kilimanjaro. But he loved Jane, and his deepest hope was that he could eventually overcome what held him back and be the man that she deserved.

Through the next couple of days, Jane spent most of her spare time with her family while they were in town. He saw them once more when he went to Jeff and Marla's for a visit. Lana remained polite but said little to him. However, the more time he spent with Walter and Louisa the more he liked them—and they seemed to like him. On the day that they were all scheduled to fly home, Jane called him at the hospital to see if they could meet him on his lunch break at the cafeteria, before she took her family to the airport. "Sure, why not?" he said, loving any opportunity to be with Jane—especially in the middle of a long shift.

Jane took her sister and her parents to the hospital and to a back hallway that led into the emergency area, a place where she had met Alex many times. They'd only been there a minute before Alex peered around the corner. He waved at them and held up a finger to indicate that he'd be another minute, then he disappeared again. She hoped that their time together would go well. She'd been praying for Lana's heart to be softened toward Alex. She'd been technically appropriate toward him, but Jane knew her well enough to catch the subtle undercurrents of disapproval. Jane wanted Lana to be able to grasp even a small degree of what a good man Alex was.

"So he really does work here," Lana said with the tiniest hint of something skeptical in her voice.

"Did you think he made it up?" Jane asked, keeping her voice light. She felt as if Lana was trying to somehow discredit him, but it was too subtle to address.

A couple of minutes later Alex came down the hall, dressed as usual in hospital scrubs.

"Hello, Alex," Louisa said, kissing his cheek.

Walter shook his hand and said, "Good to see you again."

"And you," Alex said as they moved on together down the hall.

Lana glanced toward his ID badge and said, "So, you really are a doctor."

Alex looked directly at her and said, "I'm pretty sure they made certain I could use a stethoscope before they issued the ID badge." He lifted the badge and pointed to it as he added, "Of course, it does say 'intern' right here, which keeps anyone from trusting me completely without a second opinion."

Jane fought to keep from smiling and was glad for a distraction when they heard from behind them, "Make way, Doctor. We're coming through."

They all turned to see two nurses pushing a bed down the hall. As they moved aside for the patient to go by, Jane noted it was an elderly woman, not looking at all well.

"Mrs. Bean," Alex said and moved into step with the nurses as he took the old woman's hand. Jane and her family followed behind. "I see they finally got that suite upstairs ready for you."

"So I hear," the woman said with a slight laugh.

"Now, you remember what I told you. They've got great rice pudding here, so you make sure they get you some every day. And Dr. Johansen is the best in his field; he'll take good care of you."

"Thank you, Doctor," Mrs. Bean said. "You've been so sweet."

"A pleasure, Madame," he said with a smile.

They stopped moving when it became evident that Mrs. Bean and her escorts needed to go a different direction. Alex said to one of the nurses, "Have Johansen page me before he talks to her."

"Of course," the nurse said.

"And—"

"And I'll get some rice pudding," she interrupted Alex with a smile.

"Thank you," Alex said and then led the way to the visitor elevator.

Lunch in the cafeteria was pleasant and relaxed. Jane enjoyed seeing Alex interact with her parents and was pleased with how comfortable they seemed together, but she hated the way that Lana said practically nothing, which was so out of character for her. They were pretty much finished eating when a doctor dressed in surgical garb passed by and stopped to visit with Alex. He introduced everyone, then spoke to Dr. Allred for a few minutes about some case they had previously consulted on. Jane loved listening to Alex use medical jargon that she didn't begin to understand. And she loved the way that Alex so clearly loved his job.

When it was time for Alex to get back to work and for the rest of them to leave for the airport, Jane was surprised to have Alex kiss her quickly on the lips in front of her family. But she certainly didn't mind. "I'll see you later, then," he said to her, then he exchanged heartfelt farewells with her parents, who both hugged him and told him to take good care of Jane. He promised fervently, then turned and offered a hand to Lana. "It's been a pleasure. Glad you could make it."

"Yes, of course," she said and returned his handshake.

Alex squeezed Jane's hand and walked away. Jane watched him go, wondering if she would ever stop feeling so in awe of him.

* * * * *

A week after Jane's family left town, Alex's mother surprised him with a phone call, telling him that a friend of hers had some air miles that needed to be used and she was going to get a free round-trip ticket to anywhere in the country. She was coming to visit for a few days. Alex was ecstatic. It felt like forever since he'd last seen his mother, and the thought of having her meet Jane made him almost jittery.

"Guess what?" he said to Jane that evening while he was having dinner with her at Jeff and Marla's home. "My two favorite women finally get to meet."

"Your mother's coming?" Jane asked, sounding as excited as he felt. She'd spoken to Ruth on the phone a number of times, and Alex had told his mother every detail of his feelings and experiences with Jane. They'd practically become best friends, without ever having met face-to-face.

"She is," Alex said and explained the situation. Marla eagerly offered to let his mother stay with them, and Alex was pleasantly surprised. His mother had only come to this town once before, and that was when he'd gotten his medical degree. She had used the bed in his apartment, while he'd slept on the couch, but he felt sure that this would be much more enjoyable for her.

Jane was more excited than nervous when she went with Alex to pick his mother up at the airport. She recognized her immediately from pictures she'd seen, but she was much more lovely in person. Her full figure and dark hair were greatly enhanced by a natural glow about her, as if she were the happiest person in the world and her happiness was destined to contagion. Jane watched as Alex laughed and pulled his mother into his arms, lifting her feet off the floor. When their greeting was finished, Ruth turned to look at Jane. "And this is the incredible woman who has captured my son's heart." She eagerly embraced Jane as if it were the most natural thing in the world, then she eased back and put both her hands on Jane's shoulders. "You're even more beautiful than your pictures."

"I was thinking the same about you," Jane said, and Ruth hugged her again.

"Oh, she's precious," Ruth said to Alex.

"Yes, she is," Alex said, and they went to retrieve Ruth's luggage.

The days of Ruth's visit were wonderful, and they all had a marvelous time together. Jane quickly grew to love Ruth Keane, and it was evident that Ruth thought Jane was the best thing that had ever happened to her son. Jane enjoyed seeing firsthand the closeness Alex shared with his mother. She felt certain that was a good sign as to how he might treat his wife one day. When Ruth had to return home, Alex had a tough time, but he told Jane he was grateful to have *two* good women in his life.

— 6 —

With all their company gone home, and the competition behind them, Jane found herself feeling down. She would no longer be sharing rehearsals with Alex, and the time for his move to Michigan was creeping closer. With his student loans paid off, he was able to buy a newer used car that he could trust to get him to Michigan. Seeing the car made the reality sink in more fully. He was getting ready to leave the state.

"It's not a black Ferrari," he said, "but we're getting closer."

As the days drew nearer to his scheduled departure, Jane found it difficult to even think about his leaving, let alone talk about it. He'd become the center of her life in no time at all, and now they would be separated by hundreds of miles. Tight budgets and tight schedules would make it difficult to see each other, and she felt almost terrified of being without him at all. When he finished his final shift at the hospital and started packing up his things, she felt as if her world might end.

While they went together to a movie and out for pizza afterward, she did her best to hide her grief. But she knew that he could see through her when he said, "It's going to be okay, Jane."

Tears trickled down her face before she had a chance to think of holding them back. "It doesn't feel like it will ever be okay."

Alex reached across the table to wipe her tears with a napkin. He was startled when she said, "Let's get married, Alex."

He took a long moment to study her expression before he said, "You're serious."

"Yes, I'm serious. How can we live like this? We can get married, and . . . I'll finish school at—"

"Whoa," he said. "What are you saying? That we just elope and—"

"Maybe," she admitted.

"No. Not a chance. What happened to the practical, responsible woman I fell in love with?"

"Her heart is breaking," she whimpered.

"Which is the very reason you should not be making life-altering decisions. Your family would never forgive me."

"Of course they would."

"Eventually . . . maybe. But far worse, I'm not sure you would ever forgive me. You may think you mean it now, but you're talking with your emotions. It's nonsense. You're going to . . . what? Settle for less than a temple marriage because you don't want to be separated for a while?"

"A while? Unless we get married, it could be years before we ever live in the same city again."

"Okay," he took both her hands, "but . . . we can at least wait until you get your degree . . . and until I can take you to the temple."

"Is that ever going to happen?" she asked with anger tainting her sorrow.

Alex pondered the question for a long moment, and with firm conviction he said, "Yes, it will. But we need some time. You need to get your degree, and I need some time to . . . work some things through. We'll get past this, Jane. We will."

Jane looked into his eyes and wanted to believe him. But at the moment, the thought of being without him was made worse by the fear that for all his good intentions, he would forever hold himself back from embracing what meant most to her. And yes, he was right, she could never settle for less than a temple marriage. Perhaps a part of her feared that once this separation occurred, things between them would never be the same. But maybe they needed just such an occurrence—as difficult as it may be—to truly test the limits of their relationship, and their love for each other.

As Alex prepared to move, there were only two people beyond Jane and her aunt and uncle that he felt the need to say good-bye to formally. One was Coach Abernathy, and the other was Brent. They'd both been very good to him through his years of living in this town, and he told them so. He also thanked them for coercing him back onto the team and giving him the opportunity to meet Jane. They promised to keep in touch, but he wondered if they ever would.

Jane found herself counting the hours left until Alex would be leaving. When he was packed and ready to go, he came to the house to say good-bye. Since his apartment had come furnished, everything he owned fit in his car. When Jane saw it filled with bags and boxes, she couldn't hold back the tears. After he'd said good-bye to Jeff and Marla, thanking them for taking him in the way they had, Alex and Jane stood together in the entry hall of the house, just holding each other for minutes that she lost track of. She wept and held to him as if she might never see him again. When he finally eased back enough to look at her, she saw tears in his eyes as well.

"I'll call as soon as I get there," he said. "And I'll e-mail every day."

"And I want a real letter at least once a week," she said.

"I promise," he whispered and kissed her. Jane whimpered as she became consumed by a kiss unlike anything they had ever shared before. In it she found all of her own desperation reciprocating from him. She wanted to never let him go, but he eased back and said, "I love you. Don't you ever forget that."

"I promise," she said softly. "I love you too."

Alex opened the door and then, as if he'd changed his mind, he pulled her into his arms and kissed her again, even more desperately. "I think maybe it's a good thing I'm leaving town," he said, holding her far too close.

Jane watched him get into the car and drive away, then she went upstairs to her room and cried harder than she ever had in her life. She found Marla beside her, giving her a mother's comfort in her mother's absence. She didn't offer any advice or wisdom that would sound trite in the face of such intense emotion. She just stayed close to Jane and let her cry.

Alex called as promised, and true to his word, e-mails came every single day. At least once a week she would get a handwritten letter or card in the mail. She wrote to him equivalently, and every Sunday he called her while he had a timer set for half an hour. It was the highlight of her week. She hated to hear that he really didn't like where he was living, and that many of the people he worked with were difficult. On top of that, most of them lived questionable lifestyles in one way or another. He had mixed feelings about the trauma he was seeing at this particular hospital. It was giving him great experience, but seeing the emergencies that resulted from crime and violence daily were difficult to get used to.

"I don't think you're ever supposed to really get used to it," she told him.

"Probably not," he admitted, but it was still tough.

Jane did her best to stay busy and get through school as quickly as possible. About four months after Alex had left the state, Lana called her out of the blue, apparently to chat. Jane couldn't help feeling suspicious. They caught up on what everyone in the family was doing, then Lana said, "So, how's Alex?"

"He's fine. I hear from him one way or another every day."

"It must be difficult being so far away," Lana said.

"Yes, it is; it's very difficult." Jane sensed that this conversation was not what it appeared to be. She just knew Lana too well. She decided to take it head on. "If you're trying to call and talk me into breaking it off, it won't work. The more time that passes, the more I realize how much I love him."

"Okay, but . . . is love really enough? Love without trust will never last."

Jane gave a sardonic chuckle. "And what makes you think I can't trust him?"

"Can you?"

"Yes!" she said firmly.

"Oh, come on, Jane," Lana said. "You haven't seen him in four months. How can you really be sure that he's living the way you think he's living?"

"What are you implying?" Jane asked. "You think because he doesn't go to church that it automatically makes him . . . what? Dishonest? Unfaithful?"

"Maybe he is."

"And maybe he's not. You know," Jane said, "your assumptions are nothing more than prejudice, plain and simple. You're basically saying that the challenge in Alex's life makes him a bad person. Our parents did not raise us to be that judgmental. Jesus certainly wasn't that judgmental."

Lana ignored the analogy and asked, "So you're absolutely sure that you can trust him?"

"Absolutely."

"It's too bad you can't . . . go see him."

"Yes, it is, but not for the reasons you're implying. I would love to go see him, but I can't afford it. I don't have time to drive there, and—"

"And you'd need a place to stay."

"That's right."

"Okay," Lana said, "so what if I pay for it?"

"Pay for what?"

"What if I buy you a plane ticket and a motel room for a couple of nights?"

Jane didn't know whether to feel furious or ecstatic over such an offer. While the thought of seeing Alex made her heart beat faster, Lana's motives made her sick. She knew that Lana's husband made a very good living, and her offer to pay for the trip was valid, and wouldn't put any strain on Lana's household. It was tempting to take the offer, motives or not. But she still couldn't believe what she was hearing.

"You are unbelievable," Jane said. "You think I'm going to drop in and surprise him and find some evidence that he's not what he seems to be?"

"Maybe."

Jane remained silent long enough to say a silent prayer that she could be free of this anger she felt toward her sister. She finally said in a calm voice, "Okay, Lana, you're on. I accept. You get me a round-trip ticket and a room. I will be sure to stop by his place, completely unexpected, and delve into his life in every way possible, discreetly of course. I wouldn't want him to know what I'm up to. And I'll be sure to pay close attention to his behavior to see if he's nervous or upset about my coming, and then I'll give you a full report."

"Okay, it's a deal," Lana said, apparently not picking up on Jane's subtle sarcasm. She seemed completely confident that Jane would prove Lana's point by doing exactly what she'd said.

It took Jane an hour after she got off the phone—and some

serious prayer—to stop feeling angry. Then it occurred to her that she'd just been given a wonderful blessing: the opportunity to see Alex. She knew from their daily e-mails what his schedule and lifestyle were like. She knew where to find him and how, and she even knew his schedule at the hospital. She would surprise him and they'd have a wonderful visit. She would prove Lana wrong and have a great time doing so. She quickly made arrangements to miss work for a few days, and to have somebody get notes for her on the one day of classes she would miss.

On the plane to Michigan, Jane actually began to wonder if Lana might be right. She prayed for the discernment to be able to know if Alex was everything he seemed to be. She was prepared to be confronted with some kind of evidence that he was uncomfortable with her surprise visit, that perhaps he was hiding something from her. Determined to be observant but not suspicious, she forced herself to put it out of her mind and simply anticipated being with Alex. She wasn't sure yet if she would go searching for him at the hospital or at home; it depended on how tired she was when she arrived, and how long it might take her to find her way around. Either way, she hadn't felt this happy in months.

* * * * *

Alex heaved a grievous sigh and stepped away from the thirteen-year-old boy that he along with another doctor—his mentor—and several nurses and aides had been working on for nearly an hour. As if through a fog he watched the doctor turn to look at the clock as he said, "Time of death, 3:47 P.M." He met Alex's eyes and added softly, "You did good, kid. It's just one of those things."

Alex only nodded, wondering why he felt the urge to cry. It was far from the first time he'd observed a senseless death. When violence senselessly took the life of a child it was especially difficult, but for some reason this one was hitting him hard. Perhaps it was simply one of those final-straw moments. He'd done little since he'd arrived in this city but work, sleep, and eat. The work was often rewarding, but it was also exhausting—physically and emotionally. And he regularly had no choice but to become involved in situations that were either heart-breaking or gut-wrenching—or both. He'd gotten to know people he worked with, and people who lived in his apartment building. But there was no one in this town he could call a friend. He was tired. He was lonely. And it seemed he'd felt that way for endless weeks.

Alex snapped his gloves off and tossed them into the trash. He looked once more at the body, the blood, the signs of trauma, then he turned and left the room, wishing it wasn't a swinging door so that he could slam it. He slumped into a chair against the wall in the hallway and pushed his hands into his hair. The time left on his shift seemed like eternity. He wondered what Jane was doing. He missed her so badly that it hurt. Maybe she'd been right. Maybe they should have gotten married. And maybe they could have if he'd been the kind of man she deserved. He cursed under his breath and leaned his head back against the wall, sighing loudly as he stretched out one leg. He wanted to just crawl into bed and sleep for a month. He knew that wasn't an option, but he just didn't know how he could muster the strength to keep going. *Please God,* he muttered silently, *help me find a reason to keep going.*

Alex was startled to hear his name and realized that he must have drifted off for a minute. "Dr. Keane?" a nurse's voice repeated. "Are you okay?"

"Yeah, I'm fine," he said, focusing on her face. "Did you need something?" he asked and stood up, pulling off the bloodied gown he was wearing over his scrubs. The nurse took it from him while he wondered if there was more trauma on its way.

"Not at the moment," she said. "You have a visitor."

Alex felt his brow furrow, wondering who on earth would visit him. He couldn't think of one person in this town who would even notice if he disappeared off the face of the earth—except for people who worked here, and they certainly wouldn't be visitors. The nurse motioned down the hall. Alex turned to look in that direction and felt certain he was hallucinating. When he realized he wasn't, he felt as if he might have gained some empathy for a coronary patient. His heart had never pounded so hard in his life.

When Jane had arrived at the hospital, she paid the taxi driver and went into the emergency-room entrance. The receptionist at the desk was kind when Jane told her she was a friend of Dr. Keane's and would like to see him if he wasn't busy. She expected to be told that they would have to take her name and ask him, but another woman behind the desk, who was obviously a nurse, said, "You must be Jane."

"That's right," Jane said. "How did you know?"

"I've seen your picture—a number of times."

Jane couldn't help smiling. A guy who was flirting at work wouldn't be showing off his girlfriend's picture. The nurse said she would check and came back less than a minute later to say, "He's just sitting in the hall. Come on back."

Jane hesitated a few yards away when she saw him. His entire countenance smacked of exhaustion and discouragement, and there was something in his expression that encouraged her to believe he'd just encountered something especially difficult. She watched the nurse talking to him and couldn't help noting the large amount of blood on the gown he pulled off and handed to her before he turned and looked in her direction. She wondered what kind of a day he'd had, and hoped that her visit would make it better, and not worse. Perfect joy surged through her every nerve as she absorbed the change in his countenance. He was so clearly glad to see her that she felt as if she'd melt into the floor.

"Jane," he mouthed more than spoke as he rushed toward her and she moved into his arms.

"Oh, Alex," she muttered, holding to him as tightly as he held to her. She heard him laugh near her ear and felt him lift her off the ground. He set her down and looked into her eyes. She caught the distinct glisten of tears clinging to his lashes before he kissed her in a way that erased her every doubt concerning his devotion. He kissed her again and she felt every part of herself that had ached for him and missed him come completely back to life.

"What are you doing here?" he asked, touching her face, laughing again.

"A miracle happened. I was able to get a plane ticket and a motel for a couple of nights." She laughed. "Where else would I go?"

"Oh, thank you, God," Alex muttered and hugged her again. "I have never been so happy to see anyone in my entire—"

"Dr. Keane," a different nurse said, peering around the corner.

"Sorry to interrupt but we've got some stitches in room one, and a possible domestic violence in room four."

Alex took a deep breath. He didn't want to deal with it, but at least he felt like he could—which was a big switch from the way he'd been feeling a few minutes ago. "I'm all over it," he said. "Just give me a minute."

"You got it," the nurse said and went back around the corner.

Alex looked at Jane with regret. "Sorry, but . . ."

"It's okay. I didn't know if I'd get to see you at all before you got off, but . . . I took a chance."

"I'm so glad you did."

"Hey, while you're finishing up here, I was thinking I'd cook you some dinner. What do you think?"

Alex grinned. "It sounds heavenly, but maybe I should take you out to dinner."

"We'll do that tomorrow," she said, and his grin broadened. "You have tomorrow off, don't you?"

"Yes, I do," he said with exaggerated delight.

"Okay, so how about if I take your car? I'll go get dinner started and come back to get you when you're off."

"If you're sure," he said.

"I'd love to," she insisted and followed him to his locker where he retrieved his car keys and handed them to her. He told her where to find the car and gave her simple directions to his apartment that was less than a mile away.

"I'll see you soon," she said and kissed him before she left him to his work.

Jane felt thoroughly delighted, almost spiteful, as she found Alex's car exactly how she'd expected it. What had Lana believed she would find? Empty beer bottles? A woman's belongings? Coming into his apartment, she was even more thrilled with the evidence—in fact, she was moved to tears. The one-bedroom apartment was much nicer than where he'd lived before. It was mostly tidy, as she'd expected, beyond the bed being unmade, a few dirty dishes in the sink, and a little clutter here and there. But everywhere she looked, there were pictures of herself. He'd taken pictures of her before he'd left, and he'd asked her to send more. But she'd not imagined that he'd put every single one of them in a frame. The picture of the Salt Lake Temple was on his bedroom mirror along with the pictures of his dream house and Ferrari—and a snapshot of herself.

Setting to work on her intended chore to cook something for dinner, she soon realized there wasn't much food to work with. She opened a drawer in search of some paper and pencil to make a grocery list, recalling that she'd passed a grocery store on her way here. In the second drawer she opened, she found tithing receipts. *Too bad Lana couldn't see this,* she thought. Then she smiled to herself, simply grateful for the blessing she'd been given to be here—even if Lana's motives had been pathetic. "The Lord works in mysterious ways," she said aloud and began examining the contents of the fridge to see what he needed. After making a quick trip to the grocery store, she returned to his apartment and put together an easy enchilada recipe that she knew from memory. While they were in the oven she fixed a green salad, set the table, and tidied up a bit. Then she went to the hospital and moved to the passenger seat where she waited in the car for only a few minutes before Alex came out. He got into the car and reached over the emergency brake between the bucket seats to kiss her as if he'd not seen her in years.

"Oh, you really are here," he said. "I can't believe it."

"I really am," she said. "But we need to hurry; dinner is in the oven."

Once they were seated across from each other, enjoying a leisurely meal, Alex said, "So tell me about this miracle that brought you here."

Jane told him about Lana's proposition, and she was relieved when he found the humor in it. "And you didn't find any booze in the fridge or anything?"

"Nothing," she said. "Not that I was looking."

"Of course not," he said and took her hand to kiss it.

"I really do trust you, Alex."

"Well, I'm glad," he said, "because I really do try to be trust-worthy."

"I don't know what the deal is with Lana," Jane said, more concerned than angry.

"How's her marriage?" Alex asked and Jane felt something click inside. She knew that Lana's husband wasn't all she'd expected him to be. As far as Jane knew it wasn't anything serious, but it certainly was not an ideal marriage. Maybe that was the problem.

"Hard to say," was all that Jane said before she changed the subject. "So what are we going to do while I'm here?"

"Absolutely nothing," he said. "We're going to talk and eat and talk, and once in a while I'm going to kiss you."

"How delightful." She laughed softly. "My motel is only a few blocks from here, so it won't take me long to get here for breakfast."

"You don't have to spend your vacation cooking."

"Who said I was cooking? I bought some Raisin Bran."

Alex laughed and just luxuriated in her presence.

"So how was the ER?" she asked, and the change in his expression alone answered her question. "Tough day?"

"Yeah, it was."

"You looked pretty bad off when I first saw you. May I ask what happened?"

Alex felt deeply comforted by her question—not because he wanted to talk about it, but he felt grateful to have someone care about what had happened today, and to realize that she knew him well enough to perceive what was beneath the surface.

Thinking of the event behind his discouragement, he found it difficult to come up with the words. He leaned back in his chair and ignored the food left on his plate. Jane took his hand, and he just said it. "Uh . . . a kid, thirteen, I think. He came in with multiple gunshot wounds—probably gang related. We worked on him for an hour, but . . . we couldn't save him."

Jane read between the lines, and a deep sorrow overcame her. She thought of the mother who had lost a child today, and the senseless-ness of such a loss. And then she thought of the medical personnel—specifically Alex—who had invested all of their experience and energy into saving a life that couldn't be saved. He'd told her in his daily e-mails about certain cases he'd dealt with, and how difficult the work could be, but there was something different about seeing it in his face.

Alex watched Jane's eyes become moist, and he waited for her to say something like, 'I'm sure you did all you could,' or 'Some things just can't be changed.' And while she would have been right, he'd grown tired of the catch phrases that were an attempt to brush away the horror that was encountered in this business. He could never tell her what it meant when she said, "I'm so sorry. I can't even imagine how difficult that must be . . . to work so hard and then . . . watch someone die who shouldn't be dying."

Alex swallowed his rising emotion and pressed her hand to his lips. "It is hard," he said, "but it's nice to have someone care . . . and understand."

"Is it harder than you expected?" she asked gently.

Alex kept her hand in his and passed the other one over his face before he admitted, "Yes, but . . . well . . . I knew it would be hard. I didn't go into this field because I like to see people suffer. I did it because I believed that I could make a difference, that I could ease the suffering. And I do; I really do. In that respect, it's very gratifying. But . . . the reality of such trauma is . . . unsettling at times. Sometimes I feel like a kid who enlisted in the military, certain he'd change the world and come back a hero, then when he's confronted with the reality of war, he's horrified at his own naïveté and . . . he'll never be the same."

"Do you regret it?" she asked. He looked puzzled somehow, and she clarified. "You've worked hard to get here. Do you regret the choice?"

"Not in the slightest," he said. "I know beyond any doubt this is where I'm supposed to be." He kissed her hand again and added, "I just might need you to remind me of that on occasion."

"I'll do that," she said and kissed his hand in return. He smiled at her, and she added, "So, when I left they said you had some stitches and a possible domestic violence. Was it?" When he didn't answer right away she hurried to say, "If you don't want to talk about work, all you have to do is say so."

"No, it's fine," he said. "It's nice to have a way to . . . decompress, I guess you could say. I usually do that in my e-mails to you. It's good to be able to do it face-to-face. I just don't want to weigh you down with my burdens."

"It's a pleasure to share your burdens, Alex."

"You are truly amazing," he said.

"Not really. I just love you, which is not difficult at all."

"It's the other way around."

She smiled. "So . . . share your burdens of the day with me and then we'll brush them away and you can start fresh next time."

"Well," he said, "the stitches were on a six-year-old boy who had stuck his hand through a glass door. Once we got the initial shot over with to numb the pain, he was fine. Cute kid."

"How *do* you get a kid through the initial shot?"

Alex smiled. "I usually give them my stethoscope and let them listen to my heart while I do it."

"How very clever."

"Well, sometimes. This kid didn't go for it, but we made it through. In a way it was harder on the mother, which is typical. Mothers have a hard time watching needles go into their children."

"I think I can understand that." She hesitated a long moment. "And the other? *Was* it domestic violence?"

Alex's face darkened. "Beyond a doubt. But it wasn't easy to convince her to admit it. They always come in claiming to have fallen down the stairs, or something equally ridiculous."

Jane felt a little taken aback by that word 'always.' How many times had he already dealt with such things to put it that way? He'd briefly mentioned domestic violence in his e-mails, but she was feeling closer to the reality by hearing it directly. Sensing that it was good for him to talk about it, she urged him to keep going. "What did you say to convince her?"

"I told her that I didn't go to school all these years to become a fool, that I knew what injuries caused by a fall looked like, and this wasn't it. This looked more like a fist fight—with someone who had a lot more strength than she did. I could also tell by the way she was behaving. People do not act terrified to tell you that they fell down the stairs."

"Was she hurt badly?" Jane asked, feeling a little queasy at the thought.

Alex briefly squeezed his eyes closed before he said with a voice that was slightly raspy, "Uh . . . she had severe contusions all over her body, and . . . two broken bones in her face. They were prepping her for surgery when I left."

"And the man responsible?" Jane asked with an edge of anger.

"Well thanks to Marina, she—"

"Marina?"

"One of the nurses who is gifted with such things. She's the one who really got her to open up. Thanks to Marina this woman is pressing charges and filing a restraining order. Many women refuse."

"It's tragic," Jane said.

"Yes, it is."

She gave him a wan smile. "It makes me grateful for what I've got."

"What you've got is a cold supper," he said and took her plate to stick it in the microwave, along with his own. When he brought the plates back to the table, he said, "On a brighter note, I helped bring a man back to life who went into cardiac arrest. He's in cardiac intensive care, and he's going to be fine. And I pumped the stomach of a woman who OD'd on sleeping pills. She's in the psych ward, and she's going to get the help she needs."

"Look at you," Jane said, "saving lives all over the place." She reached across the table and kissed him. "The rest of the world can have your medical expertise, as long as I can have the rest of you."

"It's a deal," he said, and they finished their meal.

Through the forty-eight hours that Jane was in town, Alex felt himself come back to life. He was tempted to tell her that maybe they *should* get married and stop living this way, but he knew the requirements for that, and he just wasn't ready to face certain inner demons. So he just enjoyed her presence while it lasted and coped with letting her go, knowing that it was only temporary.

Jane had a difficult time saying good-bye to Alex, but she reminded herself to be grateful for the time they'd had together. She called Lana the minute she got home and told her what she'd found—or rather hadn't found. Lana said little. Jane thanked her for the vacation, and they didn't talk again for weeks.

Two months after her trip to Michigan, Alex called to tell Jane that he'd been saving days off, as well as putting away some money. He was coming to see her, and he would be coming for a week. He would be staying with his friend, Brent. Jane was so completely thrilled that the initial cloud-nine experience of meeting Alex began all over again. When he finally arrived, she jumped into his arms and they both laughed as he twirled her around, then he kissed her in a way that reminded her of their first kiss.

"That's another one to tell our grandchildren about," she said. He laughed and picked her up again.

Throughout his week in town, Jane was able to get out of some shifts at work, and she didn't do anything that wasn't absolutely necessary so that she could spend every possible minute with Alex. Just being with him rejuvenated and replenished her in a way that nothing else could.

On Sunday Jane invited him to go to church with her. She didn't have to even guess that he didn't want to go; he came right out and told her so.

"And when is some magical transformation going to take place that will make your feelings different, Alex? You've got to at least make some effort at getting over this. Have you done anything since we've met to really work on this? Have you made any effort at all?"

"I hung that picture of the temple on the mirror in my new apartment."

Jane gave him a wan smile then asked, "Will you go to church with me, Alex? Maybe you'll realize it's not as bad as you remember."

Alex sighed and couldn't find an argument. "Okay," he said. "I'll go to sacrament meeting with you."

Jane beamed like she'd just been given a new puppy for Christmas. Alex borrowed a tie from Brent and actually found himself praying that he could get through this. Walking into the church building with Jane's hand in his was one of the hardest things he'd ever done. He kept telling himself as the meeting progressed that this was not a big deal, that he could handle this. But the memories came into his mind so profoundly, and with such emotion, that he felt as if the room would collapse on him.

Jane kept Alex's hand in hers through the meeting, grateful beyond words to have him there. He didn't take the sacrament when it was offered to him, for reasons that she understood and respected. Then the talks began, and he seemed to be interested in what was being said. She was just beginning to feel that maybe they'd finally made a huge step in the right direction when he whispered in her ear, "I'll wait for you outside. Stay as long as you want."

He got up and left, and Jane debated whether or not to follow him and leave everyone wondering what the problem might be. Deciding she didn't care, she left the chapel as well and found him outside the building pacing back and forth on the lawn near where he'd parked the car. She resisted the urge to feel angry at him for dashing her hopes and tried instead to imagine the pain he must be holding inside that would make it so difficult for him to just sit through a church meeting.

"I'm sorry," she said.

"I should be the one apologizing, Jane. I should be . . . more than this . . . for you. Sometimes I really wonder if I have what it takes to be worthy of you."

"I don't wonder about that at all," she said. "I only wonder what can be done to get beyond this . . . together." She sat on the curb and motioned for him to join her. "Why is it so hard, Alex? Talk to me."

He sighed and sat beside her. "It's just . . . the memories, the hurtful things people said, the looks we would get, and . . . realizing that he'd been living a double life. I can't count how many times I sat in church after the whole thing blew up, wondering how long it had been going on. The . . . *hypocrisy* . . . just makes me . . . *sick*."

"Okay, that's all understandable, Alex, but . . . this is Christ's church, and if you really understand Him and what He did for us, then . . . you should be able to give that burden to Him."

She talked for a while about the Atonement, and shared her testimony of how it could take away the pain and grief that had been inflicted upon him by his father. He listened; he was polite. But Jane wondered if he'd really heard her. Resigning herself to being patient, she told him she loved him, and they went home to have dinner on the table by the time Jeff and Marla returned from the block of meetings. They said nothing negative or judgmental toward Alex, and she was grateful for their acceptance. She simply prayed that one day, somehow, he would be able to get beyond this.

When it came time for Alex to go back to Michigan, saying goodbye was almost as difficult as it had been before. But now she had enough experience to know that she could survive being without him. Still, she hated it. They kept up the usual schedule of communication, and she knew in her heart that her love for him was true and sound, just as his was for her. But she didn't actually see him again until he came to town for her graduation. He was only able to stay a couple of days, and since her whole family was in town as well, they didn't get much time alone together. It was nice, though, to have him meet all of her family, and they all seemed to like him, except for Lana who told Jane privately that her opinion of the situation hadn't changed. Still, she was polite to Alex, and the overall experience was positive.

Jane went back to California and lived at home for a few months while she submitted what seemed like a hundred resumes. Knowing that Alex would soon be transferring to a different hospital somewhere else in the country in order to broaden his experience, she talked to him about the cities where she might apply, hoping that they could be married, or at least live close enough to see each other. But he was vague about his plans, not seeming certain about where he wanted to go. He told her that she should just pray about it and see what worked out. So she did. A few days later, Ruth Keane called to tell her that there were a couple of openings in the Salt Lake area. Without telling Alex, Jane applied for both of them, realizing as she did that if she truly wanted to be with Alex, this would be perfect. She knew he was very close to his mother, even though they'd hardly seen each other through these years of medical training. She felt sure that if he had a choice, he would choose to settle down close to his mother, even though he'd never said as much. Her theory felt eerily right when she was offered a job teaching first grade at a school less than twenty minutes from where Alex had grown up. She took the job and did a little research before she called Alex.

"Guess what?" she said after the usual catching up on trivial things.

"You got a job?"

She laughed. "Very good. Guess where?"

"Somewhere next door to a hospital, I hope," he said.

"Not quite next door, but close. In fact, the school is in the same city with a hospital that is well reputed for medical breakthroughs and advancements. It's a teaching hospital . . . and   . . ."

"And what?"

"It's a reputable trauma center, Alex. The perfect place for an emergency physician with your gift."

"You've been doing research," he said, feeling stunned.

"Yes, I have."

Alex realized his heart was pounding. He'd been hesitant to commit to any particular city, partly because until his residency was completed, he could be doing a lot of rotations and be living out of a suitcase at least part of the time. And nothing had felt right. Knowing that Jane was far more likely to feel the guidance of the Spirit than he was, he had just prayed that she would be guided to a place that might be right for them to eventually settle down. Or at least a place where they could be together temporarily, until they found a place to settle down—together. But he had to admit that somewhere deep inside he feared that eventually the Spirit would guide Jane away from him. If she felt guided to a job in a place that just wasn't right for him, then what? Now he felt suddenly nervous as he waited for her news. His mind filed through the hospitals he knew of that would fit the criteria she'd just listed. Was it one where he'd considered applying to finish his residency?

"And?" he pressed when she didn't go on.

"You'll never guess."

"Okay, if I'll never guess, then stop torturing me and just tell me."

"Well, first I want to tell you that I flew there for the final interview, and I loved it. It just feels like home. I think I could stay there forever and be perfectly happy, so with any luck you'll be able to feel at home there too."

"That would be a plus," he said with light sarcasm.

"While I was there I found an apartment, and when I got back I finally did what I've been wanting to do for years."

"You bought a new car?"

"I did," she said and laughed. "Well, a newer used one. And I'm packing it up, getting ready to go . . . to my new home."

"Where there's a cutting-edge, teaching hospital."

"That's right."

"Okay, I give up. I can't stand it."

"It's the University of Utah Medical Center, Alex," she said, and he sucked in his breath. "It's less than a ten-minute drive from your mother's house. The school is twenty minutes in the other direction, and my apartment isn't far from your mom's place. She helped me find it."

Alex became too emotional to speak. It had been a trip to that very hospital, as a youth in need of stitches, that had helped spur him into this career. Deep inside, he'd pondered the idea that being able to work there, and living close to his mother, would be ideal. But it was a thought he had kept to himself. He knew that residency positions—and permanent ones—were not necessarily easy to come by, and this was no guarantee that he would be able to get a position there anytime soon. But he had some marvelous incentive.

"You okay?" she asked.

"Yeah," he managed with a quavering voice. "That's just so . . . Wow. It's perfect, except . . . I don't know if I can get on there."

"They have an opening," she said. "I already made some calls and arranged for someone to mail you the applications and stuff. Of course you know there would be exams to take, and such. But it's worth a try."

Again Alex had trouble speaking. It all just seemed too good to be true. But once again God blessed him with a tremendous miracle. The position fell into his hands and within weeks he was preparing to move back to Utah—back home. He wondered what he'd ever done to deserve being so incredibly blessed. It occurred to him that maybe God was trying to make it clear that His hand was in Alex's life. But something deep inside told him that eventually something had to go bad. It all just seemed too good to be true.

— 7 —

Three Years Later

Alex got into his black Ferrari and drove away from the hospital, winding down the hill on a road that had become comfortably familiar. At the bottom of the hill he turned and headed west, attempting to keep the setting sun out of his eyes. Turning into the Avenues of Salt Lake City, the neighborhood where he'd grown up, a series of massive trees shielded him from the blinding light. The drive from the hospital parking lot to his mother's driveway was an easy five minutes, barring any road construction or heavy traffic. His visits home were frequent enough that the car seemed to know its own way, gliding to a smooth stop in the narrow driveway beside the little brick house where Ruth Keane had lived for over thirty years. Alex got out of the car and habitually patted the door as he closed it, as if to offer some form of affection to the vehicle. He loved the car, plain and simple. At the age of fourteen he'd taped that magazine picture of a black Ferrari on his bedroom mirror, and he'd taken that picture with him to college. Through all those years of education, internship, and residency, that picture had kept him believing that it would all be worth it. He'd worked hard to reach a point in his life where he could afford to drive such a car. To him it was a symbol of all he had achieved. And he would never forget the look on his mother's face when he'd first pulled the car into this very spot to take her on a test drive. He might as well have shown her an academy award by the way she squealed with delight and jumped up and down like a child. But she'd always been that way. One great constancy in his life was this amazing woman who had stood behind and beside him in all he had done. She'd believed in him, guided him, and lectured him when he'd needed it. And even when he'd not met her expectations in certain aspects of his life, she had never stopped loving him. As busy as his life had become, he was grateful to have school behind him and now be established with his career right here in his home town so that he could see his mother nearly every day. He never stayed long, but at the end of a shift he could hardly keep himself from going through the side door into the kitchen, just to see how she was doing and absorb some portion of the light that radiated from her. Ruth worked at home and was rarely not there when he came; of course he kept her informed of his shifts at the hospital, and she worked her shopping and appointments around them. She often told him that she wouldn't want to miss a visit from her favorite son.

Alex went to the mailbox and flipped through today's mail as he carried it into the house. He found a few things with his name, but they were all junk, and he tossed them into the outside garbage can that was near the door. Swinging open the screen door, Alex couldn't deny the security he felt in the sound it made on its hinges. Prior to college, he had no memory of ever living anywhere else, since his parents had purchased the home when he'd been less than two years old. The house and yard were both small, but they were surrounded by century-old trees that added to the quaintness and security of home. Ruth kept the house immaculate, and the yard was always well-groomed and filled with flowers through the warm months of the year.

The screen door slammed closed behind Alex, and he tossed the mail onto the counter.

"I'm in here!" Ruth called from the other room. Alex grabbed an apple from a silver fruit bowl on the table as he headed toward her office, a tiny room just off the dining area where she did her work. Through his early childhood, Ruth had been a stay-at-home mom, putting all her efforts into caring for Alex and his two sisters. Then Neil Keane had turned their lives upside down by turning his back on everything he'd always claimed to believe in. While Neil was living with some other woman, Ruth went to work waiting tables to keep her children fed. Alex clearly recalled hearing his mother crying late at night, and then there was the day she had told them she was going to find a way to be able to make the money they needed and still be there when her children came home from school. It didn't happen right away, but eventually she was led to an opportunity to type medical transcripts for a local clinic. Alex remembered sitting at her side and watching the words appear on the paper from the keys of an electric typewriter. He'd felt deeply fascinated with the medical terminology, and he'd always wanted to find out what those big words really meant. When he'd first told his family that he wanted to be a doctor, his older sisters had laughed, insisting that they could never afford medical school, and he wouldn't have the diligence to see it through. But Ruth's eyes had lit up and she'd told him firmly that he *could* do it, and they would find a way. When he'd learned that good grades could result in scholarships, he began to focus more intently on his school work. Any scholarship he could earn would mean less work for himself, and less stress for his mother. He knew she'd take on an extra job to see him through if it became necessary, but he wasn't going to stand for that. She already worked far too hard, in his opinion.

Ruth had long ago graduated to the latest computer technology in order to do her work, and that's where Alex most often found her. It was somehow comforting to find her sitting in that chair, typing so fast that her fingers were almost a blur. He always enjoyed seeing what she might be wearing. Her wardrobe mostly consisted of bright-colored, comfortable skirts and light-weight sweaters and blouses. It was as if she always wanted to feel beautiful and comfortable at the same time. Her feet were usually bare. Today she wore a pink blouse and floral skirt. As usual, he was wearing scrubs. She rarely saw him in anything else.

"Hi," he said and took a bite out of his apple. Her graying dark hair was curled back off her face and hung to the top of her shoulders. She had an indefinable beauty about her that had always been there. She reminded him of the movie stars of the fifties with her full, rounded figure and a way of carrying herself that radiated self-confidence perfectly balanced with humility and a love of life. In that respect she was so much like Jane.

She clicked on the 'Save' icon then turned and grinned at him. "How's my favorite son?"

"I'm your only son," he reminded her for the millionth time, as if she might not know.

"Still my favorite," she said as if she had asked him if the soup needed more basil. "How was your day?" she added.

"Not bad," he said, sitting in the only other chair in the room. "How about yours?"

"Good," she said. "Did my visiting teaching this morning. Sister Jensen is still pretty sick with the chemo, but she's in good spirits."

"Thanks to you," Alex said and took another bite.

Ruth made a noise of disagreement and looked down. "I haven't done anything."

"Except visit her more than any other person in the ward, cook meals for her family once a week, and call her three times a day."

Ruth brushed off the facts in her typical way and changed the subject. "So, tell me about the emergency room excitement. Anything good?"

"No life-threatening emergencies today," he said. "Some stitches, a broken arm, an elderly woman with pneumonia who is going to be just fine. There was a severe stroke, but the victim was DOA."

"Someone elderly?" she asked with compassion, as if she were imagining the person's loved ones facing a death that had likely been a complete shock.

"Early seventies, I think."

"Still too young."

"Yes," he agreed, then went back to his list. "And we had one severe case of dysphagia, and the patient had to have an esophagogastroduodenoscopy."

"Trouble swallowing, eh?" she said, and he smirked. "And just had to have an EGD?"

"Just seeing if you still know your stuff."

"I knew those words and what they meant long before you did." She pointed a finger at him and attempted a scolding glare, but her eyes smiled. "And don't you forget it." She stood and reached up a hand to rough up his thick, dark hair.

"How could I?" he asked, following her into the kitchen. "It's just nice to know someone who speaks the same language."

"Indeed," she said, leafing through the mail he'd left on the counter. "Oh look!" she said with excitement. "*Fun* mail." She held up a white envelope that was obviously some kind of announcement. "It's not a bill and it's not junk."

"That *is* pretty amazing," Alex chuckled and leaned against the counter, folding his arms over his chest while he finished eating his apple and his mother opened the announcement.

"My cousin's daughter is getting married," she said with a little smile on her face as she read the card in her hand, then her eyes widened and lit up brilliantly. "Oh, good heavens!" she said breathlessly and pressed a hand over her heart.

"What?" he demanded, wondering what other information on a wedding announcement could possibly provoke such a reaction.

"The reception is at the house."

"The house?" he echoed, completely baffled when she didn't explain.

"The house." She laughed. "*The* house."

"Okay," he drawled, and motioned with his hand for her to go on.

"It's the Barrett house. The one we've driven past so many times, but I've never been inside."

"Oh, *that* house," he said, and his mother reached for his right hand.

She looked at it and said, "You don't wear that ring."

He gave her a comical scowl. "You know very well that it doesn't fit me; it never did. But I told you when you gave it to me that even if it did I wouldn't wear it. It's really not my style."

"It was my great-grandfather's ring; it's an opal."

"I know, Mother, but it . . . looks like one of those mood rings from the seventies."

Her disappointment over his attitude was evident when she said, "That ring is the only thing I've ever owned that connects me to any of my ancestors. Alexander Barrett was an amazing man; that's why I named you after him. You need to understand how important that ring is to me."

"Yes, Mother," he said tenderly and tossed his apple core into the trash can. "You told me all of that when you gave it to me. That's why I always carry his ring with me everywhere I go." He reached into his right pocket and opened his hand close to her face. Lying in his palm were a couple of quarters, a pair of nail clippers, and the ring.

"Oh," she said, and her entire countenance changed. Moisture brimmed in her eyes as she picked up the ring and admired it closely. She looked up at him. "Forgive me," she said.

"There's no need to apologize, Mother. I'm sorry that I think it's ugly, but that doesn't mean I can't appreciate its value."

Ruth smiled and put the ring back into his hand before she said brightly, "The wedding is at his house; Alexander Barrett *built* this house after he came west with the Saints. My great-grandmother, Katherine, came much later with a different company. They were married and raised their family in that house. From what I understand, they endured many hardships and sacrificed a great deal so that we—their posterity—could live in this beautiful place, and have all the blessings that we now have." She sighed. "I've always wanted to see the inside of the house, but I've never been close enough to the relatives who own it to dare pay a visit. I'd heard that it had been completely restored in the last few years. And now we can go to the wedding and see the house." She looked up at him. "You will go with me, won't you?" She glanced at the calendar. "It's two weeks from Saturday."

"I'd love to," he said.

"Do you think Jane would like to go?"

"I'm sure she'd love it—especially if I bribe her with dinner. Why don't we all go out to dinner afterward and make an evening of it."

"Sounds delightful," she said and sat down at the kitchen table. "How is Jane, by the way?"

"She's good." Alex sat across from her and felt it coming just by the look in her eyes. His mother hadn't brought up marriage in a long time, but he knew she couldn't go *too* many weeks without working it into a conversation.

"Have you set a date yet?" Ruth asked.

"A date for what?" he asked with a smirk.

"You know very well what. You told me well over a year ago that you and Jane were officially going to be married, but I'm still waiting. Is there a problem?"

Alex cleared his throat more loudly than he'd intended and looked away. He reminded himself that she was his mother, and she had a right to know what was going on his life. She'd never been nosy about his personal life—just concerned. And maybe she had reason to be. But it had been a long time since they'd shared much beyond trivial conversation, and he felt suddenly uncomfortable. While a part of him wanted to change the subject and save it for another day, something unexplainably powerful compelled him to talk about it now. He cleared his throat again and kept his eyes down as he spoke. "Jane wants to get married in the temple."

"Good for her," Ruth said, as if she'd never heard this before. "She's the best thing that ever happened to you—beyond me, of course."

"Of course," Alex said with a tense chuckle.

"Why is that still a problem?" Ruth asked. "You quit smoking before college. And unless something's changed, you haven't had a drink for years."

"Nothing's changed; I haven't touched the stuff since I met Jane."

"That's good then. Is there something else? You told me once that you pay your tithing in spite of not going to church."

"Still do," he said.

"Okay, so . . . you're minding your manners with Jane, I hope."

"Of course I am," he said, wishing it hadn't sounded so defensive. "I have my problems, Mother, but that's never been one of them."

"So . . . if you're worthy to go to the temple, why don't you just do it?"

"I'm not presently guilty of any grievous sins, Mother, but I haven't been to church in years; you know that."

"And why is that?"

Alex finally looked at his mother. "I don't understand why it's so important. I can be a good man without going to church or being married in the temple."

"And you can be a better man if you do."

"Like my father?" he countered with sarcasm.

Ruth's eyes turned brittle. He expected her to comment on the grief his father had brought into their lives. He knew how hurt she had been by the man's hypocrisy and betrayal. But she looked at him hard and said with a voice that clearly came from her soul. "When are you going to grow up and stop putting your own accountability at his feet?"

Alex barely felt the question penetrate his brain before he abruptly stopped it from going to his heart. He couldn't recall having a conversation at this level—on this topic—for many years, and he wondered why it was happening now. He retorted in a voice that was hot and quiet. "The man paraded himself before the community as a fine, upstanding, card-carrying Mormon—while he secretly had a girlfriend on the side. He *left* us—high and dry!"

Ruth drew in a deep breath; he could see her visibly attempting to remain calm. "You're not telling me anything I don't already know, Alex." The sadness that accompanied her words made him stop and ponder how much grief was tied into the facts he'd just stated. "I'm not disputing there was a time when he deceived and betrayed us. I'm not disputing his hypocrisy in living a double life. But that was a long time ago. He was excommunicated. He worked his way back and was baptized again. He's a different man now, and you need to learn to accept that. One day you're going to have to forgive him."

"Have *you* forgiven him?"

"Yes," she said with no hesitation.

Alex sighed and looked away. "Well, I don't know if I can."

"And that's hurting you—not him. But it's also hurting Jane—and me. How long will you deny yourself—and those you love—the blessings of the gospel because you're holding a grudge?" He said nothing while he debated over whether he should feel angry or humbled. He quickly decided against the anger, knowing his mother wouldn't put up with it. He also knew that she was right, even before she added in a gentle voice, "Don't let your father keep you from living the best possible life you can live, Alex." She reached across the table and took his hand. "Alexander," she said and looked into his eyes with an intensity that took his breath away. "You know that I love you. I always have; I always will. There's nothing you can say or do that will change that. You also need to know that I want more than anything for you to be truly happy, to be free of the residue of grief you're holding onto. You have a right to be angry over what he did; I was angry too. But you need to forgive, let go of the anger, and move on."

Ruth took a deep breath and tightened her hold on his hand. "Alex," she said in little more than a whisper, "I've not said anything about religion for many months now. You know that I'm not going to nag you over such things."

"You never have, I know," he said.

"But . . . right now . . . there's something I feel compelled to say. It's been on my mind for days, and I've prayed for the opportunity to say it without upsetting or offending you."

Alex recalled the times he'd become upset or offended by talk of religion and wished he could undo those conversations and take them back. Knowing he could only control the moment, he simply said, "Say whatever you like, Mom. It's okay. I'm sorry for being a jerk about it in the past."

Ruth smiled and touched his face with her other hand. "You have a good heart, Alex, and a strong spirit. I want you to know that whatever life may bring, my love for you will always be there. It's eternal, Alex. In spite of your father's bad choices, we were married in the temple, and I have honored those covenants. You were born under that covenant, Alex. You and I are sealed together, forever, as long as we live for those blessings. I can see why it's easy to look around at this world we live in and wonder why living religion makes much difference. Religious people struggle and suffer every bit as much as anybody else—maybe more in some respects. But I want you to know, Alex, that I live my religion because I know beyond any doubt that it's true, that it's what God wants me to do. A great many people endured unspeakable suffering to give us all that we have. We live in a time and place that makes it so easy to worship as we please, and I can't take that blessing for granted. There is a joy and peace associated with living the gospel fully that I can never explain to you. Until you take the steps and cross certain thresholds of your own accord, you will never be able to fully understand what I'm talking about. I don't know when you might be ready to make such choices, but I believe one day you will."

"And what if I don't?" he asked. "What if I'm just not cut out to be the man that you think I am? What if I'm not the man that Jane thinks I am?"

"I know better," she said firmly.

"How do you know?"

"Alexander," she said, and he realized that was the second time in this conversation she'd called him by his full name. It was rare, and he knew she was serious when she said it that way. "It is the only thing I want in this life. I have everything else I could ever ask for. My only wish is to see my children within temple walls, to see you live a life that honors the covenants your father broke. I don't want it as some measure of my own success as a mother, or to somehow compensate for your father's mistakes. I want it because I know it's the only source of *true* happiness." She sighed and gave a faint smile. "Enough said. Just think about what I said, okay?"

"Okay," he said and smiled back. For a long moment they just stared at each other, as if she were attempting to silently communicate something to him that could not be spoken with words. He wasn't certain what that something might be, but he undoubtedly felt her love for him. He knew that he could face anything as long as she loved him. And he knew that she always would.

The mood was broken when Ruth glanced at the clock and said, "I bet Jane is waiting for you."

Alex glanced at his watch. "She probably is." He stood up, and his mother did the same. "However," he said, wanting to ease the tension between them, "I think we need a dance before I go."

Ruth laughed as Alex eased her into a simple waltz around the kitchen. He loved dancing with his mother, and it was something he did often. He knew that she too loved to dance, that she had instilled that love in him, but she had spent nearly twenty years alone. Waltzing with his mother was his way of expressing how very much he loved her, and he hoped that she knew what it meant to him.

When she laughed again and declared that she was getting dizzy, he stopped dancing and hugged her tightly, relishing her embrace. For a long moment the world just seemed to stop, and he could almost literally feel her love soak into him.

She stepped back and smiled. "Run along now. Thanks for stopping by; it's the highlight of my life."

"No, it's the highlight of *my* life."

Ruth laughed softly. "You have a beautiful woman waiting for you ˉvho loves you, who—"

"And I have a beautiful woman standing right here who loves me too."

"Now you're flattering me." She opened the door for him. "Tell Jane hello for me, and you treat her well, now. She's an amazing young woman."

"Yes, she is," Alex agreed. "Maybe I should wise up and marry her."

"Maybe you should," Ruth said.

Alex pressed a quick kiss to her cheek and left the house, taking note of the distinct sound of the screen door closing behind them as she followed him out. Ruth waved from the porch as he got into the car. He waved back and drove away.

Through the ten-minute drive to Jane's home, Alex contemplated his mother's words. It wasn't the first time she'd said them, but it was the first time he'd really heard them. He wondered what had been different today as opposed to their previous conversations about religion—and his father. He couldn't quite pinpoint the difference, but for the first time in his life he found himself asking questions that he'd previously been too angry—or perhaps afraid—to ask. Was his hesitance in committing to temple marriage truly a result of his father's hypocrisy? Was he using his father's mistakes as an excuse to avoid his own accountability? Was he limiting his own happiness by not forgiving his father? Or was there something more, something deeper, something more difficult to define? A heaviness descended over him, making it clear that such questions would not be easily answered, but perhaps it was time he started trying to answer them—instead of avoiding them.

Alex pulled the car into the driveway of Jane's home. Technically, it belonged equally to him. When they'd officially made the decision to be married, they'd also decided to buy a house. He ate many of his meals here, most of his belongings were here, and he spent all of his free time here, but just like in college, he was sleeping in a tiny apartment elsewhere because Jane wanted to be married in the temple, and he was stubbornly holding back from any active involvement with religion. Alex sat in the driveway for several minutes wondering why Jane had committed herself to someone like him in spite of such attitudes. He finally concluded that the best way to answer that question was to ask her.

Alex walked in the door and hollered in a silly voice, "Honey, I'm home."

"Hi," she said, clearly glad to see him as he walked into the kitchen to find her cutting up a tomato. Her blonde hair hung in gentle waves around her shoulders. She wore a navy blue jumper with ABCs embroidered on it in bright colors. "I know you," she added. "You're that famous doctor."

"Famous?" he chuckled. "Famous for what?"

"Famous for loving me," she said with a ring of laughter in her voice. "Dr. Alexander Barrett Keane. That is you, isn't it?"

"It's me," he said. "But you're the famous one, I think. How was kindergarten?" he added before he kissed her in greeting.

"It was great. I'm really glad I got promoted from first grade. We learned the letter K," she said proudly. "And we made kites with crepe paper tails."

Alex chuckled. "Did you fly them?"

"We tried but the wind wasn't so good. How was the ER?"

He repeated what he'd told his mother while he washed his hands and started tearing the lettuce into little pieces.

"Did you see your mom?"

"I did," he said.

"And how is she?"

"She is almost as amazing as you are," he said.

Jane made a dubious noise. "Other way around."

Alex wiped his hands on a towel, then pulled Jane into his arms. "Let's dance," he said and led her into a vibrant twirl, making her laugh.

"We're in the kitchen."

"Great wood floor," he said and guided her into an elegant waltz, making it clear that neither of them had lost their touch.

"I'm in stocking feet."

"It won't hurt when you step on my toes."

"I've never stepped on your toes." She laughed again.

"Oh, that's right," he said. "It was me who stepped on *your* toes."

"I don't recall that either," she said, and he just smiled, looking into her eyes the same way he always had, since that very first waltz. "We have no music," she commented.

"Who needs music?" he asked.

After silently waltzing while they shared an intense gaze, Jane said, "We haven't danced for a while. It used to be like breathing."

"Still is," he said, guiding her through a series of complicated steps while neither of them missed a beat. "Remember the day you found out I was your partner for the dance competition?"

"How could I ever forget?" she said while they continued to dance, circling around the kitchen island. "That was the same day I found out you were going to be my partner forever."

Alex stopped dancing abruptly; she tripped, but he held onto her and kept her facing him. "How did you know that?"

"I just . . . knew," she said.

Alex contemplated the question he'd been pondering in the car. "Is that why you put up with me?"

Jane smiled. "I'm waltzing in the kitchen with a tall, dark, handsome, broad-shouldered young doctor who helps me cook, does my laundry, reads poetry to me, and he's not a bad kisser." Alex smiled, and she added, "Is that what you mean by putting up with you?"

His expression sobered, and he asked, "But in spite of all that, you want something I'm not giving you. That's why we're still living in separate houses." Jane stepped back and looked down. "I got you there. Why do you stick with me, Jane? Maybe I'm just not the man you want me to be."

Alex felt almost startled when she met his eyes with the same kind of intensity he'd felt from his mother only a while ago. With a conviction that took his breath away, she said, "I've seen your potential, Alex; I've felt it. I pray every hour of every day that you will be able to see in yourself what everyone who loves you can see."

"And what is that?"

"That everything good about you would only be better if you could overcome whatever is eating at you and live the life your mother raised you to live."

While Alex was pondering that, the timer on the stove rang and Jane hurried to turn it off and drain the pasta that had been cooking. While she was rinsing it in a colander, Alex asked, "Will you marry me?"

She turned abruptly to look at him. "Already said yes." She lifted her left hand to display her engagement ring.

"Don't you ever get tired of people asking you when the wedding will be?"

"Yes, I do," she said, but there was no malice in her voice. She set the pasta down and stirred the sauce that was in a pot on the stove. "But I just tell them when we're ready we'll send out the announcements."

"I think you're a saint, you know." She just shrugged, and he added, "Maybe we should send out some announcements."

Again she looked at him, almost sharply. "I hate to point out the obvious, Alex, but I'm getting married in the temple, and you can't get a temple recommend if you don't go to church."

"Well then," he said, folding his hands behind his back, "I guess I'd better start going to church."

Jane took a step toward him. She touched his face as if to check for fever and looked closely into his eyes. "No, I'm not sick," he said.

"So . . . what brought this on? The last time you went to church you practically started hyperventilating halfway through the meeting."

"Oh," he looked away and sighed. "My mother said some things that . . . got me thinking."

"Okay," she drawled, "but . . . your mother has said things before that have just gotten you . . . ticked off. What was different?"

"Truthfully," he said, "I don't know. I asked myself the same question, but . . . there was something about the way she said what she did. It was as if . . . she thought she might never see me again."

Jane intensified her gaze on him, and he quickly added, "No, that's not it really. It was more subtle than that. It's just . . . I don't know. There was something about the way she said it that . . ."

"Or maybe something's changed in you?" she guessed. "Maybe the time was right."

"Maybe," he said. "Anyway, I'm trying to tell you that . . . I'd like to start going to church."

Jane smiled but said nothing.

"Well . . . you could show a little more enthusiasm," Alex said.

"I'll show enthusiasm when I find you actually sitting beside me in sacrament meeting for several consecutive weeks."

"Is that a dare?"

"It's a wish, Alex. And when it comes true, I will be the happiest woman on earth."

Alex actually felt choked up as he said, "Well if anyone deserves to be happy, it's you. I'll see what I can do about that."

She looked into his eyes again, as if to gauge his sincerity, then she threw her arms around him and hugged him tightly. "I love you, Alex."

"I love you too, Jane. And I'm grateful for your patience, truly I am."

"It'll pay off one of these days," she said, then added in the same tone, "Dinner is ready. Let's eat."

8

Alex slept little that night as he pondered the conversations that had taken place with his mother and his fiancée, and the feelings inside of him that had resulted. He actually pulled out a Book of Mormon and read for a while—something he'd not done since his youth. More accurately, it was something he'd not done since his father had left with another woman. Instinctively he believed that the journey for him to get to the temple without the emotional burdens that had held him back would not be easy. But for the first time in his life, he felt prepared to begin that journey, and he was grateful for these two incredible women in his life who would be there for him no matter what.

It was dark when Alex got up and left for work. His shift began early and he arrived to find it unusually busy. He was pleased to see that Liz and Shelly were two of the nurses there. They were pleasant and easy to work with. Dr. Ray Baker was also on duty. He and Alex had become fast friends when he'd initially come here, and he most enjoyed the shifts when they worked together. In the first few hours there was a car accident with two injured victims. Thankfully, they would both be fine. There were a couple of screaming babies. One had an ear infection, the other strep throat. There was a bad cut to a hand from a saw, which was referred to a surgeon. And then things quieted down a little. After the local clinics were open for the day, the sick children and minor injuries usually went elsewhere.

Things became a little too quiet, and Alex found himself feeling sleepy. He was about to tell one of the nurses he was going to lie down and to get him if he was needed when a call came in from paramedics that were on their way in with a heart attack victim.

Female in her fifties. Called 911 reporting chest pain. When the emergency team had arrived, she was gone. They were attempting to revive her en route, but the radio report already let him know the patient wasn't going to make it. Still, according to protocol he waited for the ambulance to arrive so that he could officially declare the death, since Baker was momentarily busy elsewhere. Alex watched the ambulance pull up on the other side of the doors, and there was no attempt to hurry as they removed the patient and wheeled the gurney through the automatic doors.

"Sorry, doc," one of the medics said. "She was gone before we got to her. We did everything we could."

Alex absorbed the information as an emergency room doctor who had witnessed death more times than he could count. Then he got a look at the patient's face, and life as he knew it came to a dead stop. "No," he muttered under his breath, then again more loudly. "No."

"Dr. Keane?" Shelly asked with obvious concern. "What is it? What's wrong?"

"God help me," he murmured, touching the victim's face, her throat, her arms, desperately searching for any sign of life. But there was none. He felt a burning in his chest, then heard a sob erupt from his own mouth.

"Dr. Keane?" He heard two different voices say his name, as if from a distance, reminding him that he wasn't alone. He turned to look at the paramedics, the nurses, Dr. Baker, all staring at him with horror in their eyes.

"Who is it?" Liz asked.

Alex touched Ruth Keane's lifeless hand and felt tears trickle down his face. "It's my mother," he said and rushed into an empty room to be alone before the full extent of his grief could explode into the open. He lost track of the time as he sobbed and struggled to breathe and forced himself to keep from screaming loud enough to bring the entire staff running in to invade his privacy.

Alex found himself sitting on the cold floor of a vacant trauma room, his back against the wall, his head in his hands, unable to accept what the evidence had told him. He was all cried out and blanketed by shock, unable to move, or even think. A gentle hand touched his arm and he looked up to see Liz's kind face close to his.

"Dr. Keane," she said tenderly. "I've cleaned her up and she's in the next room, if you'd like to sit with her for a while."

It took Alex a long moment for her meaning to fully penetrate his clouded brain. "Thank you," he said, struggling to get to his feet. She held to his arm to help him.

"Doctor Reynolds is on his way in to cover your shift."

"Thank you," he said again, walking slowly from the room while she kept his arm in her hand as if she feared he might fall over. He hesitated at the door of the room where he knew his mother lay, and he was grateful for Liz urging him forward. He gasped when he saw his mother again. She really was dead, gone. He couldn't believe it. A heart attack? She had regular physicals. She'd never had any signs of heart problems. He just couldn't believe it.

Liz guided him to a chair that was placed close to where Ruth lay. "Can I get you anything?" Liz asked. "Are you hungry? Thirsty?"

"Just some . . . water," he said, his voice raspy.

She left and returned with a drink of water, saying gently, "I'm so sorry, Dr. Keane. I don't know what to say. We're all kind of . . . in shock . . . on your behalf I guess. None of us even knew her, but . . . for you to find out this way. It's just . . . I don't know what to say."

"It's okay," he said when he realized she actually had tears in her eyes. "Thank you."

"Is there anyone I can call for you, or . . ."

"Uh . . ." Alex rubbed his forehead, attempting to put together a cohesive thought. Jane. He needed Jane. He felt for the cell phone clipped to his belt. "Uh, no . . . thank you. I can do it." Then he realized that Jane wouldn't answer her cell phone while she was in class. "Actually . . . could you call the school . . . where my fiancée works and . . ."

He told her Jane's full name and which school to call. "Just . . . have her call my cell phone."

"I'll do that," she said. "You stay as long as you need to. I'll check back."

"Thank you," he said again and watched her leave the room, leaving him alone with this lifeless form that just yesterday had hugged him tightly and had spoken words of wisdom to him as if . . . as if . . . "Oh, help," he muttered to the empty room. What had he

said to Jane? *As if she might never see him again?* Had he really said
that? Had he really *felt* that?

Alex felt his cell phone vibrate and gasped. He grabbed it and
looked at the caller ID. It was Jane. He pushed the button to turn it
on, but then he couldn't make himself speak.

"Alex?" she said, her voice frantic. "Alex? Are you there?"

"Yeah . . . I'm here," he said.

"Alex, what's happened? They called the office; they said to call
you . . . that it was an emergency."

Alex cleared his throat and squeezed his eyes closed, not knowing
how to make the words come out. Fresh tears trickled down his face.

"Alex?"

"Uh . . . it's my mom. Um . . . she's gone, Jane." He sobbed then
pressed a hand over his mouth.

"Gone?" she cried. "What do you mean?"

He forced his grief back. "She . . . uh . . . had a heart attack." He
heard Jane gasp but he pressed forward. "The paramedics brought her
here. She was . . . DOA." He groaned as it came out of his mouth.
How many times had he said that and felt nothing? How could he say
it about his own mother?

"I can't believe it," Jane muttered, and he could tell she was
crying. Her tears prompted more of his own.

"I can't either. I . . . I . . . don't know what to say."

"Are you at the hospital?" she asked.

"Yeah. I'm . . . with her."

"I'll be right there," she said and hung up. Alex took hold of his
mother's hand, pressed his face against the bed where she lay and
wept like a lost child. He was still there crying when Jane sat beside
him and put her arms around him. He took hold of her and cried
harder, well aware that she was crying with him. When he finally
calmed down, he told her more of what had happened, even though
there wasn't much to tell. He was grateful for Jane's levelheadedness as
she helped him make arrangements with a mortuary and phone each
of his sisters to tell them the dreadful news.

Through the next few days, Jane hardly left Alex alone for a
minute, except when he was with one or both of his sisters. He slept
at his mother's home, which was where his sisters stayed as well. She

got a substitute for her kindergarten classes and held Alex's hand through the funeral and all that led up to it. While he felt endlessly grateful for her presence and her ability to think on his behalf, he felt somehow on the periphery of a perspective that everyone except himself seemed to have. He listened to his sisters and Jane analyzing Ruth's death, the timing, the things she'd said to each of her children over the last few weeks, and they all seemed convinced that it had been Ruth's time to go, that her death had been in God's hands. And while they were all obviously grieving, missing her, struggling with the loss, they all claimed to feel a great deal of peace. Well, Alex didn't feel peace. When he allowed himself to feel at all, he could only feel either a deep festering heartache that threatened to eat him alive from the inside out—or a smoldering anger. Preferring the anger over the heartache, he squelched any hint of sorrow with an anger that boiled inside of him but had nowhere to go. When his father showed up at the viewing, Alex barely managed to hold himself together.

"What's wrong?" Jane whispered, taking hold of his arm.

"That's my father," he whispered back.

Jane discreetly observed the man who had caused so much grief for Alex. He was alone, and she wondered if he'd purposely come without his second wife out of respect to the family. She was actually looking forward to meeting him, then Alex said quietly, "Let's get out of here."

He urged her away from the receiving line, and she couldn't help noticing that his father watched them leave, appearing visibly disappointed. But Alex wouldn't even make eye contact with him, and he didn't return to the receiving line until she verified that his father had left the building. For Alex's sake, she was glad that his father didn't actually come to the funeral. Or if he did, he kept himself well hidden in the crowd.

Alex managed to keep his emotions in check through the funeral, and then through all that had to be done to settle his mother's estate. Her will was very clear, her life insurance good, her home and papers in perfect order. He was grateful that his sisters were able to stay a few days after the funeral, but it wasn't nearly enough time to go through their mother's things or make any big decisions related to the home. So they settled what was important, locked up the house, and asked a neighbor to keep an eye on it. He would also see that some boys in the neighborhood would keep up the yard to earn some extra money.

Once Alex saw his sisters onto their separate flights to leave the state, he attempted to face life without Ruth Keane in it. He and Jane both went back to work on the same day—a Monday, more than a week beyond his mother's death. He felt as he'd felt since it had happened: dazed and lost, as if he were viewing life through a fog. At first walking back into the ER was tough, due to his memories of seeing his mother come through those doors on a gurney. But he quickly got busy and was grateful for an ongoing string of emergencies that didn't give him time to think. He managed to get through the first day relatively well, but the next day there were too many lulls, too much time to think, and then a car accident victim came in. He frantically worked on her for nearly an hour, but he wasn't able to save her. Seeing this young woman's life fade away, he felt a volcano of grief inside of him threatening to erupt. He went into the personnel lounge, grateful to be alone, and cried for several minutes before he was able to force the grief back beneath the barrier that held it in control.

He was still sitting in the lounge, his head in his hands, when one of the nurses—a tall brunette named Lida—came in.

"Sorry," she said, getting something out of the fridge. "I hope I didn't intrude."

"It's fine," he said and came to his feet. "I need to get back to work anyway."

"Hey, don't leave on my account," she said and put a hand on his arm to stop him.

Alex looked at her hand on his arm, then at her face, and felt completely surprised by what he saw in her eyes. Lida had been subtly flirtatious with him ever since she'd started working here less than a year ago. And he had completely ignored her subtle comments and gestures that seemed to imply she was after something. Even if he were available—which everyone he worked with knew he was not— he would never date someone he worked with. And he would never date a girl like Lida. But suddenly the situation was no longer subtle. If he had any doubt as to her intentions, they were erased completely when she said, "I can tell you're having a rough time, Alex. If there's anything I can do . . . anything at all, just say the word." Her eyes turned coyly downward then slowly assessed him on their way back up to meet his.

In his typical straightforward manner, he said, "That sounds a lot like some kind of come on."

She smiled slightly. "It is if you want it to be."

Alex couldn't believe what he was hearing. Forcing back the temptation to get angry, he simply said, "You must know that I have a fiancée, since everybody around here does."

"Yes," she said. "I also know that you've been engaged an awfully long time; obviously it's not working out." Her voice became almost sultry as she tightened her grip on his arm. "Maybe she's just not the right woman for you, Alex."

Alex looked into her eyes and was surprised to realize he was actually weighing her proposition. She'd hit a nerve. Maybe Jane wasn't the right woman for him. Maybe he was wasting Jane's time. A voice somewhere inside seemed to say, *You're not worthy of a woman like Jane. The cheap, tawdry lifestyle Lida is offering is more suited to a man like you.*

Alex brushed the idea quickly away. Whether Jane was the woman for him or not, he knew it wasn't in him to stoop so low as to become involved with a woman under such circumstances. He could never give her what she was after, and she could never give him what he needed. He might be depressed, and in some respects he was probably a fool. But he would never be *that* stupid.

"Whether or not she is the right woman for me has absolutely nothing to do with you. I'm not interested. And I would prefer that you call me Dr. Keane."

He savored the angry astonishment on her face for just a moment before he left the lounge. He'd barely taken a couple of steps down the hall before he was met by the ER director. "You okay?" she asked.

"Yeah," he insisted. "I'm fine; just needed a break."

"Hey, maybe you need some more time off."

"No, what I need is to keep busy. I'm fine." He moved past her, forcing himself to stay busy through the remainder of his shift. He found himself dreading the end of the work day. While it was always good to see Jane, and though he was grateful to have her in his life, he felt as if he'd become very poor company. There was way too much silence between them, with nothing to say that hadn't already been said.

He was on his way out the door when Shelly stopped him and said, "Hey, we're having a little thing at our house tonight to celebrate my husband's birthday. Why don't you and Jane come over. It might do you good to get out. And there will be plenty to eat."

Alex had to admit, "That sounds nice. I'll see what Jane's doing. I guess if . . . we show up then you'll know we're coming."

"Fair enough," Shelly said.

"Do you want us to bring anything?"

"Nope, just yourselves. Hope to see you later."

* * * * *

Jane stood in front of the open kitchen cabinet, attempting to motivate herself to pull something out and start cooking supper. She sighed and closed the cabinet doors, wondering what point there would be in her efforts. She had little appetite, and she knew Alex would more than likely stir his food around on his plate rather than eat it. It hadn't been so many days ago that he'd expressed a newfound conviction in making positive changes in his life. She'd felt such hope; she'd truly believed that he'd finally come to his senses, that he really would do what he needed in order to marry her in the temple. And maybe he would have. But Ruth's death had changed everything for Alex. She'd never seen a human being so thoroughly lost, so utterly grief stricken that he could barely function. She suspected he was doing okay at work, but in her presence he was like a shell. And she didn't know what to do about it.

From the first moment she'd laid eyes on Alexander Keane, she'd felt completely drawn to him, as if a part of her spirit had been searching for him her entire life, and one look at him had created some kind of magnetic force that was impossible to turn off. From that very first moment she'd felt responsible for him somehow. Her excitement in learning all they had in common had been offset with her disappointment that he didn't live the values he'd been raised with. But she'd rarely allowed discouragement into the picture.

Through much prayer and pondering, and fasting more times than she could count, she had always felt a deep peace in her heart that Alex would come around, that he would somehow, someday, be able to put away the hurt festering inside of him and learn to trust God again enough to believe that he was worthy of the blessings he was denying himself. He'd come so far—and now this. Having his mother taken so suddenly, at such an untimely age, was the worst possible thing that could have happened to Alex's floundering faith. But it *had* happened, and there was nothing she could do about it. She could only stand by him as she always had and pray that they would be granted a miracle, that God might put something into Alex's path to help him understand how thoroughly blessed—and amazing—he really was. But something deep inside her wondered if she could ever stand by him long enough. She'd spent four years in his life, eager and willing to be married right from the start, and she felt no closer to seeing him go to the temple than he had been when they'd met. If anything, he'd regressed severely since his mother's death. In her heart Jane had to ask herself some hard questions, and she couldn't deny the possibility that Alex would simply never come around. She cried long and hard as the reality of the situation settled into her. She knew she couldn't go on this way. Something had to give one way or another, or she was going to snap.

Jane was startled by the phone ringing. The caller ID let her know it was Alex, likely just leaving the hospital. She wiped her tears and composed her voice before she answered.

"Hey gorgeous," he said, and she caught the subtlest hint in his voice that the real Alex Keane still existed in there somewhere. Perhaps there was still a grain of hope, but she hardly dared believe it.

"You've got the wrong girl," she said lightly. "I'm seventy-three years old. I have curlers in my hair, false teeth, and I'm wearing a ratty bathrobe and fuzzy slippers."

He actually chuckled. "No, no, no," he said. "I have x-ray vision and I can see through this phone and that's not you."

"Just give me forty years or so."

He chuckled again, but it felt forced. "I know who you really are. You're Miss Layton, that amazing kindergarten teacher."

"Okay, so you're onto me. What do you want?"

"You know Shelly . . . one of the nurses?"

"Yes."

"Well, she's having a thing at her house tonight . . . for her husband's birthday. We're invited. She said it would be good for me to get out. You want to go?"

Jane knew that Shelly and her husband weren't members of the Church, but that was all she knew beyond the fact that Shelly was a good nurse and a very sweet woman. She felt sure it would be good for Alex to get out, but she wasn't sure he would be up to it.

"Do *you* want to go?" she asked.

"I'm easy either way, but . . . it would include dinner, so we wouldn't have to cook."

"Well . . . let's go then. Maybe she's right. Maybe it would be good for you to get out and do something besides stare at the wall."

"I don't just stare at the wall," he insisted. "Sometimes I stare at you."

"I think you need to get out," she repeated. "I didn't know what to cook, anyway."

Jane ended the call and changed her clothes, praying that the evening would go well, and praying even harder that they would be blessed with a miracle—something that would touch Alex's heart and give him peace over his mother's death, and his own life.

* * * * *

Alex walked in the door and couldn't see Jane anywhere in the main living area, then he heard water running in the bathroom. He leafed through the mail, since all of his important mail came to this address. Beneath a small stack of junk mail and bills he found a large white envelope that was obviously some kind of announcement. In his memory he heard his mother clearly say, "Oh look! *Fun* mail."

Alex squeezed his eyes closed. For a long moment he indulged in the memory of their last visit, wishing he'd known that death was waiting in the wings. His thoughts quickly became too painful, and he forced them away, focusing instead on the 'fun mail' in his hands. It was addressed to Dr. and Mrs. Alexander Barrett Keane, and the address was handwritten in an elegant script. Obviously this was someone who had heard they were long ago engaged and had assumed that the wedding had taken place. He found it odd that his full name had been used, and he also thought it strange that it wasn't an address label. Who hand addressed announcements these days? Alex opened the announcement and scanned it. When he realized why it looked familiar, a sick knot gathered in his stomach. He was startled to hear Jane say, "What have you got there?" He hadn't even realized she'd come into the room.

"Uh . . . a wedding announcement."

"Who's getting married?"

"I have no idea. I think it's . . . my mother's cousin's daughter . . . or something like that."

Jane tried to figure why Alex looked so upset over a wedding announcement from someone he didn't even know. Realizing she had no idea, she just asked, "What's the problem, Alex? You look as if you've seen a ghost."

He looked up at her, visibly startled. "Maybe," he said. "Sort of."

"Tell me," she urged gently.

"My mother got one of these. She opened it while I was there . . . the last time I saw her."

"Oh, I see."

"She really wanted to go; she asked if we would go with her."

"Even though we don't know these people?"

"Well . . . I think it's more the house than the people that she wanted us to see."

"The house?" Jane echoed.

"The house . . . where the wedding reception is being held. It was . . . built by her great-grandfather."

"The ring you carry around; *that* great-grandfather?"

"The very same. He was my mother's hero; I never really knew why, for certain. But this was his house, and apparently it's been fully restored. And she never saw the inside."

"I bet she can see the inside now," Jane said with a bright tone in her voice, but Alex's expression made it clear he found no compensation in such a theory. "We should go," she added. "It might be fun to learn a little something about this hero of your mother's—or at least to see his house."

"Maybe," Alex said and tossed the announcement onto the table. "I'll hurry and clean up."

As he moved toward the bathroom, Jane called, "Are we supposed to take anything?"

"Just us, she said."

While Jane waited for Alex to take a quick shower, her mind began wandering through the present situation and the way she felt about it. She wondered for a moment if she should just relent and marry Alex civilly. Perhaps if they were married they could work toward the temple togther. But the thought barely entered her brain before she knew—just as she'd always known—that it wasn't the answer. Perhaps for some people that would be the right course, but she had prayed about this issue over and over, and she'd always known beyond any doubt that temple marriage was her only leverage. For some, dangling such a carrot might not work, but Alex loved her and she knew it. She also knew that he was a man of integrity, and he would not go through the motions of religion just to please her. He wouldn't go to the temple until he was truly ready, and that's when she would be ready to marry him. Still, it felt so ludicrous to be living this way. She told herself as she had a million times to just be patient, but in that moment a formless sense of urgency overruled anything resembling patience. Analyzing her feelings more deeply, she felt certain that if she didn't give him some kind of ultimatum, their relationship could go on this way forever.

As they drove across town to Shelly's place, Jane felt that if she didn't say something she would burst. It was as if some force beyond her control was forcing the words into her mouth, as if it were now or never.

"Alex," she said gingerly, "there's something I need to say. I apologize if the timing is bad; I know things are rough right now. But hear me out, okay?"

"Okay," he said in a bored tone, keeping his attention on the road while he drove.

"We can't keep living this way, Alex. We're not getting any younger. If we're going to have a family we can't wait forever." He looked at her sharply, and she added a gentle plea. "We should be living as husband and wife, Alex. Think about the things your mother said to you before she died." He turned away, and the muscles in his face tightened. "Think about the things you said to me before she died. Do you think your mother would—"

Alex interrupted angrily, as if he couldn't bear to think about anything related to his mother. "Do you think I like living this way?" he snapped. "It takes a great deal of willpower to keep my distance from you when we're sharing practically everything except the same bed."

"Well, obviously it's not too difficult for you," she countered.

"What makes you think so?"

"Because solving it doesn't give you enough motivation to get over what stands between us. It's readily evident that remaining celibate is easier for you than living your religion."

"I live my religion," he retorted hotly. "I'm a Christian man, and I treat the people around me accordingly."

"I can't dispute that," she said more gently. "You're a man of integrity, Alex, and I'm grateful. I appreciate the fact that you won't go through the motions of going to church just to make me happy, because that would be worse than your not going at all. You're a good man and that's why I love you. But you're missing the point, you know?"

"And what point is that?"

"How can you truly be a Christian if you refuse to go to *His* church and *His* temple?" He scowled at her, but she pressed forward with her point, refusing to be intimidated. "There are many Christians in the world who don't know any better. But you were raised with the truth, the *whole* truth, and you're not living up to that. Your mother wanted nothing more than to see you embrace the gospel and live it so that you could be truly happy." She saw his face tighten even further and knew she'd struck a nerve—perhaps too sensitive a nerve.

"Why do you put up with it, Jane?" he asked, sounding both angry and sad.

"Because I love you."

"Well, like I've said before: you must be a saint."

"I'm not a saint, Alex. I'm human, and I can't keep living like this."

Alex looked at her abruptly. "What are you trying to say? Whatever it is, just say it and get it over with."

Jane drew a deep breath. Knowing it was right didn't make saying it any easier. "I'm not going to keep waiting, Alex, if it's only a futile wait. If I had any indication at all that you were actually working toward the goal, it might be different. But I have no reason to believe that you are any more ready than you were four years ago. If anything, since your mom died, it's worse. And I'm not going to live this way."

She waited for some kind of response, but all she got was silence, while the muscles in his face tightened further. Knowing she'd said some difficult things, she figured it was best to just let them settle in. "That's all I have to say," she concluded, hoping she hadn't said too much.

"Well good," he snarled. "Now maybe we can enjoy what's left of the evening."

Nothing more was said before they entered Shelly's home. Alex was kind and amiable to people at the party, but Jane knew he was in a foul mood, and he hardly even looked in her direction. After dinner the men and women ended up splitting off when the men were all lured into the den where some game was on TV. The women all ended up in the front room where the conversation mostly focused on having babies and raising children. *Just what I need,* Jane growled inwardly. Being reminded that she was the only one in the room not yet a mother was like lemon juice in a paper cut. Insignificant to the big picture perhaps, but it still hurt.

When Shelly got out a bottle of wine, Jane felt mildly uncomfortable. She gracefully refused and noticed that she wasn't the only one in the room who didn't drink. It was far from the first time she'd encountered such a situation. She was more concerned with what they might be passing around in the other room, and how Alex might respond, given his present state of mind. She told herself that he hadn't had a drink for years and surely he wouldn't back down on that now. Half an hour later she decided she'd had enough of this girl talk and came to her feet, pleading the need to go home and grade papers. The women were all very sweet, especially Shelly, who thanked her for coming and offered compassion for Ruth's death.

Shelly walked with Jane to the den where the men were all laughing boisterously. She was relieved when Shelly interrupted them and said to Alex, "Hey there, Doctor. Jane needs to get home; you're going to have to give it up."

Jane's heart began to pound before she consciously realized that Alex was holding a drink. She quickly told herself that maybe he was just *holding* it, if only to feel less uncomfortable with the guys. Then she watched him swallow the remainder of a dark golden liquid before he set the empty glass down near a liquor bottle on the coffee table and came to his feet—somewhat unsteadily.

"Thank you, Shelly," Jane said quickly and hurried toward the front door. "Tell Alex I'll meet him at the car. I need some fresh air."

"Thanks for coming," Shelly said, apparently unaware that anything was wrong.

It took Alex several minutes to finally show up at the car. He seemed relatively steady on his feet—but not completely. He said nothing as he pointed the remote at the car and the doors unlocked.

"Give me those," she growled and grabbed the keys from his hand.

"What are you doing?" he demanded as she got into the driver's seat.

"I'm driving. What does it look like I'm doing? You've been drinking, Alex. You can barely walk straight. If you think I'm going to risk my life by riding with you behind the wheel, then you're a bigger idiot than I thought you were."

Alex snarled something under his breath and got into the passenger seat. They drove a few minutes in silence before he said, "Go ahead. Say it and get it over with."

"Say what?"

"I've been drinking and you're angry. You probably have a right to be. So just say it and get it over with."

"Why should I when you probably won't remember it in the morning?"

"I'm a little tipsy, Jane. I'm not drunk."

"How comforting that you know the difference," she said with sarcasm.

"Just say what you have to say."

"Fine," she said. "You're pathetic, you know that?"

"Yes I am," he said almost proudly. "But maybe I've got good reason to be pathetic."

"Oh, so I'm supposed to feel sorry for you? Is that it? Your father abandoned you, your mother's dead, and your sisters live too far away to know what a poor little lost boy you really are. But you know what? I'm not going to marry you because I feel sorry for you. You have barbed wire around your heart, Dr. Keane, and until you let God past the fence, there's no way you're going to ever let me past it. I'm tired of fighting it; I'm tired of waiting. I love you, Alex, but I'm not going to live this way. I'm sorry for your loss—I truly am, but it doesn't give you the right to treat me badly, and if you don't have enough character to handle your grief without liquor, then you're engaged to the wrong woman."

"Maybe I am," he said with an underlying cruelty in his voice just as Jane pulled up to a four-way stop. Alex wished it hadn't come out sounding so cutting when he saw the hurt in her eyes. She hesitated and glared at him for a long moment, then looked both ways and moved into the intersection. Looking in Jane's direction, Alex saw the truck coming. He sucked in his breath when he realized it wasn't even slowing down. Heedless of the stop sign, it was coming straight at them. The seconds became eternal as the sound of glass breaking and metal being crushed resounded through his brain. Then everything went black.

— 9 —

Without opening his eyes, Alex came awake surrounded by a sense of familiarity. And yet something wasn't right. The sounds and smells, even the voices, all felt deeply comfortable, but it took him a long moment to figure out what was wrong. When it struck him, his heart rate quickened—and a beeping noise in the room corresponded. This was where he *worked,* not where he was supposed to be coming out of a deep sleep. Forcing his eyes open, his first thought was, *So this is what it's like from the other perspective, looking at those bright trauma room lights.* And then he remembered. The intersection. The truck. The deafening sound of the crash. Jane was driving. That beeping in the room quickened further.

"Jane!" he screamed from deep inside but it came out as a strained whisper.

He felt a hand on his arm, and heard a familiar voice. "Alex, it's all right. You're going to be fine."

Alex forced his eyes to focus on the face close to his. "Baker," he whispered. "The things you do to get me here during your shift."

Ray gave a brief chuckle that ended up sounding more like a little sob. Alex noticed his chin actually quivering and the dread inside of him tightened. "Where's Jane?" he demanded quietly.

"She's in the next room," Ray said quickly.

Well, that didn't tell him anything. Alex hurried to express his most prominent thought. "If you tell me she's dead you might as well just give me something lethal right now because I—"

"She's not dead, Alex," Ray said gently.

"Then what's wrong?" Alex asked. Ray hesitated and Alex insisted, "Just tell me and get it over with." It occurred to him that there might be something seriously wrong with himself, as well. But he was more concerned about Jane.

"We really don't know how bad it is at this point. They're prepping her for surgery. She's got some broken ribs, perforated lung. That's all we know for sure. There's internal bleeding. I'm sure she'll be fine." He added the last with a forced smile, and Alex recognized something in his eyes that didn't agree.

Alex groaned as he tried to grasp what was happening. *He couldn't believe it.* The prospect of losing Jane after losing his mother was simply more than he could bear. But a numb kind of shock hovered somewhere between his conscious thoughts and his emotions. Or maybe it was just the pain in his head. He couldn't recall ever being in this much pain. Still, if the physical pain could keep him from feeling the emotional reality, maybe it wasn't so bad. He wondered about Jane. "Was she in a lot of pain?"

"She . . . hadn't regained consciousness before she went in. Hadley was on; she's with him. He's one of the best. You know he'll do everything he can."

Alex managed a slight nod then asked, "And what about me? Am I going to live?" The ring of sarcasm didn't begin to express his wish that he truly might not have to live long enough to know whether or not Jane would survive this new horror in their lives. And maybe she would be better off without him.

"I'm afraid you are, buddy. As far as we can tell . . ." He hesitated as noises outside the room made it evident a patient was being rushed to the OR—obviously Jane. Alex tried to tell himself this wasn't real, that it was all just a very bad dream. But the pain in his head was a good indication that it *was* real. He focused again on Ray, who continued his report. "Well, you're covered with contusions, but nothing appears to be broken. You got a nasty laceration there on the right side of your forehead, but I don't think the scar will be too noticeable." Alex touched his forehead and found several stitches that almost reached into his hairline. "We're sending you to radiology in a few minutes to make sure everything's okay. And I've ordered a CT scan. Apparently your head hit the side window pretty hard. We're going to keep you for a day or two and make sure there's no swelling in your brain."

Alex absorbed everything he was being told and attempted to will away the sickness smoldering in his stomach when he thought of Jane. Realizing that Ray was still beside him, a hand on his arm, Alex took a shot at breaking the tension by saying lightly, "So now everyone I work with knows everything about my medical profile?"

Ray forced a smile, but his chin quivered again. "We'll be discreet; I promise."

"If we're going to be fine, then why do you look like you're going to cry?"

Ray chuckled tensely and looked away. "I confess it shook me up pretty bad . . . seeing you come in that way . . . and Jane too. It gave me some empathy for how you must have felt when you saw your mother come in here . . . already gone. And I . . ." His voice broke. "I . . . just don't know how you can take this on top of losing your mom and . . ." He sniffled loudly. "Sorry."

"It's okay," Alex said, taking his hand. "I don't know how I'm going to take it either; it's nice to know I'm not alone."

The following hours were the worst of Alex's life. Never had he known such helplessness, such despair, such fear. And the physical pain he was in didn't help. Once he was brought back from radiology, they offered something for the pain, and he told them exactly which drug he wanted and how much of it. He didn't want to be too out of it until he knew where things stood with Jane. He was officially admitted, and they were going to move him to a room upstairs, but he asked if he could stay in the ER. It was slow and there was plenty of space, and at least here he knew that the staff would be honest with him and keep him informed.

Alex was relieved when Dr. Baker let him know that he had no broken bones, and the CT scan looked normal, but they were still going to keep him for at least twenty-four hours to make sure he was okay. While he waited to hear about Jane, he tried to give in to the fogginess in his head created by the medication. He longed to feel relaxed, but he didn't want to go to sleep. He was startled when Baker came into the room, and he realized he'd dozed off.

"She's out of surgery," Ray said.

"Is she going to be okay?" Alex demanded hoarsely.

"They're taking her to the fourth floor."

"ICU," he said, and Baker nodded. "Is she going to be okay?" Alex repeated.

"As far as I know she's stable; that's *all* I know. I'll keep on top of it, and you'll know as soon as I know. Okay? Now try to relax. Maybe I should give you something stronger."

"No, I'm fine," Alex said, not wanting to sleep.

Ray left the room, and Alex groaned as he pondered the reality. He couldn't believe it! This had to be some kind of nightmare! He felt himself relaxing, and the next thing he knew he was coming awake, his head pounding horribly, his every muscle aching. And Ray was sitting next to the bed, looking solemn.

"What?" Alex demanded.

"I got off a while ago, but I stuck around. I promised that I'd let you know."

"So let me know."

"It looks like everything's going to be okay, except . . ."

"Except?" Alex growled.

"She's comatose, Alex. She hasn't responded at all since she was brought in."

Alex squeezed his eyes closed against the news. He listened while Ray told him a medical summary of everything that had been done, what the tests had shown, and what they were doing for her. He listened with a growing sense of horror. He knew well the unpredictability of a coma. She could come out of it in hours, days, weeks. Maybe years. Maybe never.

"Get me out of here," Alex said, sitting up with a groan.

"You really need to stay down."

"I'm fine. I need to be with her. Just . . . get me in a wheelchair and get me to her room. They have a recliner in there, I'm sure. That's where I want to be. Just get me there, and then you can go home and get some sleep."

"Okay, buddy. Take it easy."

Alex realized he was in a hospital gown and asked for his clothes. Baker found them in a bag of personal items, but told him they had bloodstains, so he found Alex some clean scrubs and standard issue hospital socks, and he helped Alex get into them. He helped Alex into a wheelchair and took him to the medical ICU. Alex felt horrified when they entered Jane's room. He didn't have to ask any questions about what she was hooked to and why. He knew very well what all of it meant, and it made him sick.

"You need anything else?" Ray asked, situating the wheelchair close to the bed.

"No . . . but thank you," Alex said, "for everything."

"Have them page me if I can do anything; I mean it."

"Thank you," Alex said again, his eyes focused on Jane.

"I'm going to let the floor nurses know that you're here, so someone can keep an eye on you."

Alex ignored the last. All he could see, and hear, and feel, was Jane. His sweet Jane. He asked himself what she had ever done to deserve something like this. And then he had to ask himself what he had done to bring this on. If he hadn't been drinking, she wouldn't have been driving. It would have been him on the side of impact, not her. He replayed the moments leading up to the impact. How clearly he could see her glaring at him before she looked both ways and drove forward. If they hadn't been arguing, maybe she would have gotten through the intersection a few seconds sooner. Oh, he was such a fool! Such an absolute fool!

He sat there for a short while before a nurse came in to ask him how he was doing, and he realized it was morning. He wondered what Ray had told her by the way she moved the recliner as close as possible to Jane's bed and insisted that he get in it. He took a careful trip to the restroom while she waited close by, then he got into the recliner and tried to get comfortable. A while later he was brought some breakfast and was threatened that he must eat it.

"You may be a doctor here," the nurse said, "but you don't scare me. Now eat this so you can have the strength to help her get through this."

Alex glanced at her ID badge. "Carol," he said. "You must be accustomed to dealing with stubborn patients, Carol."

"Yeah," she said, "and stubborn doctors. Now eat it, and take this." She set a little white cup with a pill in it on his tray.

"What is it?"

"It will help the pain, and it will help you relax. Dr. Baker ordered it."

"What is it?" he demanded.

"You're so smart, you figure it out," she said and left the room.

Alex managed to eat a portion of his breakfast, then he just held the little cup with the pill, debating whether he preferred to be awake and look at her, or be asleep and oblivious to the horror. He was still contemplating when Shelly walked into the room, barely keeping her emotions under control as her eyes took in Jane, and then him.

"I couldn't believe it when I got here and they told me what had happened. And on the way home from my house. I just . . . just . . . ."

"Now stop that," Alex said. "If you cry then I'll start crying and . . ." He forced back the temptation to do just that, knowing his headache couldn't handle it.

"Is there anything I can do?" she asked, wiping at her eyes with a tissue. "Can I help you call people or—"

"Oh, good heavens," he muttered. "I need to call her parents . . . my sisters."

"Can I help?" Shelly asked, gaining control of her emotions.

"Yes, actually you can."

She found his cell phone in the bag with his personal things, and thankfully it hadn't been damaged in the accident, since that's where all of his phone numbers were stored. Once he had the phone, he said, "Okay, thank you. I think I can handle it now."

"I'll check back during my break," she said and left the room.

Alex found himself uttering a quick prayer as he looked up the number for Jane's parents and pushed the button so it would dial. He hadn't prayed at all since his mother had died, and before then it had been rare. Louisa Layton answered the phone, and he glanced at the clock, realizing it would be an hour earlier there. Still not too early, he hoped.

"Hi, it's me, Alex," he said.

"Alex. How are you?" she asked.

"Not well," he answered. "I'm afraid I have some bad news."

"Oh no," she said. "No, no. What's happened. Please don't tell me that—"

"She's alive," Alex hurried to say but he heard her whimper, as if she feared what might follow such a statement. "There was . . . an accident. She's in a coma."

"Heaven help us," Louisa muttered tearfully. "What happened, Alex?"

"It was an accident," he repeated. "A truck . . . ran a stop sign . . . didn't even slow down."

He could hear her crying as he went on to explain the details of Jane's physical condition.

"And what about you, Alex? How are you?"

"I'm fine," he said. "I . . . hit my head pretty hard, and I'm bruised up, but . . . I'm fine. I just wish that . . ." He couldn't hold back his own tears. "I just wish it had been the other way around, for all our sakes."

"Don't say such a thing," she said like his own mother might have. "Listen, I'm getting on the next possible flight. I'm sure Walt will be coming with me. Where can we find you?"

"U of U," he said.

"Where you work?"

"That's right. She's in the medical ICU . . . on the fourth floor. I'll be here too." He went on to tell her that it might be easier to catch Trax downtown than to find a place to park at the hospital. The train would take them to a bus that would easily shuttle them right to the hospital door.

After Alex hung up the phone, he pressed his face into his hands and sobbed, ignoring the pain it amplified in his head. When he finally got it out of his system, he forced himself to call his sisters. He insisted that he didn't need them to come, that there was nothing they could do. But it was nice to know they were willing. He told them he'd keep them posted.

An hour later when the noises of the equipment hooked to Jane began to make him crazy, he finally took the pill he'd been given and was grateful to soon fall asleep. He woke up to find Carol checking Jane carefully. She saw him awake and said gently, "You missed lunch, but I let you sleep. I saved a sandwich for you. I'll get it."

"Thank you," he said, having to admit he felt hungry. And the pain medication was giving him some mild nausea that he hoped food would alleviate. He made another careful trip to the restroom, then he ate his lunch, all the while acutely aware of Jane lying there, unconscious, bruised, and looking dead. A nurse from the floor where he was supposed to be found him.

"I talked to Carol," she said, "so I knew you were being taken care of. But we have an appointment at radiology."

"What for?"

"Another scan to make sure your brain is all in one piece."

"Don't count on it," Alex said and got into the wheelchair so she could take him down.

Once he was returned to Jane's room, he found his stuff to make sure his wallet was there. He found it in the bag with his clothes and felt a little taken aback to see the blood on them. Looking at the position of the stains, he realized that most of it was Jane's blood, not his. He felt sick to his stomach at the thought and stuffed the clothes back into the bag. A while later he was told that the scan looked good, and he was being officially released.

"But I assume you'll be staying," Carol said.

"Yes, and I'll be keeping the wardrobe until somebody can bring me some clothes."

"Not a problem," Carol said. "Just make yourself at home."

Alex put the recliner in a sitting position and sat close by Jane's side, holding her hand in his, praying with all his heart and soul that she would come through this, that he would be forgiven for his stupidity. Alex had uttered quick prayers here and there throughout his life, more since he'd met Jane. But never had he prayed like this! He prayed with all the energy of his soul that Jane would recover from this nightmare. Feeling unworthy to ask for such a miracle from God, he prayed that, if not for him, she would recover for her family, her students, and all who loved her and were blessed by her goodness. Alex felt tears on his face just before he heard someone enter the room. He hurried to wipe them away before he turned to see who it was, then everything inside of him turned cold—and angry.

"What are you doing here?" Alex demanded of his father, resisting the urge to swear at him.

"Your sister called me," he said. "I thought you might need some company . . . some support."

"Not from you, I don't," Alex snarled.

Neil put up his hands as if to ward off any further anger. "Alex, listen to me. I didn't expect you to be happy to see me, and the last thing I want to do is upset you any more, but—"

"Then leave," Alex said, his voice low and gravelly.

Neil sighed loudly. "Just . . . give me five minutes. Listen to what I have to say, and then . . . if you want me to leave, I'll leave. And if you never want to see me again, I will honor that."

Alex liked that promise. Still, five minutes seemed like an awfully long time to tolerate his presence. "Okay," he said, "talk and get it over with."

Neil showed visible relief just before he looked at the floor. "I know you have good reason to be angry with me. What I did put a lot of difficulties into your life at a very tough age." He looked up at Alex. "But that was nearly twenty years ago, Alex. Your holding this bitter grudge against me is going to hurt you most of all—but not only you."

"You're not telling me anything I haven't been told before."

"Then listen and do something about it. I'm asking your forgiveness, Alex. You don't have to be a part of my life if you choose not to, and I wouldn't blame you a bit. But you need to let go of it. Give it to God, Alex, and—"

"You've got a lot of nerve bringing God into it. Your hypocrisy in such things ruined my life."

The regret in Neil's expression was evident, but his voice was firm. "No, Alex, you allowed my hypocrisy to ruin your life. No matter what anyone or anything in this world dishes out to you, eventually you have to grow up, take accountability for your own choices in the matter, and get on with your life. I made a stupid mistake, but believe it or not, there are reasons. How can you possibly judge what I did when you have no idea what was going on in my heart?"

Alex felt something stab at him as he heard words that he'd once said to Jane in regard to his own poor choices. Still, there was a great distance between not going to church, and cheating on your family and leaving them. "Forgive me if I don't wholly agree," Alex said with subtle sarcasm. "There is nothing that can justify what you did."

"I'm not trying to justify it, Alex. I admit that I made a mistake—a big one. I'm not trying to blame anyone else for my choices. It took me years to come to that, but I did it. And I want to put my family back together."

"I'm not sure that's possible. If my sisters want you in their lives again, that's their choice, but I don't think that's a possibility for me."

"Again?" he echoed. "Alex, I never stopped being a part of your sisters' lives."

Alex didn't know whether to feel angry or just terribly confused. Neil went on to say, "After the dust settled from the divorce, I made arrangements with your mother to spend time with you and your sisters. Your mother made it clear that it was an individual choice for each of you as to whether or not you wanted to have any involvement with me. You made it extremely clear that you not only didn't want anything to do with me, but you would deeply resent it if your sisters ever saw me. So we kept in touch without your ever knowing. I think there were many times when you just assumed they were with friends, and they were with me."

Alex sighed and closed his eyes, not certain how to take such news. Before he could contemplate it too deeply, Neil continued. "You didn't want me in your life, and I respected that. Every once in a while I believe your mother or one of your sisters would ask you if you wanted to see me, and you made it clear that you didn't. So I stayed out of your life; eventually I stopped trying."

"And what makes you think anything's changed? Why start trying again now?"

"Because now you don't have a mother around anymore. I thought maybe you could use a father."

Hearing his words triggered a sudden, unreasonable emotion deep inside. He quickly forced anger to take its place. "This is all very tender," he said with harsh sarcasm, "but your keeping in touch with my sisters does not automatically make you a hero. What did you ever do for them, for Mom, for me that would make *me* want to continue this conversation? You left us *destitute* while you went traveling with your *girlfriend*."

Neil drew a loud, deep breath, as if he were trying hard to stay in control. "Yes, I did," he said firmly. "I was wrong. I was selfish. And you have every reason to feel the way you do about that. But that was years ago. I made restitution for that a long time ago, and—"

"*What* restitution?" Alex demanded.

"There is no reason for me to give you an accounting of what I have done for the family in the last fifteen years. But since you asked, where do you think those nice prom dresses came from? And your sisters' wedding receptions? Your mother didn't pay for that stuff with her income. Once I had a few years to realize what an idiot I had been, I worked on getting the child support caught up, and I paid it diligently until you were all adults."

"And why did my mother never tell me any of this? She didn't keep secrets from me."

"She kept this one, because you were *so* angry that she couldn't even bring up my name without your flying off. Yes, we talked about it, Alex. We talked quite regularly, amiably. She forgave me. She was . . ." His lip quivered and his voice broke. "She was one of my best friends. Even though I had betrayed her and wronged her and put her through enormous grief, she forgave me."

"Well, she was a better person than me."

"She *chose* to be a better person. *You're* the one who chooses to debase your own character by holding onto your anger and not be willing to graciously accept what I have done for you and your sisters all these years."

"*Me?*" Alex's voice resounded with bitterness as he felt his anger deepening. "You have done nothing for me. *Nothing!*"

Alex saw something in his father's expression change. The determination in his eyes turned to a sorrowful resignation as he said, "I never wanted you to know. Your mother wanted to tell you, but I begged her not to. I didn't think it mattered. I figured that my knowing was enough. I didn't want you to think that I was trying to buy something back that I'd lost through my own stupidity. But maybe I was wrong; maybe I should have told you."

"Why don't you tell me whatever it is and get it over with," Alex said. "It's been more than five minutes."

"Fine. But I want you to know that paying for your education was not some attempt to buy your love or forgiveness."

Alex sucked in his breath and held it until his chest began to burn. "That was *you?*"

"Yes, it was me. When I was promoted to CEO, some investments I'd made in the company paid off very well, and I received some significant bonuses. I had everything I needed, and I wanted to use the money to help my children. But don't go suddenly changing your tune because you just found out that I actually *did* do something for you. I wasn't a father to you, Alex, when you needed one most. I tried to be, but I had broken trust with you, and I couldn't blame you for not wanting to have anything to do with me. But that was a long time ago. I want to be there for you now . . . to help you through this." He sighed and moved toward the door. "Your sisters know where to find me if you change your mind."

Neil Keane left the room, leaving Alex so stunned that he nearly melted into the chair. *He couldn't believe it.* All things combined, he felt as if the world as he knew it had somehow ended. In a matter of days he had lost his mother, and he'd very nearly lost Jane. While he couldn't bear the thought that she might never come out of this and regain her health, he couldn't imagine such a miracle ever happening. And now. *Now,* he'd been confronted by his father in a way he'd never thought possible. Alex had believed so fervently for so many years that Neil had chosen to remain completely out of their lives, that he'd done nothing for them, given them nothing to help them through the course of their lives. Neil's absence in all things had fueled Alex's anger and bitterness toward him. And now, everything that had seemed distinctly clear, and black and white, was extremely gray and hazy.

Alex pondered the conversation with his father for a couple of hours but came to no conclusions. His mind was swirling with so many thoughts, his heart with so many feelings, that he could barely believe he was the same person, living the same life that he'd lived up to this point. Neil Keane's words had somehow been the final straw, breaking something inside of him that had been close to snapping when Jane had ended up in a coma. A part of him wanted to be blindly angry at his father, a position he was wholly comfortable with. But something deeper felt too weary to be angry. It was as if he'd spent more than half his life harboring this anger, and he was simply too tired to carry it any longer. Still, if he didn't feel angry toward him, how was he supposed to feel? Indifferent? Not likely.

Late in the evening, Alex finally found the motivation to call his sisters. He called Charlotte, who lived in Texas. He felt more prone to talk to her first, knowing she wouldn't put a religious slant on the issue. She'd stopped going to church before he had, and if anything she had been more specifically angry with God, whereas Alex had felt more angry toward religious hypocrisy. He knew that Charlotte's anger had softened in her maturity, especially since she'd had children. But he also knew that she clearly understood how he felt.

"Hi," he said after she'd answered the phone.

"How are you?" she asked, her voice balmy with compassion.

"Not well," he said. "As if it weren't bad enough, I got a visit from my father."

He heard Charlotte sigh loudly. "That might be my fault. I told him what had happened."

"I see," Alex said, wondering if he should be angry with her, but again, he felt too weary to be angry. "Silly me," he added with subtle sarcasm, "but I had no idea you even had contact with him."

There was a long pause, as if she were considering her words carefully. "Listen, Alex," she said gently. "I know you have a lot weighing on you right now, and I don't want to add to it, but I really think it's time you knew the truth."

Alex felt the temptation to become angry overriding his emotional exhaustion. He forced his voice to remain calm. "So, does that mean . . . if you're going to tell me the truth now, that you've been lying to me up to this point?"

"Not lying, Alex. We simply . . . avoided telling you the whole truth because you made it clear a long time ago that you didn't want to hear it."

Alex had trouble holding his anger back now. "Are you trying to tell me that—"

"Calm down, little brother," Charlotte said in a tone of voice she'd not used with him for many years. "Just be quiet and listen to what I have to say, and try to take the anger out of your head enough to really hear it. I cannot even count the times that we have attempted to tell you Dad had changed. You refused to hear it, refused to even talk about it. You would always say things like, 'Don't even mention his name to me,' or, 'I have no desire to know what he's doing.' You also made it clear that *our* association with him would be tantamount to high treason in your eyes. So we just agreed not to talk to you about it. We all hoped a day would come when you would get over your anger toward him and we could get it all out in the open."

Alex felt his anger slowly melting into a stark sense of humiliation. His voice was more calm as he asked, "Who is we?"

"All of us. Me, Becca, and Mom."

"Mom was . . . in contact with him . . . all these years."

"That's right."

Alex cleared his throat and swallowed a huge lump of pride. "So . . . what he told me was true, then."

"What did he tell you?"

"That . . . he'd helped pay for things . . . through the years. Your weddings and proms."

"Yes, it's true. And he's helped us both through some tough financial times."

"And . . . he paid off my student loans, but . . . I didn't know it was him. He didn't want me to know it was him."

"Wow," Charlotte said softly, "I didn't know that. I knew he wanted to find a way to help you, but he was certain you would be angry if you knew it was him."

"I was told it was . . . an anonymous donor, that it had to do with my grades, my performance record. I never even considered it being . . . him, because I had no idea he had anything to do with any of you." His voice quavered. "Why didn't you tell me?"

"You didn't want to hear it, Alex."

"Okay . . . I was . . . a snotty, angry teenager when he started showing up again, saying that he'd changed his life. I've grown up."

"Not about that, you haven't," she said, and he felt as if he'd been slapped. "It hasn't been that long since both Becca and I each tried to talk to you about him. And you slammed the door before we even had a chance to knock on it."

While Alex was struggling to breathe, attempting to comprehend the choices he'd made that had brought him to this point, he wished the earth would just open up and swallow him whole.

"Talk to me, Alex," Charlotte said gently.

"I . . . don't know what to say," he managed.

"Just . . . think out loud. Come on, I'm listening."

"I . . . I just . . . I don't know." He groaned and pushed a hand through his hair harshly before he moved the phone to his other ear. "When I think about what he did to us . . . I just . . . it makes me so . . . angry."

"I'm not trying to discredit what he did, or your right to feel angry over it, Alex. But people make mistakes. And whether or not they ever make restitution or ask for forgiveness, it's our moral responsibility to forgive."

Alex took a long moment to accept those words coming from Charlotte. He knew she wasn't speaking from a religious perspective, because it wasn't a part of her life. For her, this would be a logical deduction, most likely based on psychological information.

"The only way to heal is to forgive, Alex. The marvelous thing about *our* father, is that he *has* changed. He's admitted that he was wrong. He's worked hard to make restitution. Many people who've been hurt never get that kind of response. We're very blessed that way."

Again, Alex had to contemplate what she was saying. She had no interest in religion; she'd spent most of the last several years being angry with God, and now she was talking about being blessed. He felt compelled to ask, "So, you've forgiven him?"

"I have."

"And you've healed as well? I mean . . . you were pretty angry and snotty yourself."

"Yes, I was. And many times I've wondered if I set a bad example for you."

"I made my own choices."

"Yes, you did. But maybe having a big sister who made bad choices made it easier for you to do the same. That's all in the past, however. We need to move forward now. It's completely up to you whether or not you want to have anything to do with our father, but I'm telling you that he's really a decent guy. There are reasons he did what he did. It doesn't make what he did right, but you can't stand outside of someone's heart and judge why they do what they do, or deem that they are unworthy of forgiveness. That will only hurt you. And quite frankly, I am tired of seeing you suffer over what you refuse to let go of. Everyone who loves you can see it, Alex. Why can't you?"

"I don't know," he had to admit, feeling his mind become even more foggy. "I . . . didn't realize I was such a jerk. What am I—"

"You're not a jerk, Alex. Don't go making this black and white. You're a decent guy who just has trouble with this one matter. And it's caused you more grief than it's caused anybody else."

"But that doesn't mean it hasn't hurt other people. I can see that; I've seen that for a long time, actually. I just didn't know what to do about it."

"You're a good man, Alex. If you weren't, a woman like Jane wouldn't have stuck with you for so long."

Jane. He chuckled bitterly. "Yes, Jane. It's my fault this happened, you know."

"How is that?" she asked with compassion.

"We were at a party; I was drinking. It was the first drink I'd had since I met her, so it didn't take much to make me tipsy. She insisted on driving, and she was ticked off. I can't blame her. It was just . . . losing mom threw me so completely out of kilter, and . . . then Jane said some things that made me wonder what on earth I was doing with my life. Somebody offered me a drink, and I took it. I wanted the world to go away." He sighed and rubbed a hand over his face as the memories became all too clear. "So she was driving," he muttered. "She hesitated longer than normal at the stop sign, because . . . we were arguing. When she pulled into the intersection . . . that truck ran the sign, didn't even slow down, hit the car just behind her or it would have killed her. But . . ." He began to cry and couldn't go on.

"It's okay, Alex," she said, reminding him of their mother. "Go ahead and cry. You need to cry."

"It should have been me," he said on the wave of a sob. "If . . . I hadn't been drinking . . . I would have been driving and . . . it would have been me in a coma . . . and she would be fine. Maybe she'd be better off. I've asked myself a thousand times why she hasn't just dumped me and moved on."

"She loves you."

"She loves my potential."

"You *and* your potential," Charlotte clarified. "So . . . why don't you just . . . take a leap here and . . . catch up to your potential."

"What's the point?" he growled. "She'll probably never come through, and—"

"Whether she survives this or not, Alex, it's up to you to take what you've been given and make the most of it. As I see it, life dishes out heartache and hardship and we have two choices. You can either make the most of it, learn and grow from it, and move on as a better person. Or you can become bitter and angry and let yourself deteriorate from the inside out."

Alex swallowed hard. He certainly knew which choice he'd made when his father's choices had dished out heartache and hardship. Had he learned anything since then? Could he be more of a man now than the snotty teenager who was still alive and well somewhere inside of him? Maybe. But at the moment he just felt too exhausted and overwhelmed to think clearly.

"I should go," he said, "but . . . thank you . . . for listening, for caring, and . . . for having the courage to say what I needed to hear. I'm not sure what to do about it, but . . . thank you anyway."

"I love you, Alex."

"I love you too, sis. I'll keep in touch."

Once he'd hung up the phone, Alex went into the little restroom attached to Jane's room. He turned on the fan and sobbed until the tears ran dry—temporarily at least. He knew they'd be back. And while he wept he prayed. He prayed fervently, deeply, furiously. He prayed that he could come to terms with all that he'd learned about his father, and he prayed that he could somehow, someway, be a man worthy of Jane. But in his heart he found it difficult to believe that such a thing was possible.

10

Alex was relieved to realize that it still wasn't too late to call Becca, who lived in Washington State, since it was an hour earlier there. While he approached the conversation with more humility than he had with Charlotte, she pretty much told him the same things that Charlotte had said. She added one poignant point, however. "Alex, your Heavenly Father loves you. There is great evidence in your life of how He has blessed you in spite of your challenges. You just need to reach out to Him, and He'll get you through this. He'll help you find peace."

All through the night, Alex drifted in and out of sleep in the recliner in Jane's room. The events and conversations of the past couple of days whirled in his mind like a full-blown hurricane with nowhere to go. He came awake to noises in the room and found the nurse meticulously checking every tube and monitor and piece of equipment that was going in and out of Jane. Even though these checks were done frequently, this was a different nurse; the shift had obviously changed. Her ID badge read Gabby. She spoke softly to him. "You're the most quiet loved one in a hospital room I've ever dealt with. Usually I'm bombarded with questions because it all looks so strange."

"I don't have any questions," he said. He knew exactly what the chest tubes were for. He knew about every monitor and every drug going into her through IVs. He knew all about the ventilator coming out of her mouth that was helping her breathe. And for the first time in his life he almost wished that he weren't a doctor. Perhaps knowing what he knew made it harder to try and accept that this was happening to the woman he loved.

"The last nurse must have been very thorough in answering your questions, then," Gabby said.

He recognized her effort to make conversation and keep the mood light. He reminded himself not to feel defensive or angry, or to take his grief out on this woman who was just doing her job and trying to be kind. "Actually," he said. "I work downstairs; I'm a doctor. ER."

She looked mildly surprised, then enlightened. "I remember now one of the nurses telling me that; I'd forgotten. Forgive me."

"It's okay. Just . . . take good care of her."

"The best possible," she said. "I promise."

Alex nodded, and she left the room. He went into the bathroom and managed to wash up a bit, but he realized he hadn't been home since the accident. He really needed a shower and some fresh clothes. But he felt so hesitant to leave Jane alone. He was still debating the issue when Gabby came in with a breakfast tray for him. "Eat up," she said. "Hospital vigils are exhausting."

"So they are," he said, feeling eerily disoriented to be on the other side of something he'd dealt with such a great deal. He'd done rotations in intensive care units a number of times. He knew the drill. And while he considered himself a compassionate man, and he'd consciously sought for a good bedside manner, he'd never fully appreciated how difficult it could be to wait and wonder. "Thank you," he added as she left the room.

"No problem," she said and smiled.

Alex finished eating, then just sat close to Jane, holding her hand. Tears streamed down his face as he pondered the regret he felt. He'd never lived up to what she'd deserved, and then his selfishness and pride had led her to this disaster. He frantically wiped the tears from his cheeks as the door came open. He was expecting a nurse; instead he saw Jane's parents. They said nothing before they were both overcome with emotion at seeing their sweet daughter on life support. Alex just eased back and gave them space and time to be close to her and accept the reality of her condition. He waited with a pounding heart for one—or both—of them to turn and angrily demand what had happened, to imply that he was responsible. And he honestly didn't know what to say. He was trying to come up with a possible response when Louisa Layton turned toward him as if she'd just now remembered that he was in the room.

"Oh, Alex," she said, moving toward him. She put both her hands on his face and asked with all the tenderness of a mother, "Are you all right?"

"Not really, no," he admitted, his voice quavering. She put her arms around him with complete acceptance, and in a way that made him miss his own mother.

Louisa gingerly touched the bruises and stitches on his face, then she looked into his eyes as if she were searching for something. At the same time, Walter put his hand on Alex's shoulder. Alex had attended a number of family functions with these people over the past few years. They had always been polite and accepting, but he couldn't recall ever having any truly in-depth conversation with either of them.

"Physically?" Louisa asked. "Are you hurt?"

"Bruised and sore," he said. "I hit my head pretty hard, but it's fine." He glanced toward Jane and heard his own voice crack as he admitted, "It should be me in that bed. I should have been driving, not her. And then it would have been me."

"You mustn't torture yourself over such things," Walter said kindly. "We can't change what's happened. We just have to deal with it the best we can."

"Oh, you poor thing," Louisa said, urging him to a chair. She scooted another chair close to it and sat down. "And so soon after losing your mother. I bet you're wishing she could be here for you."

Alex could only nod. She'd hit the head of a nail he hadn't even dared consciously consider for fear of losing complete control.

"Well, we're as good as family," Walter said. "We'll get through this."

They asked questions about what was hooked to Jane and why, and he felt grateful for a distraction from his own grief. They then asked more specifically what had happened. Alex debated leaving out the part about his drinking, but he decided on an impulse that it would be better if they knew everything, as opposed to his feeling like he was keeping some dark secret. He saw mild surprise in their expressions when he admitted he'd been drinking, but when he admitted truthfully that it was the first time in years, that he knew it was stupid, that he'd just been so thoroughly depressed, they actually seemed to understand. He was left in awe of their ongoing acceptance and silently thanked God for small miracles. If he could be completely honest with these people and still feel their favor, then perhaps there was some minuscule hope that he could get through this.

Walter wanted to give Jane a priesthood blessing. He asked Alex if he knew of anyone available who could help him. Never in his life had Alex even stopped to ponder what it might be like to have the power of the priesthood and be able to use it. He'd been given the Aaronic priesthood in his youth but had never progressed past the level of a teacher. The regret he felt as he left the room threatened to eat him alive. It only took him a few minutes to locate a doctor he was acquainted with, a man he knew to be an active priesthood holder. Alex hung back while the blessing was given, regret and fear consuming him. He longed to hear words spoken that would promise her recovery, but he heard nothing that gave him any tangible hope.

Walter insisted on driving Alex home while Louisa stayed with Jane. Alex didn't have the strength to protest, especially when he felt sure that if he didn't get a shower soon he would become offensive to anyone who came near him.

"Where to?" Walter asked once they were in the car.

"Uh . . . just take me to Jane's house. Most of my stuff is there anyway. I guess since she's not there I might as well be."

"You still have an apartment then?" he asked, and Alex wondered if it was a polite way of asking if he and Jane had maintained a chaste relationship.

"I do," Alex said and quickly added, "No problems there." He didn't want there to be any question that he had fully respected Jane in that regard. He felt sure that Walter was aware of the undertones in the conversation as much as he was.

They drove quietly for several minutes before Alex said, "You know, the two of you are welcome to stay at Jane's place, too. There's plenty of room. I mean . . . you always stayed there before when you came to town. I just didn't want you to think that you couldn't . . . because I'm there. We can . . . take turns at the hospital, I suppose . . . for as long as you can stay."

"That sounds good," Walter said. "Thank you." More silence passed before he added, "Alex, I want to share something with you. I hope you won't be offended or put off. I know how much you love Jane, and she loves you. I really do feel that we're like family."

"Go for it," Alex said calmly, while his heart pumped wildly.

"I just want to say that in spite of certain . . . challenges between you and Jane . . . I know you're a good man, and I know you would never do anything to hurt her. I just want you to know that I'm not blaming you for this, and you shouldn't blame yourself."

Alex looked out the window and struggled for a voice to respond. When he finally found it, he said, barely composed, "I appreciate that. I keep asking myself if I am to blame. I feel like I am, but . . ."

"Accidents happen, Alex. But in the big picture, I truly believe they happen for a reason. If she comes through this, then surely there is something to be learned for her, and all who love her. If she doesn't, well . . . we don't want to think about that, but . . . if she doesn't then . . . that means it's her time to move on."

Alex couldn't even go there. He recalled people saying that they knew it had been his mother's time to die, and he could never accept that. How could it possibly be Jane's time to go? She was so young, had so much to offer this world. Unable to even ponder that, he steered the subject elsewhere. "Since we're having this candid conversation, there's something I've always wanted to ask you. And now, with what's happened, I believe it's got me puzzled more than ever."

"Go for it," Walter said, the same way Alex had said it minutes earlier.

"You've known ever since you met me that I was not active in the Church, that I had some . . . challenges and . . . issues with it. Yet, you've never looked down on me. You've always supported Jane's relationship with me. Why? Surely she deserves the very best."

"She certainly does," Walter said. "And I know Jane well enough to know that she won't settle for anything less. If she had a different personality, I might have stepped in to discourage it. But I respect my children as being adults who need to make their own decisions. I also knew she wouldn't take anything less than a temple marriage. I figured that you would either come around, or she would realize you weren't going to and move on."

"I wonder sometimes why she didn't move on a long time ago."

"Obviously she has her reasons; knowing Jane, those reasons are probably more spiritual than anything else. I suspect she knows that holding on is the right thing." He sighed. "I just hope she holds onto her life with as much stubborn conviction."

Alex sighed as well. "Yeah, me too. But you haven't answered my question; not really. You're a wonderful, righteous family. You should be wanting only the best for your children."

"And we do. But don't go making us out to be perfect. We've had our challenges; we have our faults. Truthfully, Alex, I learned many years ago that we simply can't judge the heart of another. When I met you I didn't see a man who was simply arrogant or lazy about not going to church. I saw a man who had been deeply scarred."

"You're talking like a psychologist."

"No, just a man who has served as a bishop, and on the high council. I've sat through a lot of disciplinary councils, and I've heard a lot of heart-wrenching stories. I've heard and seen the damage done by poor choices in people's lives. But I've also heard and seen that in most cases there was hurt inflicted elsewhere that became the seed of those poor choices." He sighed loudly and added, "Also . . . you should probably know that . . . well, maybe Jane told you, but . . . my father was an alcoholic."

Alex was momentarily stunned. "No, she didn't tell me that."

"Well, it's not a pleasant topic for our family. He passed away many years ago; she hardly knew him, really. He had a good heart; he truly did. But he also had an ugly addiction. Still, his father and grandfather were both the same way. How can you judge such a poor choice when a child grows up believing something is normal, and not understanding that it's so destructive? How can you judge how a particular person's body chemistry responds to alcohol, as opposed to a different person who is unaffected? For years I hated and resented my father, and then I was given a rare opportunity. It's difficult to explain, but . . . I can only say that somehow the Spirit gave me the privilege of seeing life through my father's eyes, just for a moment. It changed my life." He sighed again. "So there you have it. I believe that ultimately we make our own choices, and we are judged accordingly when the time comes. But only God can judge fairly, because only He can see a person's heart. The truly wonderful thing is that we know this is exactly the kind of situation where the Atonement works its greatest magic. It's there to cover all the bad choices, the pain inflicted by others, the circumstances we have no control over, and even the sins we willfully commit. All we have to do is do our best to change those bad behaviors and give the burden to Him. In my father's case, he was never able to fully conquer his addiction in this life. But he tried. He wanted to. And I believe that counts for a great deal on the other side. It's what we do with what we have to work with that matters most."

Alex listened to Walter Layton's words and felt them go straight to his heart. He felt too overwhelmed and exhausted to fully absorb and appreciate what he was hearing, but he uttered a silent prayer that he would be able to remember what had been said, and perhaps even understand it.

"Thank you," was all Alex could think to say, but he sensed that Walter understood.

Once at the house, Walter went in with him and made certain all was well. Alex took a quick shower and went straight to bed, taking something mild to help him sleep. He was grateful to know that one or both of Jane's parents would stay with her all the time, and that they would call his cell phone immediately if anything changed.

He slept in the bed that Jane normally slept in, wanting to feel closer to her somehow. He thought it ironic that they should have shared this room a long time ago, but he'd been so stubborn. Just so blasted stubborn.

Alex woke to daylight. He immediately called the hospital—first the nurses' station in ICU to be assured that Jane's condition hadn't changed, and then the ER to see when he was on the schedule.

"You don't have to come in until Monday," Liz told him. "And if you need more time, nearly every doctor has offered to take at least one shift for you."

"Monday will be fine," Alex said, "thank you." As much as he wanted to sit at Jane's side and watch her every breath, he knew it would make him go insane. He was grateful to at least be able to work in the same building. If he planned ahead and brought some clothes and personal items, he could practically live at the hospital.

Alex got dressed and packed a bag with spare clothes and all he'd need to keep up some degree of personal hygiene. He fixed himself some toast, and while he was eating it he noticed the mail he'd opened just before they'd left for the party. The wedding announcement caught his eye and he picked it up, feeling such a deep heartache that he almost couldn't breathe. He remembered his mother's excitement when she'd opened hers, and how they'd talked about going out to dinner afterward. The wedding was tomorrow. He and Jane and his mother should have been going to it together.

With scorn he tossed the announcement back onto the table and hurried to clean up after himself before he left. Going into the garage, he was momentarily taken off guard not to see his car. He reminded himself that it was totaled, gone for good. He was surprised at how the loss of the car didn't bother him. His regret was focused on Jane, and he thought of nothing else as he got into her car and drove it to the hospital. He arrived to find Louisa sleeping in the recliner and Walter holding Jane's hand. She looked no different except that the bruises on her face were changing hues.

"Hey," he said to Walter while his eyes were focused on Jane, "why don't the two of you go back to the house and get some real sleep. I'll stay with her."

Louisa stirred from the sound of their quiet conversation. They reluctantly agreed to let Alex take a shift. Through the day he hardly left her side for more than a minute. He was grateful for the compassionate and competent nurses who were watching over Jane. He was also grateful for a visit from Ray Baker and a few other staff members from the ER, some of whom brought food. Through the long stretches of silence while he was alone in the room with Jane, he held her hand in his and pondered all he had been confronted with in the last few days. He believed it was true that coma patients could hear what was said around them. He wanted to talk to her and tell her how he loved her, and how everything would be all right. But in both respects he felt as if it might come out sounding like a lie. He knew in his heart how much he *did* love her. She was everything to him. But if he truly loved her, wouldn't he have overcome his own selfish issues long ago in order to make her happy? And how could he tell her everything would be all right when there was a fair possibility that she would never wake up?

In the middle of the afternoon, Alex was sitting close to Jane's bed, his head in his hands, when he heard someone come through the open door, wearing shoes that were not silent on the floor. Praying it wasn't his father again, he lifted his head to see who was here. Well, it wasn't his father, but it was almost as bad.

"Lana," he said, but he couldn't say anything else without sounding cynical.

"How is she?" Lana asked, taking in the horrific appearance of her sister.

"She's no different from whatever your parents told you when you last talked to them—whenever that was."

Lana sat down and just stared at Jane for several minutes, saying nothing. Alex allowed her the silence to accept what she was seeing; in fact he preferred it. He'd felt an undercurrent of disapproval from her right from the start. And he was in no mood to deal with it now. He prayed that she would just keep quiet, and he could do the same. His hopes were dashed when she said, "You look like you came through okay." Alex was appalled to realize that the sarcastic edge in her voice wasn't even subtle.

"Oh, yeah, I'm just great," he said with equal sarcasm. Silently he added, *Go ahead. Just pour some more guilt on me. That's just what I need.* When she only gave him a silent glare, Alex decided he'd had enough of this game. "Why don't you just go ahead and say it, Lana, and get it over with."

"Say what?" she asked with an innocence that was only slightly mocking.

"Just say what you're thinking and get it in the open, once and for all. I'm tired of your silent insinuations." Her eyes widened as if she couldn't believe what she'd just heard, but now that he'd started it was easy to keep going. "Let me guess. You're thinking that if it weren't for me in her life, this never would have happened. She would have been married to some decent, church-going man and have children by now, living happily ever after."

"I would never say something like that," Lana said.

"No, but I'd wager a great deal that you're thinking it. I'd wager there's a great deal you've wanted to say to me through the years that you never would—at least to my face. But you weren't afraid to tell

Jane what you thought, and you weren't afraid to manipulate her into trying to discredit me. Well, I'm tired of games, Lana, and I don't have the fortitude to play them." She still appeared silently stunned, and he went on. "You know one of the things I love most about Jane is the way that she could just say what needed to be said; there were no pretenses with her. I never had to guess or assume. So, why don't you follow her example and just get to the point."

Lana squared her shoulders and said, "Fine, I will. You're right. I've never felt comfortable with Jane's relationship with you. She is an amazing young woman, and she deserves the very best. Quite frankly, I think she's wasted the last four years of her life with the hope of something that you will never be able to give her. I think you're a loser, Alex. And now, it's obvious she was in the wrong place at the wrong time—because she was with you."

Alex wanted to feel angry. He wanted to defend himself with some smart comeback to put her in her place for being so judgmental toward him all these years. But he simply had no retort. Everything she'd said was true. And all he could say was simply, "You know what, Lana? You're probably right."

"No, she is not!" Walter said, and they both turned to see him standing in the open doorway.

"How long have you been there?" Lana demanded of her father in a tone that made Walter's eyes go wide with angry astonishment.

"Long enough to know that there's been something going on here for years that shouldn't have been going on—not in my family."

Lana countered quickly, "Alex is *not* family."

"To me, he is," Walter said, and Alex felt tears burn his eyes. "And *you* certainly are. But I didn't raise my children to treat people the way you're treating him. The problems in your marriage do not justify such an inappropriate attitude toward someone else's relationship."

"Hey," Alex said to Walter, "she's obviously upset by what's happened to Jane. And I told her to tell me what—"

"I don't need you to defend me," Lana snarled at him and left the room.

"I'm sorry about that," Walter said gently.

"What have you got to be apologizing for?" Alex asked, pushing his hands through his hair.

"I didn't raise her to be like that."

"I'm sure she has her reasons, and I wouldn't expect you to be responsible for your children's behavior." He looked at Walter. "You didn't have to tell her that I'm family to you; I think that really set her off."

"Well, I meant it," Walter said. "And we're going to get through this . . . together."

Alex felt too choked up to respond. He just nodded and hung his head, grateful when Walter said, "I'll give you some time alone. I'm meeting Louisa in the cafeteria."

Walter left the room, and Alex wondered if he'd also gone to find Lana. He was glad that the issues between them were in the open, but he wasn't so happy about having her parents brought into it. Realizing there was nothing he could do about it, his focus turned as always to Jane. He found himself praying with all the energy of his soul that she would survive this, and that somehow he could be the man that she deserved. Somewhere in the midst of his ongoing prayers, the thought occurred to him that he needed to go to that wedding reception. He made a scoffing noise, even though there was no one around to hear it. He wasn't going to leave Jane's side just so he could go to some old house and shake hands with people he didn't even know. He tried to force the thought out of his mind, but it simply wouldn't budge. He could almost imagine his mother's spirit hovering close by, insisting that he get out of this chair and go to the wedding reception. He argued with the idea in his mind, determined not to leave Jane alone. Then Walter and Louisa returned, looking much better than they had that morning, with some good rest behind them. Walter told him they'd talked to Lana, but he didn't say anything else about it. They visited quietly for a few minutes while Alex convinced himself that just because they were here with Jane, it didn't mean he had any good reason to leave and go to that stupid wedding reception. Then Louisa dug into her purse saying, "I saw this on the table and wondered if it was important." She handed him the wedding announcement. "It's obviously a relative of yours. You really should go. In spite of the circumstances, it would be good for you to get out. We'll stay here and take very good care of her."

Alex looked at the announcement while an almost eerie sensation surged through him. "I don't even know them, actually," he said. "But

my mother really wanted to go to this; she wanted to see the house."
Their expressions showed compassion at the mention of his mother,
but neither of them said anything. Alex went on to say, "Apparently
her great-grandfather built this house, and it's been restored. She
always wanted to see the inside, but . . ."

"I'm sure she's seen it now," Louisa said gently, and the words
caught him off guard.

"That's what Jane said," he murmured.

"Well," Walter said, "I'm sure she'll be attending this reception, in
her own way."

Alex wasn't sure why he suddenly felt desperate to get there. He
told himself it wasn't some ridiculous belief that he might actually feel
close to his mother's spirit if he went there, but he couldn't deny that
it had crossed his mind. Announcement in hand, he left the hospital
and hurried home to change into some nicer clothes. He made a
quick stop to buy a gift and have it wrapped. Recalling how the
announcement had been addressed, and perhaps compelled by what
should have been, he signed the card, *Dr. and Mrs. Alexander Barrett
Keane, and the late Ruth Barrett Keane.*

Making the drive toward his great-great-grandfather's home, Alex
couldn't avoid the ongoing argument in his head. He did *not* want to
go to this wedding reception. He didn't know these people, and he
wasn't necessarily fond of weddings in general. At this point in his life,
Alex disliked anything that reminded him of his mother—and Jane.
They should have gone to this thing together, the three of them. It just
wasn't right. As always, his thoughts wandered to Jane. He thought of
the torturous hours he'd sat with her, holding her hand, staring at the
monitors attached to her, the only tangible evidence that she was still
alive. Oh how he wished that her hand could be in his right now! But
it wasn't. Instead she was barely clinging to life, while his frustration
continued to mount with each passing hour. He was a doctor, for
crying out loud. He dedicated his life to stitching wounds, setting
broken bones, prescribing whatever it took to make things better. But
Alex couldn't do a blasted thing for Jane. Still, he ached to be with her
every moment, as if his presence might somehow fight on her behalf.

So why was he using his precious time to leave Jane behind in a
hospital room and go to the wedding of some distant cousin he'd

never even met? Alex asked himself that question a hundred times as his car wound toward the outskirts of the Salt Lake valley. He recalled a few different occasions when his mother had asked him to drive past the house while she'd repeated stories he'd heard many times of how her great-grandfather had built it after coming into the Salt Lake valley with the early settlers. Having been here before, he had no difficulty finding the place, but he didn't remember it being so beautiful. Perhaps he hadn't been paying attention. Perhaps the apathy he'd had over other things in his life had included this, among the many other things that he'd overlooked.

Alex parked across the street and sat in the car for several minutes, just looking at the house. It was a magnificent, three story, Victorian-style home, built from brick, with many windows, a large porch, and a beautiful yard with two incredibly huge trees. He pondered the things his mother had told him about it, and about the man who had built it, and her relatives who had lived here through the generations. He wished he'd been paying better attention—to that and many other things. Even more, he wished that his mother—and Jane—were here with him. Knowing such a wish was futile, he got out of the car, took a deep breath, and headed across the street. When candle lanterns guided him around the side of the house, he was disappointed to realize that the reception was being held outside. He gave his gift to a child, signed his name in a book, then stood in the neatly manicured yard trying to be discreet and inconspicuous. He was actually relieved to note that the receiving line had broken up, and that the couple was cutting the cake. Instead of having to introduce himself to people he didn't know, he could just hang back with his thoughts, wondering why he hadn't married Jane a long time ago. He hovered at the perimeter of the yard while the bouquet was thrown, then the happy couple prepared to leave.

Alex focused more on his surroundings and wandered idly through the yard, admiring the house from this perspective. Again he wished that his mother were here to see this. She'd have been in heaven. The analogy almost made him smile. Almost.

Attempting to avoid thoughts that would rekindle his grief, Alex moved closer to the house. Standing on a brick patio, he felt an urge to just touch the wall, as if it might somehow bring him closer to something that had the ability to give him peace. The brick felt cold, and he tried to imagine how many years it had been since the brick had been put there. Just touching it gave him a sense of constancy in a world where everything had changed for him almost overnight.

"The original brick is beautiful, don't you think?" a feminine voice said behind him.

Alex turned to see a lovely woman who looked slightly older than his mother. "It's amazing, really."

"Do we know each other?" the woman asked. "You look dreadfully familiar, but I can't place it." She held out her hand. "I'm Susan Barrett Clark."

"You own the house?" he asked.

"I do," she said with a smile as she glanced up at it. "I've debated continually over whether that's a curse or a blessing, but overall it's a great place to live." She held out her hand. "And you would be . . ."

"Ruth Keane is my mother," he said, shaking her hand.

"Oh." The enlightenment in her eyes was mixed with compassion. "She passed away recently, I heard, but I wasn't able to make it to the funeral. I'm terribly sorry."

"Thank you," he said and looked away.

"So your name is . . ."

"I'm sorry. My name is Alex Keane." Recalling how she'd introduced herself, he clarified, "Alexander *Barrett* Keane, actually."

"Ah yes," she smiled. "When you live in a house like this, you never forget that Barrett part."

"No, we mustn't forget that," Alex said.

"Forgive my asking, but . . . what happened to your face?"

"Oh." He self-consciously touched the stitches, having forgotten they were there, "I was in a car accident a few days ago."

"Are you okay?" she asked, seeming genuinely concerned.

"Oh yeah," he said. "My head hit the window pretty hard, but I've been pronounced sound."

"You're sure?" she asked as if she feared he might still be in need of immediate medical attention.

"I'm fine." He focused his attention again on the house since she didn't seem eager to leave now that they'd met. "It's beautiful. Was it difficult to restore?"

Susan chuckled. "You wouldn't believe it, but it was worth every cent. There's something about this house that . . ." she shivered as if a pleasurable chill had seized her, ". . . that stirs the soul." She apparently caught the interest in Alex's eyes when she added, "Would you like to see inside?"

"I'd love to," he said eagerly, "but surely you have better things to do right now than—"

"Actually, it was my sister's daughter who got married. The bride and groom are on their way, and I have a clean-up crew assigned. My job was just to provide the house and yard; now that's done. Come on in."

Alex followed her through a side door and down a long hall. Her love for the house was increasingly evident as she took Alex through most of the main floor, commenting on the plumbing and electrical that had been added long after the house had been built. She pointed out pieces of furniture and paintings that were original and talked about some of the challenges they had faced in the restoration. Alex was so enthralled that he hardly uttered a word. He just listened to Susan's oratory and tried to absorb every detail of his surroundings. He desperately wanted his mother to be here; she would have loved every second. He found some comfort to think of her being with him in spirit. And he missed Jane as well; he wished that she were here to see this with him. She too would have loved it.

Alex followed Susan into a study where she pointed out a huge hardwood desk with ornate handles on every drawer. "This was built into the room," she stated, "so it was refurbished right here. As heavy as it is, we didn't want to try and take it out and move it." Susan glanced around the study as if she liked this room particularly.

"It's beautiful." Alex pressed a reverent hand over the polished surface. For the first time in his life he truly wondered about his mother's great-grandfather. Had he sat in this very spot attending to his paperwork, whatever it might have been? The thought sent a chill across his shoulders, and he took the opportunity to bring up something he wished he'd asked his mother. "My mother told me there were some great stories about this house and the people who lived here through the years."

"Oh," Susan chuckled, "there are several great stories. It's hard to know where to begin."

"What's your favorite?" he asked, pushing his hands into his pockets where he could feel Alexander Barrett's ring.

"Well," she laughed softly, "of course I love knowing all that Alexander and Katherine endured to be here and be together, but—"

"Katherine? His wife?"

"That's right. She was quite a bit younger than he was, and he had the house built before they married. But I really like the story of how he had returned to Europe after the house was built—and before he married Katherine. Apparently there was a family matter that he needed to attend to, and when he returned, after being gone for many months, he found a dead body in the house."

"Really?" Alex chuckled. "Who was—"

"Susan," a young woman peered into the study, "we need you in the kitchen for just a minute."

"Excuse me." Susan smiled at Alex, and he nodded. "I'll be right back. Make yourself at home."

Alone in the study, Alex turned to survey the room more closely. Again he fingered the ring in his pocket and closed his eyes, trying to imagine Alexander Barrett here in this room, seated at this desk. He pulled the ring out of his pocket to look at it, wondering if it held some particular significance to its original owner. He regretted not attempting to find out more about it while his mother had been alive.

Distracted by his thoughts, Alex lost his grip on the ring. It slipped from his hand and rolled beneath the desk. He squatted down but couldn't see it, so he got on his hands and knees and crawled beneath the highest part of the desk to search. In the shadows he couldn't see the ring, but groping with his fingers he finally found it. With the ring wrapped securely in his hand he backed out from beneath the desk, but he misjudged the distance and bumped his head as he came up. He didn't know whether the intense pain and dizziness were a result of his recent head injury, or the fact that he hit his head especially hard. Either way, it really hurt and he wasn't thrilled with the idea of having Susan return to find him incapacitated on the floor. The thought barely entered his mind before he felt his own consciousness slip away into darkness.

11

Alex groaned and closed his eyes, hoping to avoid the stars swimming in front of him. When they didn't go away he sat hard on the floor and put his hand over his eyes in an effort to regain his equilibrium. When Alex moved his hand he focused on the ornate handle of the center desk drawer. He kept waiting for his sight to adjust. In his peripheral vision the room seemed dark, almost hazy. A stale odor struck his nostrils, and he wondered if he had a concussion. But from bumping his head on a stupid desk? Perhaps that head injury from the accident had affected him worse than he'd believed.

Alex bent his head forward and closed his eyes, certain he'd get over this strange sensation any moment. He opened them again and focused clearly on the floor. But it wasn't the same floor. Or was it? The floor in the study had consisted of brightly polished wood slats, with late evening sun shining across them. This floor was darkened by shadows, and the wood looked unkempt. As Alex inhaled deeply, the odor became more evident. Alex shot his head up, and his heart began to pound. Surely he'd gone unconscious and this was a dream.

Alex came slowly to his feet and turned to take in his surroundings. The room was the same. The window was in the same place—and the desk. The door he'd come through was the same door. But everything else was different. First and foremost, it was dirty. Neglect was evident in the thick dust, as if human hands had not touched this room for many months. And then he noticed the absence of the electrical fixtures that Susan had made such a point of showing him. They'd been added long after the house was built, she'd told him.

Alex turned full circle again, attempting to get a grip on what was happening. It was as if he'd gone back in time. The thought came so naturally that he wondered again about that concussion. Such a thing was impossible, and he knew it.

Alex's intrigue with the house momentarily overruled his questions, and he felt a desire to explore. In an effort to ease the stale odor in the room, he pulled back the drapes, then coughed when dust flew from them. He groaned as the window stubbornly protested opening. When it finally gave way he opened it wide, and the stagnant room sucked in fresh air as if it had been suffocating.

With sunlight illuminating the room, Alex examined it more closely. A sofa and a bookshelf were the only furnishings beyond the huge desk, and an overstuffed chair was near the window. Alex ran his hand over the desk and watched his fingers collect the dust particles. If this were a dream, it was certainly realistic. Maybe *he* was in a coma. Or maybe he was dead, and spending time in an ancestral home was like a holding area prior to judgment.

Gingerly, Alex moved through the open doorway and into the hall. One step at a time, he ventured through the house, noting the exact floor plan he had just toured with Susan, except that everything had changed. Occasionally he recognized a piece of furniture or a painting, but beyond that there was no similarity to the brightly restored house he had seen earlier. This place was overrun with neglect and a stagnancy that was beginning to feel eerie. There was a complete absence of plumbing or electricity, and the kitchen's modern conveniences had been replaced by a water pump, a stove unlike anything he'd ever seen before, and a healthy pile of wood.

Having explored the main floor thoroughly, Alex ventured up the stairs. Each time he opened a door he held his breath, as if he expected to find a ghost, but he only found empty rooms and more neglect. He passed a painting in the hall that caught his attention, but with all the bedroom doors closed, it was too dark to discern more than the shadows of a face. Alex pulled open the drapes at the end of the hallway and realized it was getting dark. He found an oil lamp on a table in one of the bedrooms, and matches conveniently nearby. The glow of the lamp added a little warmth to his surroundings, but he didn't like the eerie shadows cast by its wick as he moved warily back down the hall toward the painting.

When Alex saw the face in the portrait, something inside him wanted to scream and run. But all he could do was stare. In dumbfounded silence he gaped at the likeness before him, as if he were looking in a mirror. If he had lived more than a century ago, Alexander Barrett Keane would have looked just like that. The dark hair was styled slightly different, though not much. Only the old-fashioned cut of the clothing verified that this was not himself.

"This dream is too much," Alex said aloud, then wondered if he were losing his mind. He recalled learning once that different people were capable of dreaming on extremely different levels. He found it strange to consider that at some level he knew beyond any doubt that he was dreaming, and yet the realistic sensations of the dream were unlike anything he'd ever experienced. That quality of authentic awareness tempted him to believe that this was much more than a dream, yet even in the midst of it, he knew that it wasn't; he knew that with time he would wake up and find the world he knew.

After a fair study of the portrait, Alex felt his anxiety lessen until he moved the lamp down to the engraved gold plate at the bottom. Alex gasped and the lamp fell to the floor and shattered. Gratefully it doused itself rather than igniting, but in the dark silence that followed the crash, Alex could still see the name blazoned on his mind. Alexander Barrett.

While Alex groped through the dark to find another lamp, he tried to ignore what appeared to be happening. Logically he was in some kind of dreamlike state that had put him in Alexander Barrett's home, in Alexander Barrett's time. But why? And how? Was he so intrigued by this ancestor, his namesake, that he would create this fantasy in his own mind? But how could he? How could he conjure up things that he'd never seen before, never imagined existed?

He struck a match and touched it to the wick of the lamp, sighing with relief to be free of the hovering darkness. Using the light to guide him, Alex returned to the study and found the drapes blowing in a hefty breeze. He set the lamp on the desk and closed the window, which again protested. Feeling suddenly exhausted, he attempted to beat some of the dust off the sofa, then realized it had a dustcover over it. When he pulled it off and threw it aside, the sofa actually looked inviting. Certain he'd wake up to find himself someplace logical, like in his own bed, or maybe in a hospital room with a bandage around his head, Alex settled onto the sofa but left the lamp burning for reasons he didn't want to admit to. His next awareness was morning.

"I'm still here," he said in dismay. "I'd like to wake up now," he added to the empty room. Wherever he was, he'd lost his initial fascination, and he wanted to go home. He missed Jane and wondered if her condition had worsened.

It was still early morning when Alex went back upstairs to continue his exploration, perhaps hoping to find some logical explanation for all of this. He mentally tallied the rooms he'd ventured into the previous day and realized he'd seen all of the second floor, but he'd not gone to the third. Peering into rooms there, he found they were all much the same. Simple bedrooms with basic furnishings that were mostly covered, as if someone had been intending to leave.

When a particular door opened, Alex sensed something different, even before the foul odor struck him. But he simply was not prepared to find the decomposing remains of a body on the center of the bed.

"Merciful heaven," he muttered and backed out of the room. He closed the door as if it might grab him and force him to go in there again. Subtle nagging doubts blew suddenly into full-fledged fear. He was alone in a spider-infested house with a dead body that had been there a long time.

"Now what?" he muttered and lumbered down the stairs, if only to put distance between himself and that room. He had to get out of here, that's what. But how? Could he just walk out the door and leave? It was worth a try.

Alex unbolted the door and stepped outside to inhale the fresh air. He walked about the overgrown property and realized the house was surrounded by rugged ground on every side. A barn and some kind of shed were some distance from the house, but he felt hesitant to explore them for reasons he didn't want to admit to. From his point of view there was nothing else beyond mountains in one direction, and a familiar view of the Salt Lake valley in the other— although it looked completely unfamiliar beyond the actual geographical features. And the lay of the land made it impossible to actually see the city from here, even though he knew it was only a few miles away. Looking at the house from the outside, he had to admit it was the same house, situated in the same spot on the outskirts of Salt Lake City. Again he had to think this was the most incredible dream he'd ever encountered. Or maybe it was like some kind of vision. If prophets had been able to see forward in time and record what they'd seen in the scriptures, then perhaps he'd been given some kind of bizarre vision in order to see back in time. He was certainly no prophet, but it was the only explanation he could come up with that seemed even remotely probable.

When he couldn't bring himself to venture very far, Alex warily went back to the house. He hesitated before going through the door and pressed his hand over the brick, recalling how he'd touched it in the twenty-first century. It looked and felt so much the same. Forcing himself not to try and analyze this too much, he went inside, trying not to think about the body upstairs—what was left of it. He rebolted the outside door for whatever reason it had been locked in the first place. The stench of death seemed to seep into the stale air, and he felt suddenly claustrophobic. Attempting to think clearly, he came to the conclusion that he'd gotten here when he'd bumped his head under the desk. And with any luck, maybe he could undo this strange experience the same way.

Alex clapped his hands together, liking the idea. "I'll reenact what happened exactly," he said to himself and moved eagerly toward the study. "And that will take me back where I came from, and somebody else can give a eulogy for the body upstairs."

Alex reached into his pocket for the ring and was relieved to find it there. He dropped it on the floor and it rolled beneath the desk. Carefully he got down on his hands and knees to search for it. When he felt it in his hand he backed out from under the desk and purposely hit his head as he came up. He felt a little dazed, but he was still here.

Two hours and several tries later, Alex began to accept that he was staying, whether he liked it or not. And he had an awful headache. He sat on the sofa where he'd slept and fondled the ring as if it might give him the answers. Something clicked in his mind, and he bounded up the stairs to the portrait of Alexander Barrett. Sure enough, he was wearing the same garish ring—on the ring finger of his right hand.

Alex attempted to slip the ring onto that finger, knowing from past experience that it wouldn't fit. Then he stuffed it back into his pocket. He looked around again and wondered how long this dream, or vision, or whatever it was, might go on. And whatever it was, what purpose could there possibly be in such an experience? Surely he'd seen too many reruns of *Quantum Leap*—or maybe *The Twilight Zone*. And they had fried his brain. Was he simply seeing life through the eyes of Alexander Barrett? Or was that Alexander Barrett decaying in an upstairs bedroom? Frantically attempting to find some answers, an idea occurred to him, and he hurried back to the study where he pulled open a desk drawer, wondering why he hadn't thought of this yesterday. He rummaged through an odd assortment of papers that seemed pointless to the present situation. He closed that drawer and tried two others that were locked. In another was blank stationary, ink and pens, sealing wax, and engravings with which to stamp it. He became briefly intrigued by what he considered historical artifacts, then he reminded himself of his purpose. The next drawer gave him what he hadn't dared hope for.

Alex lifted the leather-bound book reverently into his hands, and it fell open to where a pen had been left between two pages. He moved toward the light of the window and tilted the book carefully to read the last words scribed in an eloquent hand.

> *It's difficult for me to leave at this time and return to my homeland, but my decision to go has been a matter of fervent prayer, and I know that the journey is necessary. There are loved ones there who need me to solve these problems. I worry for Katherine and pray that she will not have a change of heart in my absence, and that I will be able to return quickly and keep my promise to her. My deepest concern is for my father. He has endured so much, and I sense that his health is deteriorating, while we're told repeatedly that there's nothing to be done. In my heart I believe that once I leave here I will not see him again in this life. I know he is in good hands, and I must hold onto the peace in my heart that overrides my every concern.*
>
> *Alexander Barrett.*

Alex glanced through the journal and realized that every entry was signed that way. He touched the written words on the pages and felt deeply affected by the pricelessness of what he was holding. He'd never kept a journal himself, but looking at the words written by his great-great-grandfather, he suddenly felt that he should start.

Focusing again on Alexander's final entry before leaving the country, he leaned weakly against the edge of the desk. Part of him wanted to read everything in this book. He wanted to know Alexander Barrett, to know everything about him. But for the moment his mind went to the body upstairs. Reading the words in front of him, he had to wonder if the body upstairs was Alexander's father. Had he passed away following Alexander's departure? If so, why had no one noticed? Alexander had written that he was leaving his father in good hands. Obviously something had gone wrong somewhere. He recalled now that Susan had told him that her great-grandfather had left the country and returned to find a dead body in the house, and then . . . Then what? Susan had been called away, and Alex had bumped his head. Logic told him that this was simply some kind of elaborate dream, and Susan's story had fed his imagination. Inhaling the stale odor of the house, he found it difficult to believe that his imagination could be this vivid. Whether it was a dream or not, Alex knew that if he was any kind of man, he would do the respectable thing and put that body to rest. He didn't know what he was doing here, but the bottom line was obvious. He *was* here, and no one else had been since Alexander Barrett's father died. Rather than trying to analyze his present circumstances, he pushed the questions out of his mind and focused instead on just doing his best to exist in the moment.

Alex set the journal aside and took a deep breath. He was a doctor, for crying out loud. He'd survived years of medical school, studied cadavers, and spent endless hours working in a trauma center. Surely he could survive caring for the remains of this man.

Alex considered digging a hole and burying him in the yard, but that didn't feel quite right. If this house existed, then not far away was the budding city of Salt Lake, and surely there was a cemetery. He considered heading toward where he knew the city should be and search out some other human being for help, but he had mixed feelings on that. Deciding he really didn't want to walk miles for any reason, he put his focus on dealing with the dead body first. Needing to assess what he had to work with, Alex unlocked the side door and ventured first to the shed. He found a number of basic tools there, and several pieces of lumber. "Perfect," he muttered and set to work building a basic wooden box to hold the remains of Alexander's father. His thoughts wandered as he worked, but he forced his mind to avoid attempting to understand what was happening. Instead he just hummed the melody from *The Twilight Zone* and kept working.

When the box was finished, Alex went into the house and found a lightweight towel in the kitchen that he tied over his mouth and nose before he headed up the stairs, feeling like some kind of bandit from the old west, mustering courage for the big shoot-out. He squeezed his eyes shut before he opened the door to the crypt. Having lost the fear he'd experienced when he'd entered before, Alex just stared at the remains, and something in him wanted to cry. What circumstances had left this man to die all alone and remain here for months unnoticed?

Forcing back his emotions before they got the better of him, Alex forced his logic to dominate. How was he going to do this? Carefully he pulled out the edges of the bedding on all sides and lifted the corners over the body so he was able to ease it onto his back in a firm bundle. With reverence he carried it outside and put it into the box. He uttered a little prayer, then nailed the makeshift coffin closed.

Free of his burden, Alex stood and pulled the cloth from his face. He looked toward the sky and momentarily savored the breeze against his face. He returned the tools to the shed, then felt the urge to peek into the barn. He was surprised to find a horse there, and he was relieved to see that it had plenty of water and feed. Having a horse certainly helped with the prospect of getting into town without walking, except that he had absolutely no idea how to ride it—or even get a bridle and saddle onto it.

Alex returned to the house, but that stale odor struck him, and he decided there was one more thing that had to be done. He dragged the mattress that Alexander's father had died on out to the back yard and set fire to it. He waited until it burned completely and safely, then he wet down the surrounding grass with water from a nearby well. He returned to the house and found what had to be soap. He scrubbed his hands and arms good, then went through the house and opened several windows to allow the fresh breeze to replace the stagnant air. Then he realized that his clothes reeked. Venturing to what he knew was the master bedroom, Alex opened the closet and found neat rows of simple clothing that he thought would do nicely.

While he soaked in a hot bath, Alex contemplated how much he missed modern plumbing. Taking a bath had never been so much work. He'd had to heat buckets of water on the stove and carry them to the galvanized tub he'd found in a corner of the kitchen. But at the moment it was worth it. Once clean, he dressed in a blousy white shirt with dropped shoulders, narrow black pants, and a black waist-coat that he left unbuttoned. He admired himself in the mirror, wondering if he could pass for a man of this time. He wiped the dust off of a comb lying on the dresser and smoothed his hair, then he emptied the bathtub and cleaned up the bedroom a little. If he was staying, he decided that he far preferred sleeping in this room as opposed to the study sofa.

Feeling a bit chilly, Alex wandered through each room, closing the windows and drapes, grateful for the fresh air that had eased the odor in the house. Closing the last window on the third floor, he distinctly heard a pounding from somewhere below. Once he'd recovered from the way it had startled him, he rushed down the stairs so quickly that he almost fell more than once. He unbolted the door and pulled it open to see a woman with dark hair moving around the corner of the house. Her attire was consistent with the time period he seemed to be living in—or rather *dreaming* in.

Hearing the door she turned back expectantly. Alex didn't know if his nervousness was a result of seeing a woman so immediately beautiful, or just seeing another human being. Her hands went to her cheeks as if they could prevent the blood from draining out of her face. Now that Alex had made his presence known, he couldn't think how to react. Who was she? What was she doing here? Alex expected her to run, or perhaps hurl questions at him that he couldn't answer.

Instead she put a hand to her heart and stepped toward him.

"Alexander?" she said in a rich voice. *She thinks I'm Alexander Barrett.* Now what? Not knowing what to say, he said nothing. When she could come no closer she lifted a trembling hand to touch his face as she looked into his eyes.

"Alexander," she said with a certainty that sent a chill down Alex's back. It might have frozen him solid if not for the warmth of her touch. He regretted the question in her eyes as she waited for him to recognize her. She saved him when she said tentatively, "It's me. Katherine."

"Katherine," he said with genuine recognition. The woman Alexander loved, the woman he'd made a promise to. Alex's great-great-grandmother!

"Oh, Alex!" she said. "It really is you."

Not knowing how to handle this, Alex said, "If it looks like me, it must be me."

"Oh!" She laughed and touched his face with both her hands. "Brother Akins told me he'd seen you arrive yesterday, but when you didn't come to see me I felt sure he'd been imagining things. Then when I saw smoke from this direction, I wondered if it were true." She laughed again. "And it is true! You're here; you're really here. I knew you would come back!" Her face became puzzled as she added, "But . . . why did you not come to see me?"

"I'm . . . so sorry," Alex said quietly. "I . . . I don't know what to say." Well, at least that was honest. He knew he had to get a grip on this. But at the moment he just felt so thoroughly in awe of this experience. Katherine was incredible! There was something about her that reminded him of his mother. And why wouldn't she? His mother was this woman's great-granddaughter. And she was beautiful! Perhaps in another time he might not have noticed it. Perhaps make-up and a blow dryer would have marred her natural beauty. But there was no need for either.

Feeling stuck and uncertain, Alex muttered, "Would you . . . like to come inside?"

"That would be nice, thank you," she said, following him through the side door. "And I could use a glass of water, if that's all right."

"Of course," Alex said and got her one as she sat at the kitchen table.

"I can't believe you're really here," she said as he sat down across from her.

"Neither can I," he said with an ironic chuckle.

"You were gone much longer than I'd expected. I was truly worried."

"I'm . . . sorry about that. The last thing I would want is for you to be . . . worried over me."

"Are you all right?" she asked, looking at him closely. "You seem so . . . different."

"Do I?" he asked, his voice practically squeaking. Without thinking he found himself trying to explain. "Well, I got this bump on the head and . . . after that I . . ."

His explanation faded, and Katherine's eyes narrowed on him. "Amnesia?" she guessed and he could only gaze at her, feeling disoriented. "I've heard of such things. It makes people lose their memory. Is that what happened? Is that why you've been gone so long?"

Alex looked at her deeply. He shrugged his shoulders and was relieved when she took over.

"That's it, isn't it." Her eyes lightened as if the explanation gave her peace. "My poor, dear Alexander. Did you . . . forget everything?"

"There is much I . . . don't understand."

"Do you remember me?" she asked carefully.

Alex hesitated. "It's coming back to me slowly . . . in bits and pieces."

"Oh my poor Alex," she said. "Maybe you should go see the doctor."

"Oh, there's no need for that," he said. "I . . . saw a doctor . . . before I came here . . . and he said I'd be all right."

"That's good then, but . . . where's your father?"

"My father?" he asked.

"Don't tell me you've forgotten you have a father and you left him somewhere along the way or—"

"No, no. Of course not," he said. "He . . . didn't go with me."

Katherine's eyes widened with something akin to horror. "If he didn't go with you, then . . . where is he? The Nelsons said that—"

"Who?"

"The Nelsons. You asked them to pick your father up at the house the same day you left. He was going to stay with them. They came but no one was here; no one answered. They tried several times. The house was locked up, so they figured you'd decided to take him with you." Her voice became frantic. "Where is he?"

"He's . . . dead," Alex said as the picture became clear. Katherine gasped, and he hurried to explain, "I found him dead . . . upstairs when I got here . . . yesterday. You know he wasn't doing very well when I left."

"You were worried about that," she said, wiping tears from her face with a lacy handkerchief she'd pulled from her pocket. "All that pain he was having in his chest; you were worried. I just assumed that you had decided to take him with you at the last minute; that's what we all assumed."

"Well . . . he must have died very soon after I left," Alex said. "Otherwise he would have answered the door. It was probably his heart; he probably went quickly. In fact, he looked as if he'd just . . . died in his sleep. I'm sure it was . . . his time to go."

Katherine nodded and dried her eyes. "Where . . . is he now?"

"I . . . built a . . . box. He's in the yard. I guess we'll have to . . . get the undertaker to come and . . . get him."

"Of course," she said. "We'll make all the arrangements right away."

Alex nodded. Katherine gave him a compassionate smile just before she stood up. "You need to come home with me. Why, supper will be on by the time we get there. And you know Mother will be so anxious to see you. And after supper we'll talk with the bishop and make those arrangements."

"Of course," he said, wishing it hadn't sounded so hesitant. Arrangements to take care of the body in the yard would be good, but everything else was so disorienting.

"What's wrong?" she asked. "You do remember my mother, don't you?"

"I'm . . . afraid not," he said.

"But . . . you must remember some things. You found your way home."

"Yes, somehow I . . . found my way here."

"Oh, you poor dear. Come along. Perhaps seeing familiar faces will help bring everything back."

Alex followed her to the barn where she said, "You harness the buggy and . . . What's wrong?"

"I . . . don't know how," he said. She just smiled and did it while he watched her carefully so that he could do it next time.

He helped her step in then sat beside her. She put the reins into his hands, and he snapped them the way he'd seen in movies. The horse moved forward, and he was pleased to find that it was well trained and it didn't take much trial and error to figure out how to control the way they were going. And he *did* know the general direction into town. He noticed other homes scattered about as they went along.

Alex noted the setting sun as he drove and became briefly distracted by the familiarity of the horizon. Katherine filled the silence by talking about all the people that he was apparently supposed to know, and everything that had happened to them during his absence. He was so distracted by listening to her that he was startled to look ahead and see that they weren't far from the heart of the city. Impulsively he pulled on the reins to stop the horse.

"What are you doing?" Katherine asked.

"I just . . . wanted to . . . take it all in," he said, wondering how the people of this time might have felt if they could see this city the way he had seen it. The streets laid out in a grid were not a surprise, and there were many buildings and homes that indicated a thriving city of the nineteenth century. But Alex's focus was drawn to the rising granite walls in the center of town.

"The temple," he muttered under his breath.

"Isn't it beautiful!" Katherine exclaimed with a vehemence that gave him chills. "Every time I see it I just feel so . . . grateful."

"Grateful? Why?" he asked, curious to understand her perspective.

She laughed softly and said, "I should think it would be obvious. I keep forgetting that you can't remember." She took his hand. "I'm just so grateful that we can actually build a temple without threat to our lives and our safety. I'm grateful to know that when it's completed we can go there and have the privilege of every blessing of the gospel. And we can do the work for everyone we love who didn't make it." Alex gave her a puzzled gaze, and she clarified, "This is what they gave their lives for, Alex. Your mother and grandparents. My father, my grandmother. The brothers and sisters we lost. Do you have any comprehension of the joy they will feel to see this work come together on their behalf?"

Alex felt something tighten inside of him as he asked, "How . . . were they lost?"

Katherine's eyes filled with compassion, apparently for his memory loss. "Maybe you should go back and read your own journals."

"Maybe I should," he said. "But right now, just . . . tell me . . . how they were lost."

"Well," she sounded hesitant, "there was that mob attack . . . before your family headed west, and there were the ones who . . . died of exposure . . . and starvation . . . on the way."

Alex nodded and swallowed hard. All his life he'd heard the stories of the tragedies these people had endured. But never had it touched him as it did now. Suddenly it was close and personal, and he felt tempted to just break down and cry. He was relieved when Katherine went on with a bright voice. "But it's all right, Alex, because we're building a temple. And the blessings of the temple are what it's all about." She squeezed his hand and put her head to his shoulder. "Because of those blessings, you and I will be together forever, Alex." His heart began to pound even before she added, "The day that you and I are together within temple walls will be the happiest day of my life. And then, every sacrifice of those gone before us will be made right."

Alex urged the horse forward again while a tight burning hovered in his chest. The stupidity and stubbornness of his life paraded through his mind, while an undefinable weight became heavier with each thought, as if his every act of pride and foolishness had been tantamount to spitting on the graves of those who had died for blessings that he had spent a lifetime refusing to take hold of. People who shared his blood, people who had sacrificed everything in order to give their posterity—including him—a better life.

Katherine guided Alex to her home at the edge of town, and he was grateful again for her ongoing chatter that kept him from being completely overtaken by his thoughts and the depth of emotion being spurred by them. Shedding some stray tears, she talked about Alexander's father and how she was going to miss him. He said enough to agree and keep the conversation going while the heaviness inside of him continued to grow. He forced himself to focus more on the moment as he helped Katherine down from the buggy and they went inside. The house was nice but much more conservative than the one Alexander lived in. He realized then that Alexander Barrett had been a man of some means.

Alex was met by two surprises when he came face-to-face with Katherine's mother. The first was learning that her name was Ruth. His own mother had been named after this woman. The second, and even more startling, was Ruth's being confined to a wheelchair. After she greeted him with overt joy at his return, they were all seated to share a meal—a meal that Ruth had managed to prepare by maneuvering her way around in a wheelchair that was archaic from his perspective. He wanted to inquire over the reasons but felt awkward. He was grateful for Katherine's talkative nature as she explained to her mother about the death of Alex's father, and the unfortunate misunderstanding that had prevented him from being buried all these months. She also explained Alex's apparent amnesia, which prevented him from having to try and explain to one more person why he had no idea what was going on.

Once they'd finished eating, Ruth said, "Now, Alexander, I hope you learned how to do a fair waltz while you were in Europe."

Alex felt startled to have something so familiar to him come up in a situation that was entirely foreign. "Oh, I think I can manage," he said, not certain about the point she was making.

"I heard you promise Katherine that you would waltz with her at the wedding. You know how she loves to dance. You're not getting out of it, young man," she said with a bright voice and a warm smile. "If you're going to marry my daughter, you'd best know how to waltz."

"Oh, I wouldn't want to get out of that," Alex said, smiling at Katherine. He held a hand out for her and said, "How about giving it a try?"

"Right now?" she asked, beaming as she put her hand into his.

"But we don't have any music."

"Who needs music?" he asked and put a hand to her back. He attempted to guide her into a simple waltz, but it was as if his feet wouldn't do what his mind could see so clearly.

Katherine laughed softly. "You never could dance," she said, "but I love you for trying."

Alex chuckled self-consciously and said, "Let's just . . . give it some practice." He counted the steps aloud for himself in a way he hadn't needed to for over twenty years. Katherine was patient with him as they tried it over and over, and he finally managed to reteach himself how to waltz.

"Oh that's lovely," Ruth said, observing them. "I do believe you're catching on."

Katherine declared exhaustion and sat beside her mother. Ruth laughed softly and said to her daughter, "I'll never forget waltzing with your father the day I married him."

Alex knew that meant she'd not been disabled all her life. Going with the amnesia theory, he couldn't resist saying, "Forgive me, but . . . my memory is . . . well, you know and . . . I was wondering why . . . the wheelchair."

Neither of the women appeared upset or uncomfortable. Katherine simply said, "Gangrene set in . . . from the frostbite." She said it as if she expected to have him remember if given a clue.

"Frostbite?" he echoed with a sense of where this was going.

Still, he was unprepared to hear a detailed account of how Katherine, as a young child, and her mother, had been among the members of a handcart company that had been rescued by saints who were already settled in the Salt Lake Valley. Katherine and Ruth had been the only survivors from a family of seven. Ruth had been barely clinging to life when her feet had been amputated, and since it hadn't been done correctly, she still suffered with pain.

"I'm so sorry," was all he could think to say, while that tight burning in his chest mounted dramatically. Suddenly fearing he would break down, he stood abruptly and headed toward a door that obviously went outside from the kitchen.

"What's wrong?" Katherine asked.

"I just . . . need some fresh air," he managed to say with a voice that was barely steady.

Once outside, Alex staggered around the corner of the house. He dropped to his knees and pressed his head into his hands. "Oh, God forgive me," he muttered as the pain and sorrow of his life rushed through him in torrents, filling him with a suffering so tangible he felt as if he might shrivel up and die—or at least he might prefer to. He'd been such a fool! He thought of his mother and all she had given to live the gospel fully. He thought of Jane, her conviction, her love and patience. And what had he done? He'd wasted precious years, caught up in his own pride and fear, oblivious to the privileges that were right in front of his face.

Alex lost track of the time as he wept and prayed, feeling as if the earth might swallow him. He was startled to feel Katherine's hands on his shoulders. "What is it?" she asked gently, kneeling beside him.

"I'm such a fool," he said. "I've just . . . done so many stupid things, and . . . I've never stopped to consider how . . . blessed I really am."

"Oh, Alex," she said, "you're a good man. We all have weaknesses. We all struggle. But that's why we were given the Atonement, Alex. The Savior will take this burden from you. All you have to do is ask."

Again Alex lost any sense of time as he listened to Katherine bear witness of the Atonement and how it had healed her own heart—and her mother's—after all of the suffering they had endured. She spoke of the light and peace that could be found by living the gospel fully, and by accepting all that Jesus Christ had done. The more she talked, the more she reminded him of his mother, and he almost felt as if it was her holding him, comforting him, telling him all that he needed to hear. Alex just listened and wept, praying with everything inside of him that he could feel the peace and light that she described, that he could be given a second chance.

When he finally calmed down, he felt a glimmer of something inside of him that made him believe there was still a chance for him. The tightness that had weighed him down felt lighter as he clung to the arms encircling him, feeling deeply comforted. Then he heard someone calling his name, as if from a distance, drawing him back into reality.

— 12 —

"Alex. Alex!" he heard a feminine voice say in a frantic tone. "Please wake up, Alex. You're scaring me."

Alex came awake surrounded by a sense of familiarity. And yet something wasn't right. His brain felt foggy, and his head hurt in a way that reminded him of waking up in the emergency room after the accident.

"Alex?" that same voice said. He felt a hand on his face. "Alex? Are you with me? Are you okay?" He groaned and forced his eyes open, hearing that same voice let out a laugh of relief. Everything looked blurry, and he closed his eyes again, trying to place the familiarity of that voice. His mother. Was it his mother? No. And he didn't think it was Jane; it couldn't be. She was in a coma. And as much as he felt like he wanted it to be his mother, there was some relief in knowing it wasn't. If his mother was talking to him, he'd either be dead or insane. Considering his most recent experiences, insanity seemed more plausible. He groaned as he tried to make sense of what was happening.

"Oh, thank heaven," the voice said, and he tried again to open his eyes. He focused first on the ceiling above him. He knew this room, but the way it looked now made him gasp for breath. He turned his head abruptly to look both directions, taking in his twenty-first century surroundings. The movement provoked pain, and he groaned again, then his eyes focused on the face nearby.

"Susan," he said.

"You know who I am?" She laughed. "Oh, my goodness. I thought I'd lost you." She actually got tears in her eyes. "I was only out of the room a few minutes, and when I came back you were out cold."

"Good heavens," he muttered under his breath, attempting to comprehend the dream he'd just emerged from. It had all felt so real, so undeniable. And yet, here he was. Alex felt something in his hand and realized it was the ring, right where it had been when he'd bumped his head. He discreetly slipped it into his pocket.

Knowing it would be impossible in that moment to fully digest such a profound and realistic dream, he focused more on the moment. "How long . . . was I out?" he asked.

"Ten minutes at most," she said. "But . . . when I couldn't get you to come around, I called 911 and—"

"You did what?" he interrupted, well imagining how this would go over with his associates. He sat up, ignoring a subtly dizzy sensation. "Call them back and tell them I'm fine."

"But you're not fine," Susan insisted. "You told me yourself you had a head injury a few days ago, and you obviously got another nasty bump. I think you need to sit tight and let the paramedics take a look at you and—"

"I'm fine," he argued. "The last thing you need is sirens blaring in the middle of your wedding. Just—"

"I'm not letting you go anywhere until someone checks you out and says your okay."

Alex looked into her eyes and had to say, "You sounded almost like my mother just then."

"Well, if she were here she'd insist that you do the smart thing and make sure you're all right."

"Okay, fine," he said. "But call them back and tell them I'm conscious and they don't need to come in with sirens and—" They heard a siren in the distance, and he added, "Never mind."

Susan shrugged her shoulders and actually laughed.

"What?" Alex snarled.

"Well, knowing that you're all right, it really is quite funny."

"Yes, sirens at the wedding."

"Hey, the wedding reception is over," she said. "The bride and groom are long gone."

While they waited, Alex's mind was drawn to what he had experienced in his unconscious state. The memory of all he'd dreamt was more clear than any dream he'd ever had in his life. "Unbelievable," he muttered.

"Did you say something?" Susan asked.

"Uh . . . I was just wondering if you have any . . . genealogical records . . . journals, histories. Anything I might be able to look at."

"Sure," she said. "I'd be happy to share anything I've got."

The thought made Alex feel almost giddy.

When the paramedics arrived, Alex was dismayed to realize he knew one of them quite well. "Dr. Keane," he said lightly. "You sure cause a lot of trouble these days."

"Not a word about this to anyone," Alex said, attempting to sound threatening.

They checked him out and declared him to be okay, but they suggested he put some ice on the bump on his head and wait a while before driving home.

"Good," Susan said once the ambulance had left. "That will give us time to dig up some of that genealogy you were asking about." She added with a suspicious smile, "*Dr. Keane?*"

"Yeah," he said sheepishly. "I work at the ER."

"How marvelous," she said and led the way into the hall.

Holding an ice pack to his head, Alex followed her into a room where one wall was completely lined with books. He noticed on one shelf that there were several copies of the same book. Susan pulled one of them out and handed it to him. "I want you to keep that," she said. "My father had lots of copies printed so that we'd always have plenty to pass out to relatives when we came across them. He'll be glad to know his plan worked."

As Alex examined the book, an excited tremor went through him. On the dark blue, hardbound cover, it simply said *Barrett*. His heart quickened even before she added, "It includes all of the descendants of John Barrett, who joined the Church in England and brought his family here."

"His son Alexander built this house," Alex said.

"That's right."

"And John died in an upstairs bedroom while Alexander went to Europe to take care of some family matters."

Susan looked at him askance. "How did you know that?"

Alex hurried to say, "Didn't you tell me that before I passed out?"

"I didn't think I'd told you that much, but maybe I did. Maybe I'm losing my mind."

"Maybe it's an epidemic," Alex said under his breath.

Susan went on. "All of the journals and letters that were found have been typed up and put into that book. I remember my father working on it for years. It was an enormous undertaking."

"I can only imagine," Alex said, holding the book in his hands. "Thank you. This is priceless."

"Yes, it is," she agreed, and he wondered how his mother might have felt to have had such a book in her possession. He wondered if she even knew it had existed.

Alex then watched Susan as she pulled sheets of paper out of a thick folder and started sorting them. "I always kept extra copies of these things for the same reason," she said. While Alex thumbed through the book in his hands, she sorted papers and set aside a small stack. When she was finished, she slid the stack into a large manila envelope and handed it to him. "Those are copies of the most important things. When you've had a chance to get through all of that, call me and we'll go from there." She wrote her phone number on the large envelope.

"I can't thank you enough," he said. "Can I give you something for the copies or—"

"Oh, don't be silly," she said.

"Well, if you ever need a doctor and yours can't be found, feel free to call me—anytime, day or night." He took a card out of his wallet and handed it to her.

"Thanks," she said. "This could come in handy."

He visited with Susan for a while longer, amazed at how good it felt to find a closeness with someone who shared his blood. He realized then that he'd never really had any connections with extended family. After getting a hug from Susan, he finally left with the treasures she'd given him tucked beneath his arm. During the drive to the hospital, he felt stunned and disoriented as he attempted to digest what had happened to him, and to accept that it had all happened in a matter of minutes. He didn't understand it, but he knew that it had changed him. He just needed to take some time and figure exactly *how* it had changed him.

Arriving at the hospital, Alex practically ran to Jane's room. He took a deep breath, anguish mingling with relief. She was still there; nothing had changed. It felt as if he'd not been here for days. But it had only been a matter of hours. Walter looked up from a magazine and simply asked, "How was the wedding?"

"Incredible," Alex said, more focused on Jane. There was so much he wanted to tell her, so much he longed to understand. He moved slowly toward her, briefly taking note of the monitors and their evidence of her stable condition. He took her hand into his and pressed a kiss to her brow, murmuring softly, "Oh, how I love you!"

He looked at her lifeless face and listened to the sound of the ventilator as it breathed for her. His mind reached back to the bizarre experience he'd encountered during his unconsciousness. All things combined, it took every ounce of his energy to resist the urge to bawl like a baby. He was startled to feel a hand on his arm, and he turned to see Louisa beside him.

"You okay?" she asked.

He forced a smile and felt that urge to cry cluster in his throat. "Not really, no," he said.

He was afraid she might probe him with questions he didn't want to try and answer, but she only touched his face, much like his own mother would have. "Do you want to talk about it?" she asked.

Alex shook his head. "Maybe . . . another time."

He was relieved when her next question was, "Would you like to be alone with her?"

"Yes, actually . . . I would."

Louisa smiled. "You can talk to Jane about it . . . whatever it is. She'll understand."

"Yes," Alex swallowed hard, "I believe she will."

Walter and Louisa each hugged him tightly, and he assured them that he would just spend the night in the recliner and see them in the morning. Once alone with Jane, he sat close to her and touched her hair, combing his fingers through it gently. "Oh, Jane," he muttered, "if only I could tell you what's happened to me." Recalling how Louisa had said that Jane would understand, he began talking about his reasons for wanting to go to the wedding reception. He told her details of the house, and with little thought or effort he told her in detail what had happened to him when he'd bumped his head on the desk and lost consciousness. He was grateful for the opportunity to relate the vivid quality and details of the dream he'd had without the fear of being judged as crazy, or at the very least accused of suffering from hallucinations as the result of a head injury. Once he'd told her everything up to the present, he attempted to analyze what had happened, finding it easier to do so aloud, rather than letting a myriad of thoughts swirl chaotically in his brain. He lost track of the time while he talked to her, and he'd gotten over feeling embarrassed to have a nurse come to check on her and catch him talking. He would just wait until he was alone again with Jane to continue, telling her lightly that she was an excellent listener. He wondered if it was really true that a person in a coma could hear and remember all that was going on around them. He hoped so. The idea gave him comfort somehow.

"I know it was a dream," he said. "But . . . it felt so real. Of course, I know better than to believe it could be anything else but . . . in a way, it's like . . . somehow I was given some . . . incredible vision; the privilege . . . of seeing life through the eyes of my great-great-grandfather, and . . ." Alex stopped speaking and heard himself gasp before he consciously recognized the reason. All at once he felt both hot and cold, both terrified and filled with incomparable peace. It was as if the words that had come out of his mouth had come from a source beyond himself, and some power beyond his own was verifying their truth. *That was it.* Somehow, for reasons he couldn't begin to comprehend, he'd been given some kind of vision through the course of his dream. It was personal and sacred and deeply profound, and he knew in that moment that he would never share it with anyone besides Jane. He didn't ever want it to be trivialized by people who could never understand what he'd just felt. He had no idea what would make him worthy of such an extraordinary experience, but he felt grateful beyond words that it had happened.

As the enormity of what he'd experienced fully overcame him, Alex pressed his face into the sheet beside Jane and wept uncontrollably. When he finally calmed down, he kept his head on the bed, realizing that he'd been crying a long time. He wondered if a nurse had come in and found him distraught and had left him to weep alone. He pondered over whether his emotion was more from grief, or just being so overcome with gratitude. He concluded that it was both, and he felt in awe of being able to feel such heartache for the present circumstances, and still feel such an inner peace.

Alex drifted to sleep with his head against the bed. He woke up when a nurse came in, and he moved to the recliner where he settled himself for the night, coming awake each time that Jane was checked, then drifting easily back to sleep. He woke to daylight and realized that he must have slept through a couple of visits from the nurse. The room was growing light with day, and Jane looked no different. He took a quick trip to the restroom and gave Jane a kiss in greeting, wishing her lips weren't so inaccessible due to the ventilator. "I love you," he murmured close to her ear and made himself comfortable in the chair closest to her bed. It was a spot that had become alarmingly comfortable to him. A few minutes later an idea occurred to him, and he glanced at the clock, his heart beating quickly. He was just wondering if he could actually make himself go through with it when Walter and Louisa arrived. It wasn't the first time they'd shown up just when he felt the need to be elsewhere.

"Good, you're here," he said. "I . . . need to go for a while. I'll talk to you later." He hurried out of the room before they had a chance to say more than a couple of words. After going to his locker near the ER to get a few things, he shaved and washed up and was glad he'd been wearing nice clothes for the wedding the previous evening, and he still had the tie with him. He decided the button-up shirt and slacks didn't look too much like he'd slept in them.

Alex drove to a church building that wasn't terribly far from the hospital. He knew enough about LDS meeting schedules to know that you could go to practically any ward house and find a meeting beginning at nine A.M. The car clock read eight fifty-seven. He took a deep breath, recalling how the last time he'd tried this he'd practically hyperventilated before the meeting was half over. He reminded himself that a lot had happened since then; he wasn't the same man that he used to be. He uttered a quick, heartfelt prayer and recalled all the praying he'd done throughout the unconsciousness of the dream. While his mind had technically only been elsewhere for a matter of minutes, he couldn't deny that he'd somehow gained a stronger relationship with God during the dream when time had somehow stood still.

Thinking of all that Alexander Barrett and the people he loved had gone through just to be able to worship freely, Alex got out of the car, squared his shoulders, and went inside. He sat discreetly near the back just as the opening song was beginning. The hymn urged his emotions closer to the surface, and he found it difficult to keep them in check. As the meeting commenced, he felt some habitual anxiety, but he prayed fervently and felt himself relaxing. The sacrament prayers brought tears to his eyes, although he didn't partake of it personally. He felt sure he had a long way to go to be worthy of that.

As the meeting progressed, he found memories of the grief caused by his father mingling with memories of the privilege he'd been given to see life as it had been in another time. Taking in his surroundings, he pondered the beauty of the building and the sweet spirit filling it now. He thought of those who had sacrificed such a great deal so that people like him could worship surrounded by peace and prosperity. He vowed to never take such seemingly simple things for granted again.

Alex was actually surprised when the meeting ended and he realized that he'd lost track of the time, and that his anxiety had completely ceased. He sat where he was, watching churchgoers filing out of the chapel. He knew they were going on to other meetings and wondered whether or not to join them. Feeling the need to get back to the hospital, he committed himself to attend all of the meetings next week.

"Are you new here?" a man asked, and Alex looked up to see the same man who had been conducting the meeting. The bishop.

"Uh . . . just visiting, actually. I live in another part of the city, but . . . I was at the hospital and just wanted to catch a meeting nearby."

The bishop sat down beside him. "Do you work there, or do you have a loved one there?"

"Both," Alex said and hurried to explain as briefly as possible. "My fiancée . . . we were in an accident. As you can see, I'm fine, but she's in a coma."

"Oh, I'm so sorry," he said, and Alex knew he meant it. "Is there anything we can do?"

"Well," Alex chuckled tensely, completely unprepared for such an offer, "this isn't my home ward, and . . ."

"That doesn't matter," he said. "If we can help, then . . ."

"Really, I think all that can be done is being done. Thank you."

"Has she been given a blessing recently?"

"Yes, by her father, but . . . thank you."

"And you work at the hospital?"

"I do. I'm a physician."

The bishop asked him a few questions specifically about his work, then he reached into his pocket and pulled out a business card. "My home, work, and cell numbers are all on there. If you think of something we can do to help, please don't hesitate to call."

"Thank you," Alex said again. The bishop shook his hand and walked away. He looked at the card and tucked it into his pocket. Before he could get out of the chapel, he was stopped by three other people, asking if he was new or visiting, and expressing a kind greeting.

Alex sat in the car for a few minutes, attempting to accept how his feelings about attending church had changed so dramatically in so short a time. Was it the sudden, abject humility he felt from seeing Jane barely clinging to life? Or was it the perspective he'd been given through some kind of bizarre vision? Both, perhaps. Whatever the reasons, he couldn't deny being grateful as he began to comprehend what he'd been missing.

Alex returned to the hospital and was surprised to enter the room and find Walter and Louisa crying in each other's arms. His heart thumped as he quickly scanned the monitors to be certain that Jane's condition hadn't worsened in his absence. Everything appeared to be as it had been previously. He debated leaving them in peace, since they'd obviously not heard him come in, but he felt more compelled to intrude.

"Is something wrong?" he asked gently, and they both turned toward him, not looking at all embarrassed by their emotion.

Walter explained. "I guess it's just . . . one of those moments when it . . . hits you." He looked at Jane with yearning in his eyes. "It's just so hard to believe . . . that something like this could happen to your baby girl."

Louisa added tearfully. "You think things like this only happen to other people. I just . . . don't know what we'll do if we lose her, or worse . . . if she stays like this for years."

Alex couldn't deny how their words pierced his own heart with fresh pain. But he heard himself saying, "For now, we're just going to do our best to have faith that she'll come through and be all right. If the time comes to cross another bridge, we'll cross it together."

Louisa smiled through her tears and hugged Alex tightly. "You're a good man, Alex," she said, and tears he'd been fighting to hold back stung his eyes.

"Not as good as I could have been," he said, feeling regret burn his lips with the words.

Louisa looked up at him and wiped a tear from his face as it fell. "She loves you. And so do we. Don't you ever forget that."

Alex's tears increased and he moved away to grab a tissue. "Sorry," he said with a tense chuckle.

"You're welcome to join us in a good cry anytime," Walter said lightly. He then motioned toward Alex's attire and asked, "So, where have you been so early?"

Alex pressed a hand over his tie and stated, "Church. I went to sacrament meeting."

Alex expected Walter to respond with some indication that it was about time, but he simply smiled and asked, "Was it a good meeting?"

"It was, actually," Alex said, and Louisa got fresh tears in her eyes.

"Come on," Walter said, putting a hand on Alex's shoulder. "We'll buy you some brunch at the cafeteria. We all need to eat; she'll be all right."

Alex enjoyed his time with Jane's parents. While he didn't delve into any of his deep feelings or recent experiences, he did admit to them that he was ready to let go of the issues that had held him back and take some steps he should have taken a long time ago.

"In that case," Walter said, "this tragedy already has a silver lining."

Alex didn't want to admit how uncomfortable he felt with that idea. He looked down abruptly and cleared his throat. With a quiver in his voice he admitted, "How can I live with the belief that Jane has to go through this—that everyone who loves her has to go through this—because I was too stubborn to get over my problems a long time ago?"

Louisa put a hand over his on the table and said gently, "We can't question why God allows things to happen the way they do. I'm certain there's more to this than that. The important thing is that we don't lose our faith when trials come. We just have to move forward and learn all that we can."

Alex nodded, unable to speak. He wished that he'd been able to understand that when his father had left nearly twenty years ago. He knew that his mother had said something equivalent to him many times, but he'd never heard it; he'd never been able to let it penetrate his ailing heart.

Walter and Louisa left to attend a church meeting that began at one. Later that afternoon, Jane's sister Debi arrived from out of state. Only then did it occur to Alex that he'd seen or heard nothing more from Lana; apparently she had returned home. Debi would be staying a week, and then another sibling would come and spend some time. Walter had to fly home early Monday morning, and the family had set up a plan so that they could each spend time with Jane and be a support to their mother—and to him. Debi hugged him tightly when she saw him, even though they'd only met a couple of times and had shared nothing but surface conversation. Alex was grateful for her acceptance, especially after what had happened with Lana. And he was grateful to have her around, knowing that he had to go back to work in the morning, and he felt better having someone with Jane the majority of the time. They worked out a reasonable schedule so that everyone could eat and rest, and they could take turns going to the house to get some decent sleep in order to keep going. They all had each other's cell numbers so that they could share news quickly should anything change.

With Louisa and Debi hanging around in Jane's room and visiting, Alex felt mildly out of place and decided to go home. He couldn't argue with Louisa when she said that he needed a good night's sleep before he went to work in the morning. Once at home, he eagerly perused the book and the papers that Susan had given him. Looking at the names and dates on the genealogical records, he was amazed to see facts in black and white that coincided with what he'd experienced. But he was most stunned when he found the transcribed journals of Alexander Barrett included in the book. There he read about Alexander going back to England to deal with a family problem, and his return to Salt Lake City where he found his father's remains in the house, due to a misunderstanding. Alex didn't know whether to feel eerie or indescribably awed to realize that what he'd dreamt had coincided with actual events. Pondering the experience and how it had affected him, Alex cried an endless stream of cleansing tears.

When he'd gained composure, he was glad to realize that it wasn't too late to make a phone call. Talking to Susan deepened his gratitude for all that had happened and for this new connection in his life. Sharing an in-depth conversation with his mother's cousin, he felt a growing appreciation for the ancestry that Susan had been passionate about for years. He felt somehow closer to his mother as they talked, and he wished that his mother had been able to have more than a distant-relative, surface relationship with this woman.

The following morning Alex went back to work and found that he was grateful to be busy. He was able to check on Jane during his breaks, and then he spent the evening with her. On Tuesday morning while he was working, a little before ten, one of the nurses told Alex that he had a visitor. He went to the waiting room to find his sister Charlotte.

"This is a long way from Texas," he said, hugging her tightly.

"I thought that maybe you could use some support."

He chuckled to keep from crying and hugged her again. Alex took a break and escorted Charlotte through the hospital halls and to the ICU on the fourth floor. He updated her as they walked, and when they entered Jane's room, Charlotte started to cry. Alex handed her a tissue and introduced her to Louisa and Debi. Charlotte told them she would be in town for a few days and was willing to do anything they needed to help ease their burden in trying to be with Jane as much as possible. Alex left them to get better acquainted and returned to work, silently thanking God for the love and support of family. During Charlotte's stay, Alex was able to spend some time with her, and he found a silver lining in being able to gain a closeness to his sister that he'd never experienced before. While he felt some deep changes taking place within himself, he didn't necessarily feel ready to share them with anyone but Jane, and he was grateful that Charlotte didn't even bring up their father. And he didn't either. He had a long way to go to come to terms with that issue.

It was difficult to say good-bye to Charlotte, but she assured him she could return in another month or so if he needed her. He wanted to believe that this would all be over by then, but he wasn't so sure.

After doing four twelve-hour day shifts, Alex got two days off. He took time to pay bills and do laundry. And he moved out what little was left in his apartment and gave the landlord notice that he would no longer be renting it. He began staying at his mother's house for the most part, which left Jane's house for the use of her family, even though he needed to go there occasionally to get some of his things. With that taken care of, he spent every minute he could with Jane. He was present when her doctor declared that they could probably remove the ventilator soon, and he made certain he was present when it was taken out. Just to see Jane breathing on her own seemed a huge triumph, and he was glad to share that with Louisa and Debi. Then they each made phone calls to share the good news with family members elsewhere. He was with Jane when they moved her out of the ICU to another area of the hospital. The move was a great milestone, but it was also discouraging. She was healing from the injuries caused by the accident and doing well in that respect, but she was showing no signs of coming out of the coma.

On Sunday Alex was glad to be working a night shift so that he could attend church meetings in Jane's ward. He knew that his records were technically in the ward where his apartment was located, but he would be changing that. He was determined that as soon as Jane came out of that coma, he was going to marry her at the first possible moment, and they would share the home they should have been sharing a long time ago. Therefore, it was Jane's ward he chose to attend. The block meetings began at one P.M., so he was able to get some sleep after he got off early in the morning, and still get to church on time. People here were even more friendly than they'd been at the ward he'd attended the previous week. A counselor in the bishopric got some information from him right after sacrament meeting so that his records could be transferred. When Alex mentioned the situation with his fiancée, the bishop overheard and immediately pulled Alex into his office and closed the door.

"I'm Bishop Fitzpatrick," he said, shaking Alex's hand. "So, you're Jane Layton's fiancée."

"That's right," he said, certain this man would likely say something to the effect that it was about time he showed his face at church.

Instead, the bishop said, "She told me many times she was engaged to a fine man. It's a pleasure to finally meet you." Alex just nodded, and the bishop went on. "Of course we're aware of the situation with Jane. The Relief Society has been in contact with her mother, who has been at the house off and on, I believe."

Alex nodded again, wondering why he'd not heard anything about this. Then he realized that Jane's family members had been attending church meetings, and they'd likely been here at least once. He knew they'd attended an earlier meeting today so that they could be at the hospital while he was gone. The bishop continued, "It sounds like things are a little rough for you right now."

"Yeah, that's true," Alex said.

"So, what can we do to help?" the bishop asked.

Alex just came straight to the point. "I just . . . need to get my act together. I had trouble with getting myself to church. I was a disappointment to Jane in that respect. I'd like to make that right."

"Well then, you've come to the right place."

Alex was amazed at how comfortable he felt with this man as he gave a five-minute summary of his spiritual state, and a one-sentence explanation for his aversion to attending church. He admitted to the drinks he'd had the night of the accident, but declared with full confidence that beyond that he had technically been living righteously for years; he had even been paying tithing. He'd simply had trouble attending church. But he was committed to changing that now, and his goal was to receive a temple recommend just as soon as the bishop felt that he was ready. In the meantime the bishop assured him that he was worthy to take the sacrament and that he should certainly do so. He spoke briefly of the Atonement that it represented, and that this was the only possible source for him to truly find peace.

Alex left the bishop's office feeling a tangible hope that he could actually be the man Jane deserved. He prayed that she would live to share his joy in these changes he was making in his life. He attended the remainder of Sunday School following his visit with the bishop, then he went to the elders' quorum meeting, even though he wasn't an elder. He'd been ordained a teacher in the Aaronic priesthood prior to his inactivity, but nothing had changed since then.

Through the following weeks, Alex continued to attend his every church meeting, even if it meant having to trade a shift and make special arrangements, which wasn't always easy, but somehow he managed to make it work. At times he found it especially difficult to stay awake during the meetings when he'd worked all night, but he felt great incentive to be there and to be attentive. Occasionally, members of Jane's family attended church with him, and sometimes he went alone when they attended other meetings in order to balance out schedules. He'd spent time with each member of Jane's family as they'd come to aid in the ongoing vigil. They all came, except for Lana. He asked Jane's parents about the situation, and they simply said that she had some issues to deal with and let it drop. Alex felt badly that he might be to blame for keeping her away from her family, and especially from Jane, but he couldn't figure out what he might do about it.

Jane's kindergarten classes were taken over by another teacher who finished out the school year. Before school let out for the summer, each of the children in her classes colored pictures for Miss Layton, and they were hung all over the walls of Jane's room. Alex often stared at the childlike renditions of Jane and her students, drawn in crayon with great care. He thought of how she loved to teach, and his heart ached for the children she had grown to love through her work.

During his quiet hours in Jane's room, Alex continued to immerse himself in the family history that Susan had given him. His gratitude and awe deepened steadily as he learned more and more about the people who had come before him, and the sacrifices they had made to make the gospel a part of their lives. Many times he wept as he read, feeling a deep regret for the way he had taken those blessings for granted. But with time, he felt that burden lifted. He was making changes in his life now, and he knew in his heart that he was on the right path and that God was with him.

Inspired by the writings of his ancestors, Alex bought himself a journal. He considered using a computer, but he'd been so touched by seeing Alexander Barrett's hand-written words, and he liked the idea of being able to carry the book around with him. He felt a desire to leave something of himself for his own posterity. While he sat with Jane he recorded his recent experiences and feelings, and the changes he was making in his life.

Alex kept regular contact with Susan, and a number of times she met him at the hospital, bringing him a meal from the outside world, or stopping by just to lift his spirits. They shared long conversations about their common ancestry, and he couldn't deny that she was one more miracle in his life.

Several times each day, Alex took Alexander Barrett's ring out of his pocket and examined it closely. Holding it in his hand, it was easier somehow to feel close to its original owner. He'd learned from reading the man's history that the ring had been a gift from his father, given to him not long before they—along with other members of their family—had been baptized in England before coming to America to join the Saints. Alexander had worn this ring through great hardship and persecution, and through his years of living in the Salt Lake Valley. As an old man he had given the ring to one of his grandsons with whom he'd felt a special closeness. That grandson was Alex's grandfather, Ruth Keane's father. Ruth was an only child and had always loved the stories of her great-grandfather, and so her father had given the ring to her. And now it belonged to Alex. He felt deeply privileged to own such a possession, but even more so to have been allowed to come to know this man through the history he had written, and through the miraculous experience that had allowed Alex to get a glimpse of life through this man's eyes.

Jane continued to improve steadily. The feeding tube in her nose was the only sign that she wasn't just sleeping peacefully. The bruising had healed completely, and technically she appeared to be completely healthy. Physical therapists worked with her every day so that her muscles wouldn't lose their strength. And Alex prayed every hour of every day that this would not end in tragedy. He imagined how it would be to tell her that he'd been going to church, and of the deep soul searching, study, and prayer he'd been practically obsessed with through these weeks. He told her everything during their time alone, but he longed to see her eyes focused on him as he spoke, to hear her response, to feel her arms around him.

Once in a while Alex forced himself to ask the really tough questions. How could he cope if he lost her? Or worse, as Louisa had once said, if she remained this way for years? As difficult as it was to think of her dying, it was even harder to think of her going on this way indefinitely. At least death would bring closure, but this helpless waiting was already beginning to tell on him and on everyone else who had committed time to being at her side.

Louisa had to go home for a couple of weeks, but Jane's siblings filled in, and Alex found the opportunity to get to know each one of them on a level that was gratifying and made him feel increasingly blessed to have been taken in by this great family. He longed to be an official member of the family, and wished that he'd been smart enough to make that happen a long time ago. He was also able to get to know his sisters better. Every couple of weeks one of them would come and stay for a few days. They worked here and there to go through their mother's things more thoroughly, and he was amazed to find another copy of the same Barrett book that Susan had given him. His mother had owned this book all along. He felt somehow closer to her as he thumbed through its well-read pages and found places that she had actually marked. He got another copy of the book from Susan and gave one to each of his sisters, feeling deeply gratified to know that they each had this priceless record of their family.

Through their visits Alex found a new level of healing in relation to his mother. He came to know for himself that it truly had been her time to go, and he was grateful for the peace he felt that somewhat assuaged his grief. He still missed her, but he knew she was where she needed to be, and that she was still mindful of him and his struggles. He wouldn't be surprised to learn that she'd had something to do with pulling strings to arrange the miracles that had come into his life.

Alex and his sisters talked about many things, but still the subject of their father didn't come up. And he preferred it that way. In his heart, Alex knew that his feelings toward his father had to be faced before he could ever consider getting a temple recommend. In pondering the situation, and praying for guidance, Alex realized that he'd been able to make the steps he'd made thus far by separating them from his father's actions completely. But he couldn't separate them from the effect they'd had on his spirit. And he could never be spiritually at peace until he found peace with all that had happened. He just wasn't quite sure how to go about it.

Alex met regularly with the bishop, sharing his deepest feelings and concerns. The bishop came to the hospital at least once a week with one of his counselors, and they would always give Jane a blessing. Alex longed to be able to have the authority to give her a blessing himself, but he knew it would take time to earn such a privilege. He was grateful, however, that the bishopric occasionally gave him a blessing as well. In spite of the state of his own life, he felt deeply privileged to still be blessed by the power of the priesthood. He couldn't deny the comfort, strength, and courage he gained from those blessings.

Nine weeks beyond the accident, Alex went to his usual appointment with Bishop Fitzpatrick, feeling especially discouraged. He hated living in limbo this way and wondered how he could keep going. He sensed a growing weariness in Jane's family as well. Since she was medically doing very well, they were discussing options from here forward. She couldn't remain in the hospital much longer, since there was no need for hospital care, and her insurance benefits would run out. Alex dreaded the idea of not having her in the same building where he worked. But worse was the reality that Jane's family wanted her moved to California where they could watch out for her and be at home. Alex understood their reasoning, but it broke his heart. If she were his wife, it would have been entirely different. He would have taken her to their home and arranged for someone to be with her when he couldn't be. As it was, her parents had the legal right to make this decision. They were kind and compassionate regarding his desires, but he couldn't dispute *their* desire to have her in their home.

Alex expressed his present concerns with the bishop, who had become a dear friend through the past several weeks. He couldn't keep from shedding tears, but it was rare that they shared a visit when he didn't.

The bishop said gently, "You know, of course, that through prayer and the guidance of the Spirit, you can know what's right and feel peace over it."

"Yes, I know," Alex said. "And I've asked for exactly that, over and over. But I just can't feel it. I feel like this is all wrong, that we're supposed to be living as husband and wife, having a family. But obviously that's my own desire." He blew his nose and tossed the tissue in the wastebasket. "I'm not sure I know how to feel the Spirit at all."

"Now, I don't believe that," the bishop said gently. "You're understandably discouraged, but I've seen and felt a great deal of evidence that the Spirit is with you, Alex."

Alex felt pleasantly comforted by the comment and completely unprepared for the next thing the bishop said. "In fact, I think you're ready. What do you think?"

"Ready? Ready for what?"

The bishop chuckled softly. "To be ordained an elder, of course. And to go to the temple."

Alex sucked in a sharp breath and put a hand to his chest. "But . . . I thought it would take . . . longer, like . . . a year, or something."

"Your commitment to living the gospel is evident, Alex. I know your heart, and I've felt the strength of your spirit. I've given this a great deal of prayer. I believe that it's time."

Alex felt tears of a different kind trickle down his cheeks. He wiped them away and muttered, "I . . . can't believe it. I . . . don't know what to say."

"Give it some thought, and prayer of course. And let me know when you feel that you're ready."

Alex nodded, knowing that he did need some time. He didn't want to take these steps without feeling that he could truly put the past behind him. Attempting to sleep that night, he pondered the possibility of actually crossing this line that Jane—and his mother— had longed to see him cross for years. He thought of what it might be like to have the power of the priesthood, to be able to give Jane a blessing himself. He wondered what it might be like to partake of the blessings of the temple. Then he thought of going to the temple without Jane at his side and he turned his face into the pillow and wept uncontrollably. When his tears ran dry he prayed with all the fervor of his soul to know the steps that he should take, and if he was ready to take them. He continued to ponder the issue in his heart through the next few days. Sitting in sacrament meeting, as the bread and water were passed, Alex felt a subtle but undeniable warmth fill every cell of his being. He wept silently and discreetly as he comprehended without a doubt that God had forgiven him for his sins, and even for his stubbornness and stupidity. He knew in his heart that it was time to move forward. He couldn't fathom going to the temple without Jane, but he did feel ready to receive the Melchizedek priesthood, and to get a temple recommend. Beyond that, he'd simply have to go through the temple when he felt the time was right. And whether or not Jane went with him simply had to be in God's hands.

13

After the meeting, Alex told the bishop he would like to make arrangements to move forward; there was just one more thing he needed to take care of. That evening Alex called Charlotte and got straight to the point. "Can you tell me how to get hold of our father?"

"Why?" she asked skeptically.

"Because I want to talk to him. Is there a problem with that?"

"Not if you promise to be nice."

"I promise," he said.

"Okay," she drawled, "is there anything you want to tell me?"

"After I've talked to Dad, I'll catch you up to speed. I promise."

"Okay," she said and gave him their father's phone number and address. He lived about half an hour's drive from where Alex lived now. After ending the call with Charlotte, Alex stared at the information he'd written down and prayed fervently for the best way to handle this. He tried to talk himself into calling, so he could just say what he needed to say without having to face him. But in his heart he knew this needed to be done face-to-face. He debated calling to warn him, but decided against that as well. Figuring there was no time like the present, he got in the car and drove toward the address he'd been given, praying continually as he did. He found the house more easily than he'd expected, considering the winding roads of the neighborhood it was in. For several minutes he just sat in the parked car, looking at the house, trying to talk himself into getting this over with. The lights were on so he assumed that someone was home. He didn't want to interrupt anything, but he just had to go to the door and take it on the best he could.

Alex muttered one more quick prayer and took a deep breath before he rang the bell. A woman he'd never seen before answered the door. He hurried to ask, "Is this the Keane residence?"

"It is," she said with something in her eyes that made him feel as if she could see his soul. "And you must be Alex." Alex took a sharp breath, but before he could ask she simply said, "I recognize you from your pictures."

He forced a smile and said, "I hope I'm not coming at a bad time, or . . . interrupting anything, or . . ."

"Not at all," she said. "We were just loafing around. Please." She motioned with her hand. "Come in. I'll get Neil."

"Thank you," he said and stepped inside, noting that the home was very nice without being gaudy or showy. He felt increasingly nervous and prayed this wasn't a mistake. He hardly had another moment to think about it before his father appeared, looking as stunned as he might have expected.

"Alex," he said, "it is you." The woman who had answered the door appeared beside him. "Uh . . . this is my wife, Roxanne. Roxanne, my son Alex."

Roxanne offered her hand and a timid smile. "It's such a pleasure to meet you," she said as he shook her hand.

"And you," he said, trying not to feel uncomfortable with the fact that this was his stepmother.

"Come in. Sit down," Neil said.

Alex was relieved when Roxanne said, "I've got to answer a couple of e-mails. I'll leave the two of you to visit."

Alex watched her walk one direction, then he followed his father the other way into a comfortable living area with couches and a fireplace at one end, and an open kitchen and dining area at the other. The house was immaculate and smelled good. It reminded him somehow of the home he'd been raised in, while it looked nothing the same. Neil sat down on one couch and motioned for Alex to sit on another, across from him, with a large coffee table between them. Once Alex was seated, his father asked kindly, "So what has prompted this surprise?"

Alex considered the best way to answer and measured his words carefully. "Just . . . attempting to understand certain aspects of . . . my life, I suppose."

"Okay," Neil said and motioned for him to go on.

"May I ask you a question?"

"Anything," Neil said as if he would welcome the opportunity to talk to him at all.

"What are the reasons?" Alex asked. Neil looked confused, and he clarified, "You said there were reasons for doing what you did. I need to know what they are." Neil sighed loudly, and Alex added as an afterthought, "If this isn't a good time or place to talk about it, then—"

"No, it's fine," Neil said. "I've got no secrets from Roxanne. She knows how messed up my life used to be, but she loves me anyway. Now is fine. It's just difficult to . . . summarize. But I'll try." He sighed again and leaned back. "My upbringing had many challenges, things I never talked about, not even to your mother. Where her upbringing had been strong and secure, mine had been somewhat disturbing. There were things going on in my home that were inappropriate and confusing. I'll leave it at that. When I met your mother I was so in awe of her. I never realized that anyone could be so self-confident, so spiritual and secure." He gave a sardonic chuckle, and Alex couldn't help thinking how Neil's description of his mother fit Jane so closely. "And she was so genuine, no pretenses, no hypocrisy. And the life we shared was good. Too good, perhaps."

Neil hung his head and let out a long, slow breath. "At the time I never stopped to analyze why I felt the way I did, or why those feelings led me to the choices I made. I felt unhappy and uncomfortable and I allowed the weakest part of me to determine how to handle it. Then one day I woke up and had nothing. Oh, I had a good job; money wasn't a problem. But I couldn't see any reason to keep going to work. I'd lost my family. I'd been excommunicated. I had given up a perfect life for . . . nothing. The woman I had been involved with soon realized she'd made a mistake. She went back to her family. Her husband was very forgiving. To this day, I understand they're doing well. But I couldn't bring myself to go back."

"Why not?" Alex asked, wishing it hadn't sounded so cynical.

"Well, that was the golden question, Alex. I became suicidal before I finally had the sense to get some help. Working with a good counselor, who was also active in the Church, I began the road to understanding. It took a long time to put the pieces together and figure it all out. The ideas I'd been raised with had distorted my thinking much more than I'd ever imagined. I had believed that I could just put them behind me and move forward, but without understanding them, they were destroying me from the inside out. Bottom line: I didn't feel worthy of the life I was living. I felt sure there had to be some mistake for me to be so thoroughly blessed, so on some . . . unconscious level, I sabotaged it."

Alex felt a combination of grief and comprehension gather in his throat. He pondered his own reasons for delaying his marriage to Jane, and the times that his own thoughts had attempted to convince him that he was not worthy of the life she was willing to give him. He wondered if knowing this about his father years ago might have made a difference. He reminded himself that there was no point in wishing to change the past.

"I began leading the same kind of life I'd seen my own father lead," Neil continued, "although I give myself some credit for not having stooped so low as he had in many respects. And that was the same reason I couldn't go back to your mother. I felt certain she deserved better. I was afraid I'd only end up hurting her again—and you, your sisters. Your mother and I became friends. She helped me talk some things out, helped me understand. Somehow we seemed better suited as friends, in a way—at least with all that had happened between us. Roxanne helped me work things through, as well. She's a good woman. She's risen above a great deal, herself. I think she understood those dark and ugly parts of me. With time I was baptized again, and the second time around I actually felt like I deserved to be considered clean. I'd earned it." Neil sighed. "I think you know the rest."

A miserable silence ensued while Alex tried to think of something to say and attempted to keep his emotions in check. Pondering all he'd just heard, he was most surprised to realize that he felt a profound level of empathy. He actually understood *why* his father had made the choices he'd made. But it would likely take time before he could ever talk openly about such feelings.

"Was there something else you wanted?" Neil asked, but his words were kind, compassionate.

"Yes," Alex said and looked directly at him. His voice quavered as he added, "I've come to ask your forgiveness."

Neil looked stunned, completely dumbfounded. He finally said, "It is I who need your forgiveness, Alex. The suffering I inflicted upon my family was inexcusable."

"It's in the past," Alex said.

Neil looked as if he might cry. His voice cracked as he asked, "Are you saying that you *have* forgiven me?"

"Yes," Alex said with no hesitation. Neil pressed a hand over his mouth as tears distinctly pooled in his eyes. "But I want you to know that my coming to this has nothing to do with your help with paying for my education, or knowing that you gave financial help to Mom and the girls. It helps to know that you made restitution, that you cared enough to help. But that's not the reason. I've forgiven you because it's the right thing to do, because it's my responsibility to do it, and I should have done it a long time ago. I only hope that you can forgive me for being so slow to do it, for being so stubborn and self-righteous about the whole thing." Alex sighed loudly. "The things you said . . . when you came to the hospital . . . well, combined with other events, it forced me to do a great deal of soul-searching, and I found some things that were pretty pathetic. When I realized that my mother and sisters had enjoyed meaningful relationships with you all these years, I began to wonder what I'd cheated myself out of by being such an angry fool. That's it really. I was angry and too proud to let go of it. My anger has caused a great deal of grief for . . ." He heard his own voice crack and squeezed his eyes closed. "For . . . those I love most. It's held me back from many wonderful things. And that's why I'm putting it behind me, for good."

Again there was silence while Alex wondered what to do, what to say. Neil visibly gained his composure and said, "You know, by the time I figured out that I needed to forgive my father, he was dead."

"So I'm ahead on that count?" Alex said, attempting a light tone.

"On many counts," Neil said and came to his feet. He stepped around the coffee table and held out his hand. Alex looked at it, then into his father's eyes. He stood slowly and took the proffered hand, shaking it firmly. While Neil held tightly to his hand, he put an arm around Alex and pulled him fiercely close. Alex returned the embrace and couldn't hold back a surge of tears. There was some comfort in realizing that Neil was crying too. Alex savored the moments of cleansing and healing that took place as their embrace remained steady, then Neil stepped back and took Alex's face into his hands. Alex realized then that they stood eye to eye. Beyond seeing him from a distance at his mother's viewing, and that day in the hospital when Alex had been sitting down, he had never seen his father at all since he'd been thirteen.

"I have prayed for this moment every day for years, Alex. This moment is a miracle for me."

"Me too," Alex muttered and forced a chuckle. "Sorry it took me so long."

"Nothing matters now but the present," Neil said and sat down again, inviting Alex to sit beside him. "How is the present, anyway? How is Jane?"

Alex caught his father up on the situation, grateful for the emotional tension between them to be eased by some normal conversation. Neil asked Alex questions about his career and the education that had led to it.

"I need to thank you . . . officially," Alex interjected.

"For what?"

"For paying off my student loans. Those years were tough, trying to keep up good grades and keep the bills paid. What you did was a miracle for me; I just didn't know the source of the miracle at the time. It's given me a . . . broader perspective, you might say. I've tried to take the attitude that I need to give something back to society to compensate for all I've been blessed with. I regularly put in some volunteer time at a clinic for people who are homeless or unemployed, and it's been a great privilege. I simply want to thank you for what you did."

"I was glad to do it," Neil said. "It was a privilege to help pay for your education, especially knowing how committed you were to it. And now you're a doctor. Do you enjoy your work?"

"For the most part. It has its difficult moments, needless to say."

"What's been the most difficult?" Neil asked, as if he wanted to know everything about Alex that he'd missed through all these years of separation.

Alex didn't even have to think about it. "I was the doctor on duty when my mother was brought in, already gone."

"Good heavens," Neil said. "I had no idea. That's how you found out?"

"Yeah," Alex looked down. "I'd had a nice visit with her the day before and she'd been perfectly healthy, as always."

They talked on and on. Alex asked questions of Neil and discovered more details about his being CEO of a very successful software company. He was active in the Church and presently taught a Sunday School class, as well as serving on the activities committee. Roxanne was in the young women presidency, and together they worked in the temple every Wednesday evening. They had a goal set to be able to retire and serve a mission together within a few years. Alex discovered that Roxanne had also been through a divorce and had four children of her own. Neil treated her children and grandchildren as his own, and it was evident that Roxanne felt the same way about his family. It was only Alex who had been distant.

"But now the prodigal son has returned," Alex said. He'd meant it as a point of humor, but something deeply touched his heart as the words came through his lips.

"And we should celebrate," Neil said. "What should we do to mark this occasion? I don't have a fatted calf to kill, but I would love to take you to dinner or—"

"Actually, there is something I'd like to ask you, a favor. I don't know if it constitutes a celebration or not, but . . . if you could help me out with something, then . . . maybe we could go out afterward or . . ."

"Name it," Neil said.

Alex searched his feelings quickly once more, feeling assured that this was the right course. He had never imagined that it would come to this, but it was easy now for him to say, "My bishop is making arrangements for me to be ordained an elder, and . . ."

When he hesitated, attempting to gain his composure, Neil said, "If you're going to ask me if I want to be there when it happens, it would be an honor."

Alex looked into his father's eyes and said with a trembling voice, "I'm trying to ask you if you would be the one to ordain me."

Again Neil was so overcome with emotion that he couldn't speak. He finally hugged Alex tightly and muttered close to his ear, "Nothing could make me happier. It would be an inexplicable honor."

Neil invited Alex into the kitchen where they had some chocolate cake that Roxanne had made earlier. She joined them, and Alex enjoyed getting to know her before he finally called it a night and reluctantly left their home. Driving back to the hospital, Alex cried like a lost child come home. He arrived to find Jane alone and still lost in her unconscious state. He sat close beside her and told her of all that had happened this evening, of the miracles that had taken place in his life, then he slept for a few hours in the recliner before his shift in the ER began. He didn't struggle at all with feeling sleepy through the day. In spite of his ongoing heartache concerning Jane, he clearly felt the absence of a burden he had carried for too many years.

During one of his breaks he called the bishop, and within the next few days he had official interviews with the bishop and stake president. They both declared that his timing was good, since there would be a stake conference on Sunday. He was publicly sustained to become an elder, while Jane's parents sat on one side of him at the meeting, and his father and stepmother sat on the other. Later that day, Neil Keane put his hands on Alex's head to ordain him to be an elder in the Melchizedek priesthood. Walter, the bishop, the stake president, and a few men from the ward joined the circle. The experience was exquisite and unforgettable, and again Alex wondered why he had taken so long to make these decisions.

That evening he sat in Jane's hospital room with her parents while they discussed the fact that time had run out and they needed to make a decision. Unless something in her condition changed, she couldn't remain in the hospital and receive any insurance benefits. Alex was surprised when Walter said to him, "Maybe you should give her a blessing."

It took Alex a moment to realize he could do that, but he had to admit that he didn't know how. He'd longed to be able to do it, but he wasn't sure he felt ready. As if Walter had read his mind, he said gently, "I'll help you, but I think it would be appropriate for you to do it. Sometimes when the word of the Lord comes through a blessing, it helps those who hear the blessing—and those who give it—as much as it helps the recipient, perhaps more."

Alex couldn't argue with that concept, especially when Jane was unconscious. "Okay," he said, "but . . . what do I say?"

Walter told him the necessary words to be spoken at the beginning and end of the blessing. "Beyond that," he said, "just open your mind to the Spirit and you'll know what to say. It's been my experience that if something needs to be said, it will come to my mind and stay there until I say it. Simple as that."

Before they began, Louisa offered a prayer at Walter's request. In it she expressed gratitude for Alex being a part of their family, and for the steps he had taken to come to this point. She prayed that he would be guided by the Spirit as he used the power of the priesthood to bless this woman he loved so dearly. Louisa also asked, as they each did in every prayer they had shared through these weeks, that Jane would come out of this coma and be able to live a full and normal life. She asked for guidance regarding decisions that needed to be made that were difficult. When the amen was spoken, Alex could feel the Spirit in the room, and he wasn't so nervous about giving this blessing. Walter did the anointing, then Alex placed his hands on Jane's head and felt Walter's hands come down over his as he closed his eyes and prayed silently to be guided in the words he spoke. At first he went slowly, feeling hesitant and unsure, then words came clearly into his mind, and he heard himself saying that God was mindful of this situation and all who were affected by it. He said that these circumstances were in God's hands, and that in God's time Jane would be released from the bondage that she was in. Alex hesitated, wondering if that meant she would die rather than recover. He tried to focus on the moment and found himself pausing excessively long as words came to his mind that seemed to be an answer to the question he had just silently asked. The answer took his breath away, and for a moment he felt certain that he was reading his own desire into this. But the words came again, clearly, with the undeniable force of the still, small voice. He had no choice but to allow them to come through his mouth. "With the continued prayer and patience of your loved ones, you will be blessed with a full recovery. Through the course of your life you will touch for good the hundreds of children that you will have the opportunity to teach, and you will be blessed with children of your own who will grow strong and healthy and be true in the gospel as a result of your devotion to the Savior and living according to His example."

When his mind went blank, Alex ended the blessing. He slowly opened his eyes and lifted his head, but felt reluctant to move his hands, not wanting to break the incredible connection he'd felt through the course of the blessing. He looked up to see tears streaming down Walter's face, and a quick glance told him that Louisa was crying as well. He wondered if he'd done something wrong, until Walter said softly, "That was beautiful, son. It would seem that everything's going to be all right."

Alex felt tears sting his own eyes before he fully comprehended what Walter had meant, and how it related to what he'd said in the blessing. Only now did the words he'd spoken fully penetrate his mind. Knowing in the deepest part of his heart that those words were true, he sat down weakly and cried right along with Walter and Louisa. When their emotions settled, Walter said firmly, "I think we need to give it a few days. They told me the insurance would cover a few more days. If nothing's changed by then, maybe we'll at least have more information to help us make the right decision." He put a hand on Alex's shoulder and added, "Even if nothing changes, maybe she should stay here, close by. I think we need to consider it."

Alex nodded, grateful beyond words to know that they would at least give such an option some consideration. Whatever happened, he knew these people would make their decisions according to prayer and fasting, and he would do the same. If they all felt peace over something, then they would know it was the right course. In his heart he believed the right course would be letting her stay in her parents' home in California, and somehow he was just going to have to deal with that. But he now believed it would only be temporary. Eventually she would recover from this, and then all would be well.

Two days later, Alex came into Jane's room to find Louisa there, reading from her scriptures.

"What have you got there?" she asked, noting the little box he set on a table near the bed. It was shiny silver, about the size for a necklace or bracelet, tied with a white satin ribbon.

"It's a gift . . . for Jane," he said.

"Is it private?" she asked.

"No." He picked it back up and handed it to Louisa. She set the scriptures aside and took it, untying the satin bow. Before she lifted the lid he said, "I debated using it soon, but it just doesn't feel right. I feel like I need to wait for her."

Louisa opened the box and let out an emotional laugh to see his temple recommend lying on silver tissue paper. "Nothing could make her happier," Louisa said.

"I know," he replied sadly. "I only wish I'd had the sense to do it a long time ago."

"You're here now, and everything's going to be okay."

"So I've been told," he said with a little smile, but he couldn't deny within himself that it was difficult to hold onto hope when this had already been going on for so long, and nothing had changed.

Louisa carefully retied the bow, and Alex set the box on the table near the bed, imagining what it would be like to watch Jane open it. He sat close to the bed and took her hand while Louisa went to get something to eat.

"I love you, Jane," he muttered and habitually squeezed her hand. "I love you more than life. I pray that you can forgive me for being such a stubborn fool. Please come back to me. I love you so much."

He gasped when he felt her hand move in his. Never in all the endless hours he'd spent holding her hand had he felt even the slightest response. He squeezed her hand again but felt nothing, and he finally convinced himself that it had probably been his imagination. An hour later a nurse came in to take Jane's blood. Setting out what she needed, she explained, "Doctor's ordered some tests; I guess they're making arrangements to move her elsewhere, and he wants to make certain everything's okay."

"So I've heard," he said, trying not to sound as dismayed as he felt.

He stood up to stretch and look out the window and was startled to hear the nurse say, "Whoa."

"What?" he asked, turning around.

Her face lit up with a grin. "She flinched when I put the needle in." She said it as if she'd just won a million dollars.

Alex laughed and resisted the urge to hug the nurse. He didn't have to ask what that meant. He *had* felt her hand move. And she was withdrawing from pain. Both were clear signs that she was likely inching toward consciousness. Once the blood had been drawn, the nurse quickly left, exclaiming that she would call the doctor responsible for Jane's care and let him know what had happened.

"Oh, Jane," Alex murmured, taking hold of her hand once gain. "Please don't give us false hope here. Please come back to us."

When Louisa returned, he told her the good news. She immediately got on the phone to spread the word and to ask family and friends to embark on another twenty-four-hour fast. There had been many fasts on Jane's behalf, but Alex couldn't help hoping that this one would coincide with the Lord's timing, and the need for a miracle.

The following day, some tests were done, and it was definitely concluded that Jane's nervous system was more responsive. Given that, the doctor officially declared her need to remain hospitalized—an order that would allow the insurance company to continue covering her stay. Alex was grateful for the extra time at the hospital where he could be close to her, but when days passed and nothing more changed, discouragement settled in again.

On Sunday he went to church, grateful for this opportunity in his life, and for the way it replenished him. Still, he felt deeply sad and longed to have Jane at his side.

* * * * *

Jane became aware of her surroundings as if they were far away. She felt completely relaxed, just this side of sleep, unwilling to move or even open her eyes. The sounds and smells felt strangely familiar, and yet completely strange. She felt the sensation of time having passed without her, while in the same moment she felt as if only minutes had gone by since . . . since what? What did she last remember? Trying to recall, she found it impossible to put her memories in order. A seemingly endless string of dreams and voices swirled in chaos, leading back toward that moment when . . . Alex. They'd been in the car and . . . *Oh, help.* Where was she? What had happened? And where was Alex?

"Alex," she muttered and could barely hear herself.

"Jane?" a familiar voice responded with intense emotion. But it wasn't Alex's voice. Who was it? "Jane?" it repeated, and she felt a strong hand squeeze her own.

"Daddy?" she said and tried to force her eyes open. When it was too difficult she returned the squeeze of his hand.

"It's me, honey," her father said, then he sniffled as if he were crying. She heard a door opening, a familiar sound as if she'd heard it a thousand times, and yet not at all. "Louisa," he said, "she's coming around."

Jane heard her mother make an emotional noise, then she felt her other hand being taken between her mother's warm fingers. "Jane, honey," Louisa said.

"Mom," Jane said and tried again to push open her eyes. With some effort she was able to focus on her mother's face, and the tears were readily evident. "Why are you crying?" she asked.

"Oh, baby girl," Louisa said on the wave of a sob, "we wondered if we'd ever see you awake again."

Jane felt her heart quicken. "What happened?" she asked, turning to see her father, who was also crying. She couldn't recall ever seeing her father cry.

"You were in an accident, honey," Walter said. "You've been in a coma for nearly ten weeks."

"Ten weeks?" she echoed, her words still coming weakly.

She turned to her mother as if to be assured this wasn't a joke. "That's right, baby," she said. "And now you're being given a second chance at life."

The door opened again, and Jane heard her mother say, "She's awake."

A woman's voice made a squeal of delight just before a nurse's face appeared close to Jane's as if to check for herself. "Well, look at you," she said. "I'll page the doctor right away."

Walter said to her, "And would you also page—"

"Yes, I know," the nurse chuckled, "*the* doctor. I'm all over it."

Jane listened to their words as if through radio static while her brain tried to accept that she'd lost ten weeks of her life. That explained the hazy images of dreams. And the memory of being with

Alex in the car. But what about . . . She felt her heart quicken and looked frantically at each of her parents. "Alex? Where's Alex? Is he—"

"He's fine, honey," Walter said. "I'm afraid you got the worst of it. He's spent about a million hours just sitting here, holding your hand, trying to talk you into coming back to us."

"Oh, Alex," she said, inexpressibly grateful to know he was okay, but longing to see for herself. "Where is he . . . now?"

"We're not sure. They're going to page him."

Jane understood now what the nurse had said. *The* doctor. That was him. She tried to put the picture together in her mind. Alex. Her parents. Ten weeks. "Who else has been here?" she asked.

"Everyone," Walter said. "All of your brothers and sisters have been here at one time or another, and Alex's sisters. You've hardly been in this room alone for more than a little while here and there."

"Ten weeks?" she said still again, feeling like she wanted to cry but not finding herself capable. Becoming more focused on her surroundings, she asked if the bed could go higher. Her father adjusted it so she was sitting up, but she suddenly felt as if the bed would suffocate her. Just knowing she'd spent ten weeks in it gave her a sudden urgency to get out of it. The nurse came in to check on her, and Jane asked, "Can I get in a wheelchair? I just want to . . . see my face in a mirror and . . . wash my hands and . . . I just want to get out of this bed."

"Well . . . it's not standard procedure," the nurse said, "but . . . I don't see why not. You're awfully weak, and we need to be careful." While Walter helped the nurse move Jane into a wheelchair, the nurse explained, "Physical therapists have come every day to work on your muscles so you'll be able to get back on your feet more quickly, but it's still going to take a while. You mustn't be doing anything at all without help."

"Agreed," Jane said, realizing how weak she felt once she was in the chair. But it did feel good.

"What's that for?" Jane asked, pointing at the bag on an IV pole, then she realized it was connected to a tube in her nose, not her arm.

"That's your lunch, sweetheart," the nurse said.

"Oh, I just can't believe it," Louisa said as she stood back to see her daughter actually sitting up.

"Me neither," Jane said, feeling disoriented and almost afraid.

"It's a miracle," Walter said. "But then, we were counting on one. We had good reason to believe you'd come around."

"How did you know that?" Jane asked.

"We'll . . . talk about that later," Louisa said.

"Where's Alex?" Jane asked again, not certain she could remember what they'd told her.

"You know what?" Walter said. "We'll go down to the ER and see if he's there while you're getting washed up. We'll check back."

"Don't be too long," Jane said, sounding like a frightened child.

"We promise," Louisa said, kissing Jane's face and touching her hair.

Once in the bathroom, Jane was startled by her gaunt, pale expression. That alone let her know time had truly passed without her. The nurse helped Jane wash up a bit, and she was pleased to hear that her personal hygiene had been kept up, even in her unconscious state. She was told that her hair had been washed just yesterday. She was also told that her teeth had been cleaned recently, but Jane still asked if the nurse would help her do it again. Her mouth felt like stale wool.

"Did you page Alex?" Jane asked once she'd rinsed her mouth by spitting into a plastic basin the nurse held for her.

"If you mean Dr. Keane, yes I did. Well, I called the ER. They'll find him. He can't be too far away; he never is."

Jane smiled at the nurse and noticed her ID badge read Crystal. "Thank you, Crystal," she said and prayed that he would get here soon. She had to know for herself that he was really all right, and that nothing had changed between them in the weeks that she'd been absent. She'd been assured that he was physically okay, but what if he'd lost what little faith he'd had to hold onto? Had he started drinking again when faced with yet another disaster? Had he convinced himself that she would be better off without him? Oh, how she prayed that he hadn't! She loved him, needed him, needed to be with him. Getting a second chance at life just didn't seem right unless she could share it with Alex.

"Maybe I should get back to bed," she said, suddenly feeling that even this little jaunt in a wheelchair had been way too much too soon.

"That's where we're headed," Crystal said and wheeled Jane out of the private bathroom into the hospital room. Oh, how she prayed that Alex would get here soon! She needed him.

14

Sacrament meeting was about half over when Alex felt his pager vibrate. He pulled it off his belt and looked at the number. The ER. He wondered if they'd had a major accident, or if another doctor was sick or unable to work for some reason. He discreetly left the meeting and called on his cell phone while he drove toward the hospital.

"This is Dr. Keane," he said to the nurse who answered. "What did you need?" She asked him to hold on and came back to the phone saying, "I'm not sure. Dr. Baker just said to tell you he needs you."

"Okay, I'm on my way. I'll be there in ten minutes."

The ER seemed peaceful when he walked in, and he wondered what was up. He found Baker and asked, "So what's the emergency?"

"No emergency," he said with a little smile. "They called from upstairs; I told them I'd find you." His smile widened. "I think it's good news."

Alex couldn't run the long halls fast enough, and he felt sure the elevator had never been slower. He wondered if Jane had shown some increased response, or if her doctor had something hopeful to tell them. Or . . . he hardly dared hope. Could she have possibly come around? He didn't even want to indulge in such a wish. He rushed into her room and took a sharp breath to see the bed empty. For a heart-pounding moment he wondered if something awful had happened and she was gone. He wondered if Baker had misinterpreted the message. Then he heard noises in the bathroom, and the door came open. A sob of laughter erupted from his throat as a nurse pushed a wheelchair into the room. And in it sat Jane—alive, awake, and real. He felt stunned and frozen and unable to respond. She looked up and her countenance filled with perfect delight to see him. "Alex," she said, and he sobbed again. "Mom and Dad went to look for you."

Alex went to his knees in front of her, as much from a desire to get closer as from the weakness that made it difficult to stand. He laughed as he touched her face, her hair, her face again. He took both her hands into his, pressed them to his lips, then pressed his lips to her brow. He'd kissed her there a thousand times while she had remained immobile and unresponsive. But now she squeezed his hand, and he heard her whimper softly. "Oh, Jane," he muttered and forgot they weren't alone until the nurse spoke.

"She insisted on getting out of that bed; but she's awfully weak. I'm going to let you help her get back in, then I'm just going to leave the two of you alone."

Alex smiled up at the nurse and saw tears glisten in her eyes, as if she'd just witnessed a miracle. Indeed she had. "Thank you," he said, and she left the room.

"Oh, my sweet Jane," he said, touching her face again. "You're here; you're really here. I can't believe it."

Jane could hardly believe it herself. She felt so happy to see him she could barely breathe. He looked different somehow, but she had trouble pinpointing exactly what might have changed beyond the evidence of a fresh scar on his forehead.

"You were hurt," she said, touching it.

"Only a little," he murmured. "I'm fine."

"They told me it has been nearly ten weeks," she said, and Alex couldn't help but notice the weakness in her voice. "It feels like just a few minutes ago that we were in the car and . . ." Her voice quivered, and she eased her head to his shoulder. He carefully lifted her into his arms and put her on the bed, tucking the covers carefully over her before he sat beside her and eased her into his arms. For a few minutes neither of them could speak. They just held to each other and wept. Alex felt so full of awe and gratitude that he couldn't even consider getting words past the lump in his throat without the threat of completely breaking down. As it was he just cried silently and soaked in the evidence of her consciousness. "I love you, Alex," she whispered close to his ear, and he couldn't hold back a sob. For a minute he sobbed more than laughed, then he laughed more than sobbed and held her as tight as humanly possible without hurting her.

The door opened, and Alex turned to see Walter enter the room. "I didn't figure it would take you long to show up," he said to Alex. "Louisa's calling the whole world to let them know the good news."

Jane weakly reached a hand toward her father. He hugged her and kissed her cheek while Alex held her other hand tightly. He couldn't believe it. The miracle had actually happened. She would never have to be transported to another state to be cared for where he couldn't be with her. He would never have to live without her again.

With her father sitting on one side of the bed and Alex on the other, Jane laughed softly and said, "I don't know what to say. It could take a while to catch up."

"You don't have to say anything," Alex said and kissed her hand. "I'm just going to sit here and look at you with your eyes open. I'd forgotten how beautiful they are."

"Amen to that," Walter said.

Jane's doctor came in a few minutes later and introduced himself to her. "You don't know me," he said, "but I've been looking out for you for a long time."

"So they tell me," she said.

He asked her many questions and did some simple tests after which he declared that her brain function appeared to be completely normal. He told them the following day they would be moving her to the rehabilitation section of the hospital where she would stay until she could gain some strength and get enough physical therapy to be able to get around on her own. Once it was determined that she could leave the hospital, she would be getting some regular home health care and physical therapy at home until she could manage to exercise again on her own and completely care for herself.

"Within a few months," the doctor said, "she'll be as good as new."

This made everyone smile. They asked some questions and got their answers. After the doctor left, Jane became very sleepy and asked to rest, but she begged Alex and her parents not to leave her alone. With their promise she fell quickly to sleep. Alex almost felt terrified to let her do so, fearing she wouldn't wake up again. But in his heart he knew she would; she'd come through. It was a miracle.

Alex visited quietly with Jane's parents about their feelings concerning this turn of events. They each cried a little, and together they knelt in Jane's hospital room and expressed their gratitude for her recovery. When Jane woke up early in the evening, Alex soaked in her presence for a few minutes, then discreetly said there was something he needed to do. He went to the cafeteria to get something to eat, then killed some time in the ER, spreading the good news and harassing his coworkers. He wanted to give Jane's parents an opportunity to be with her, and not intrude too much on the relationship they shared.

Alex called his father, as he had a number of times since their reconciliation. But this time he was excited to give a different answer to the usual inquiry about Jane. "Well, guess what, Dad," Alex said. "She's awake, and she's going to be fine."

Neil laughed with perfect joy through the phone. "Well, that's the best news I've heard since you told me you'd forgiven me. Now all is right with the world, and we can live happily ever after."

Alex chuckled. "One step at a time, Dad. When she's up and around a little more, I want you and Roxanne to come and meet her."

"You call when it's a good time, and we'll be there," Neil said. "Are you okay? Do you need anything?"

"I'm fine," Alex said. "In fact, I'm great. Thank you."

They talked for a while longer, then Alex called his sisters to share the same news. When that was done he debated whether or not to go back to Jane's room. After being gone nearly three hours, he returned to find Jane asleep again, with Louisa sitting in the recliner, reading. The scene was eerily familiar, until Louisa whispered, "She's been asleep again for over an hour. I'll just—"

At the sound of her mother's voice, Jane opened her eyes and looked at Alex, smiling when she saw him. "Wow," he said. "I'm glad to know that I hadn't just dreamt that you woke up." Her smile widened, and his heart threatened to beat right out of his chest. He loved her so much!

"Now that you're here, Alex," Louisa said, "I think I'll go find Walter and get something to eat. He went to call some people. Are you staying tonight as usual?"

"Yeah," he said, "I have to work early in the morning. I have everything I need in my locker. I think I'll just hang out here in the recliner."

Jane smiled, then glanced around the room as if to acquaint herself with the time she'd lost. "I love the wallpaper," she said, referring to the pictures colored by her kindergarten classes.

"Yeah, it's great," Alex said. "The little bugs will all be glad to hear you're okay when they get back from summer vacation."

Walter came back in and said to Jane, "Boy it sure is good to have you back."

"Well, it's good to be back," Jane said. "But you haven't told me yet about the miracle." They all looked puzzled, as if it were obvious, and she added, "You said that you were counting on a miracle, that you had good reason to believe I'd come around. I want to know why."

Alex glanced at both Walter and Louisa, hoping they would handle this discreetly. There was a great deal he needed to tell Jane, but he wasn't sure where to begin. He left it up to Walter to say whatever he felt compelled to say.

"It was that last priesthood blessing you got." Walter took her hand. "You were given several, but . . . that last one was pretty clear, and a couple of days later you started showing signs that you were coming around."

Jane smiled at her father. "And were you the mouthpiece for this marvelous blessing?"

Walter glanced at Alex before he said, "No, Alex was."

Jane's heart began to thud as she turned to meet Alex's eyes. He stared back at her as if to convey some silent message. Now she understood what was different about him. While she was struggling for something to say, Louisa said, "We've had many miracles." She hugged Jane, then Alex, as if she'd been given her cue to leave the room. "We'll see you tomorrow, then." She smiled and winked at Alex and waited barely long enough for Walter to kiss Jane before she dragged him from the room.

Once they were alone, the room became eerily silent. He felt her eyes delving into his, as if she could find the answers to her questions without having to ask them. She finally said with a quavering voice, "You gave me a priesthood blessing?"

"I did," he said.

"I wish I would have been awake to hear it."

"Well, that would have basically defeated the purpose," he said lightly, hoping to divert her attention from a topic that he wasn't sure how to open up fully now that she was awake. "Do you remember anything?" he asked.

"I have . . . hazy memories of . . . voices, but . . . it all feels muddled and more like a dream. The only thing that really stands out is . . . a feeling . . . like I was surrounded by love and comfort."

"Well, you certainly were," he said and sat down.

"So, we're alone at last," she said, taking his hand. "And you've obviously been busy while I was gone. So tell me everything."

Alex struggled to know where to begin, then he noticed the little silver box on the table. "Why don't you open your present first."

She turned to see what he was looking at. "Oh, I noticed that earlier. Mother said it was from you, and I should wait until you were here before I opened it."

"So, I'm here," he said, handing it to her.

Jane laughed softly as she pulled on the ribbon. "It can't be an engagement ring because I already have one." She held it up to show him as if he'd never seen it before.

"No, it can't be that," he said.

"Maybe it's a bracelet to complement this one." She held up her arm and pointed out the plastic hospital ID bracelet.

"Not likely," he said with a chuckle. His heart began to pound as she started to lift the lid. He reached out a hand to stop her, saying softly, "Wait. First . . . there's something I have to say." Taking in her expectant expression compelled him to add, "But before I say anything . . ." He took her face into his hands and kissed her. Feeling her response, he was nearly moved to tears. He pushed a hand into her hair and kissed her again. He looked into her moist, dreamy eyes and murmured, "Oh, how I love you!"

She smiled. "Is that what you wanted to say?"

"Partly," he admitted, recalling where this conversation had been going when he'd become distracted by the urge to kiss her. "I just . . . need to tell you that . . . the first time we danced together, I was ready to get down on one knee and propose, and when I finally did propose, it already seemed like it had been way too long to wait to get married, and then . . . the waiting went on and on, and I know that was my fault. Do you remember what I said the day before my mother died?"

"I remember it well," she said.

"You should, because it was what we argued about the night of the accident. I asked you again to marry me; I told you it was time I got my life in order. Then we lost Mom and . . . well, you know how I fell apart, but . . . I want you to know how sorry I am . . . for all the hurt and the waiting I've put you through. I want you to know how grateful I am for your patience." Tears crept into his voice. "You can't imagine how many times I've said those words while you were unconscious, just wishing that you could hear them, that you could know how I really felt. I've ached to just hear you say that everything would be okay."

"Everything is okay now, Alex."

"Well, yes . . . I believe it is, but . . . you need to know that I learned it wasn't going to be okay all by itself. That whether you came through this or not, I needed to honor my promises to you, and stop hiding from things that were better faced up to. So . . . now that we're here, before you open the box, I want you to know that . . . in a way it is like another engagement ring, because . . . I'm asking you again . . . for the last time . . . Will you marry me, Jane?"

She opened her mouth to answer but he put his fingers over her lips. "Don't answer that yet. Just . . . open the box."

Alex watched her face as she lifted the lid. For a moment her brow furrowed as if she were puzzled, then her eyes widened with enlightenment and her entire countenance brightened just before she let out a breathless sob. She looked up to meet his eyes, as if to question the validity of what she was seeing. She opened her arms in an effort to embrace him but obviously didn't have the strength. Alex pulled her close and squeezed his eyes shut to more fully encompass her living, breathing presence in his arms and the tears of joy that were being shed against his shoulder. He could honestly say he'd never been more happy in his life. To have Jane back, and to see *her* so happy seemed all that he could ever ask for.

Once her emotions calmed down, Jane laughed and said, "Get me in a wheelchair and get me to the temple right now."

Alex laughed. "It's Sunday."

"Okay, tomorrow."

"The temple is closed on Mondays."

"So it is," she said. "Well . . . Tuesday then."

He laughed again. "I think we need to give it just a little more time than that. You've been patient this long, surely you can wait a few more months."

"I don't want to wait," she said, pressing a hand to his face.

"Neither do I, but I don't want to take a physical therapist with us on our honeymoon."

"Good point," she said with exaggerated disappointment. Then with equally exaggerated enlightenment, she added, "But once I get to a certain point, *you* can be my physical therapist."

Alex grinned at her. "That just might be a possibility."

"So get a calendar out, and let's set a date. I can plan a wedding from the hospital as long as I have a phone and my mother around."

"Okay, well . . . you'll have to talk to your mother about that. And your doctor." She smiled at him, and he added, "I take it that means yes."

Jane laughed but he could see the strength draining out of her from the energy she'd expended. "Yes, that means yes," she said, and he kissed her. "I love you, Alex," she murmured, and he kissed her again.

"I love you too," he whispered and kissed her still again.

"I want you to tell me everything," she said softly.

"Okay, but . . . I can tell you're tired, and . . ."

"I want to hear it all. If I get too sleepy I'll tell you, and then we'll pick it up later."

"Okay," he agreed.

"Start at the beginning."

Alex snuggled up close to her and started from the moment he'd seen the truck coming at them, and how he'd awakened in the emergency room. She got sleepy about the time he got to the part about going to the wedding that his mother had so desperately wanted to go to, but he promised to finish when she was up to it. She quickly slept, and he watched her in a way that was eerily comfortable until he fell asleep in the recliner. When he left the room to get to work, she was still sleeping. He uttered a silent prayer of gratitude and hurried to the ER. A couple of hours into his shift, he was told he had a phone call.

"Dr. Keane here," he said, picking up the phone.

"I woke up and you were gone," Jane said, and he laughed just to hear her voice coming through the phone.

"A man's got to make a living," he said. "But I'm not far. I'll come up on my break."

"I'll be looking forward to it."

Alex went to Jane's room on his break and found Walter and Louisa there, chatting comfortably with Jane. Her feeding tube had been removed, her hair was damp from a recent shower, and they were waiting to move her to rehab. "What a glorious sight," he said, making Jane smile. He kissed her in greeting and sat on the edge of the bed, listening as they continued their conversation. They were obviously telling her everything that every member of the family had done during her absence. Once Walter had finished his thought, he said to Alex, "She's craving things like chocolate malts and cheese fries."

"That's a good sign, I think," Alex said. "But I think you'd better take it slow. That stuff they've been pumping into your stomach didn't have any sugar or grease in it."

"Or chocolate," Louisa pointed out, making Jane laugh. Oh, it was so good to hear her laugh!

They chatted for a few minutes, then Alex kissed her again and said he needed to get back to work. Walter and Louisa were flying out that afternoon to take care of some things, but Louisa would be back in a few days to help plan the wedding and make the arrangements and preparations for Jane to go home.

On his lunch break, Alex found Jane settled into rehab, but they were doing physical therapy, and he only got to wave at her quickly. It was nice to see her wearing the T-shirt and stretch pants her mother had brought from home, as opposed to the hospital gowns she'd been wearing for ten weeks.

Alex got the information on visiting hours for rehab, since they needed to work around therapy sessions. Then he left a message for Jane with a nurse, letting her know that he'd be coming in after work and bringing someone to meet her. On his next break he called his father and arranged for him and Roxanne to meet him at a particular door. By then he had changed and freshened up. They arrived right on time, and he greeted each of them with a hug.

"How is she?" Roxanne asked as they went up the elevator.

"She's pretty weak, but beyond that, she's doing great."

"That's wonderful," Neil said. "She knows we're coming, right?"

"She knows company is coming," Alex said. "Actually . . . I haven't had a chance to catch her up to speed, so . . . this is a surprise."

Roxanne laughed softly, but Neil seemed a bit apprehensive. Approaching the door to Jane's room, Alex motioned for them to hold back for a minute. He went in and found her half reclined in her bed with a magazine open on her lap, but she was looking out the window.

"Hi," he said and kissed her.

"Hi," she said back. "Isn't it a beautiful day?"

"It is," he agreed, looking only at her.

"Did I get the right message? You were bringing company?"

"That's right. There's someone I want you to meet."

"Well, I look a sight, but . . ."

"You look beautiful," he said. "I'll be right back."

Jane felt mildly nervous as she watched Alex leave the room. In a way he was the man she'd always loved, but he'd changed during her absence. The changes were definitely positive, the best she could have ever hoped for. But he was so full of surprises that she wondered if she could take any more. She was wondering what new friend he'd made through this ordeal, when he came back with a middle-aged couple. She knew she'd seen this man somewhere before. It took her a moment to place it, then she gasped none too softly just before Alex said, "Jane, I want you to meet my father, Neil Keane, and his lovely wife, Roxanne."

"Good heavens," she said, holding out a hand, "this is a surprise." She glanced at Alex in disbelief. "A very *nice* surprise."

"It is such a pleasure to meet you, my dear," Neil said, taking her hand. He bent to press a kiss to her cheek.

"And you," Jane said.

Roxanne then gave Jane a careful embrace, saying, "You are every bit as lovely as he told us you were. We're so glad to have you back among the living."

"I'm glad for that myself," Jane said.

"We're not going to stay," Neil said, and Alex looked mildly alarmed. "We know you need your rest, and the two of you have a great deal to catch up on. We'll come back in a few days and have a longer visit."

"I'll look forward to it," Jane said.

"I'll call ahead," Roxanne said, "and you let me know what you're craving; we'll sneak it in."

"Sounds marvelous," Jane added with a little laugh. "Thank you for coming."

"I'll walk you out," Alex said, and the three of them left the room.

"Do you really need to go so soon?" Alex asked, walking with them to the elevator.

"We were anxious to meet her," Neil said, "and we have, but I think you need to take some time and let the world catch up with her before we get to know each other better."

"Fair enough," Alex said and thanked them for coming.

Returning to Jane's room, he found her still wearing that stunned expression. "Okay," she said, "sit down and start talking. You're not leaving, and I'm not sleeping until you tell me everything that's happened. Your *father*? What miracle brought *this* about?"

"Well," Alex admitted, "it actually started with an argument. He showed up here at the hospital after the accident. My sisters had told him."

He proceeded to tell her everything that had been said between him and his father that day, and how it had left him feeling. Her supper was brought in, and he helped feed her while they talked. He skipped over the events in between to tell her about his visit to his father's home, and the conversation they'd had then. He told her about his going to church, his visits with the bishop, and the path he'd found that had led him to be ordained an elder and to receive a temple recommend.

"I reached a point," he admitted, "where I knew that whether you made it through this or not, I needed the gospel in my life."

"Oh, Alex." She touched his face. "You're a walking miracle."

"Oh no," he said. "*You* are the miracle, my darling." He sighed and added, "You know, I never thought I'd say this, never thought I could *feel* this, but . . . now that you're back, and we're where we are, I'm so grateful for the things that happened to bring me to this point. I have been so blessed, Jane. I am amazed that in spite of my stubbornness, God saw fit to bless me so richly. I know that most people will never have such a profound experience as I have had, and I wonder why I would be so blessed. After what happened at the wedding I was so blown away that—"

"Wait a minute," she said, "you haven't told me what happened at the wedding. That's when I nodded off last night, remember?"

"Sorry," he said. "I talked to you so much when you were unconscious that sometimes it's difficult to remember what you know and what you don't."

"We'll get it all straightened out eventually," she said and settled her head on his shoulder. "Now tell me about the wedding. I want to hear everything."

"Well, the house was incredible, as my mother had said it would be." He told her how he'd arrived late and was able to claim Susan's full attention; how she'd given him a partial tour, and how they'd talked about his great-great-grandfather. Then he told her about his bump on the head and how he'd been unconscious for several minutes. He went on to tell her the details of Alexander Barrett's life that he had been privy to through a detailed dream, and what he'd learned about the sacrifices and struggles of the people who had given so much so that they could live the gospel freely now. Jane listened, occasionally wiping at a stray tear. And when he'd told all there was to tell, she declared that they had indeed been blessed with many miracles. By then she was exhausted, and he kissed her good-night, declaring he would see her tomorrow. Now that she was in the rehab section, they wouldn't let visitors stay through the night, and he found it an adjustment. But he knew she was in good hands.

"Hey, by the way," he said on his way out the door, "when you set a date for this wedding, you make sure you'll be strong enough to dance with me. I'm not getting married unless I can waltz with my new bride."

Jane smiled. "I'll be counting on it."

The following morning, Alex had an experience at work that was a rare, pleasant surprise amidst the usual challenges that came into the ER. He timed his break when he knew that Jane would be between therapy sessions and walked into her room to find that she had just finished her lunch.

"Hey there, gorgeous," he said and gave her a long, savory kiss.

"Oh, Alex," she said, putting a hand into his hair. "You haven't lost your touch. From that first time you kissed me when—"

"Shhh," he whispered, "don't tell anybody."

"What?"

"That I kissed you before I'd even taken you on a first date."

She laughed softly. "You were a perfect gentleman." She touched his face. "And you more than made up for it with the way it took you weeks to kiss me again."

"I didn't want you to think I didn't respect you," he said and kissed her once more. He smiled and added, "Guess what I did this morning?"

"It must have been pretty amazing by that look on your face."

"Actually, it was," he said, holding her hand in his. "I delivered a baby."

"Really?" She laughed softly. "Tell me."

"Well . . . this woman was apparently downtown when her water broke and labor came on suddenly. Somebody called 911, and the ambulance brought her in. She was only there a few minutes before the baby came. Her husband got there about five minutes later." He chuckled. "It was amazing, Jane. I mean . . . I've helped deliver babies before, but . . . I was just so struck with the miracle of life. Holding that baby in my hands, I thought about the children we're going to have, and how grateful I am that such a miracle will be possible."

"Oh, Alex," she said and wrapped her arms around him. He held her close, relishing the evidence of her being alive and well, and the strength that was slowly coming back to her.

Alex felt his happiness deepen steadily as Jane's health improved at a rate that her doctor called miraculous. With a wedding date set, announcements were ordered, and plans were made with the help of Jane's mother. Roxanne eagerly got involved as well. With their help he also got the house in perfect order in anticipation of Jane's return home. Once she came home, either Louisa or one of Jane's sisters would be staying with her until the wedding—or until she could completely manage on her own, whichever came first. Alex would continue staying at his mother's house until the wedding. While Jane was busy getting better and doing other things, he took some time to go through more of his mother's things. His sisters both came to town at the same time to celebrate their father's birthday, and also as a purposeful gathering now that Alex and their father were on good terms. Together they all went out to eat, and then to their mother's grave, where the new headstone had just been laid. Alex found the family reconciliation touching, even though it was difficult to think that he would never see his mother again in this earth life. But he felt certain that she knew the progress he had made, and that she was pleased.

While his sisters were in town, they helped him clean out the house and finish going through their mother's things. Sentimental things were divided up, and the rest was either sold or given to charity. They made the decision to sell the house, feeling it was better to keep their memories there as they were, and not to see the house change as a rental, or to hold onto it for reasons that were completely illogical.

Through long conversations with his sisters, Alex opened up about some of the changes in his life. They were both pleasantly surprised to learn that he'd been ordained an elder, and that he would be married in the temple in a matter of weeks. Before his sisters left town, Charlotte admitted that she'd been struggling with the desire to go back to church for a long time, but simply felt afraid to make the first steps. After hearing about Alex's experience, she was determined to go home and make those steps. Alex added one more miracle to the ever-growing list and counted his many blessings.

With Jane on the road to recovery, Alex knew he needed to break down and buy another car. He'd been driving hers, but she would soon need it herself. He'd received an insurance settlement from the totaled Ferrari and had put the money in the bank with mixed emotions. Those feelings came back to him as he used the money now to purchase a new car. With purpose, he sought out a vehicle that was nice but more conservative and practical. He was going to be a family man now.

The day Jane came home from the hospital was one of the happiest Alex had ever known. He and Louisa helped get her settled in, and he was grateful for the time Louisa had put into arranging the schedules and equipment for home health care, and the regular visits of a physical therapist. Jane was still very weak, but she could get around with some minimal help, and she'd come far.

A few days later he took her to church in the ward he'd been attending throughout her absence—the ward she'd attended before the accident. People were so excited to see her that she felt a bit overwhelmed. Once the opening song was being sung and they were sitting side by side, Alex looked at her to find her crying. He didn't have to guess the reasons as she discreetly wiped her face with a tissue. Still, she whispered to him, "I have dreamed of this day since our first date."

Lightly he whispered back, "You dreamed of recovering from a coma?"

"You know what I mean," she scolded gently.

"Yes," he said seriously, looking into her eyes, "I know what you mean. I'm sorry it took me so long."

"It doesn't matter," she said. "You're here now, and I'm the happiest woman alive."

Jane discreetly observed Alex throughout the meeting, recalling well the one time she had talked him into going to church with her, and how tense he'd been right until he'd left the chapel abruptly. She kept expecting to see some sign of tension or anxiety, but he was completely relaxed as he sang the hymns, took the sacrament, and listened to the talks being given. By the way people greeted them before and after the meeting, it was evident that many ward members had gotten to know him during her absence. She felt so thoroughly blessed by this ongoing evidence of the changes in him that she felt sure she would burst from happiness.

As days passed and the wedding drew closer, Alex watched Jane steadily gain strength. She had reached a point where she no longer needed a physical therapist; she was able to do daily exercises on her own that she'd been taught in order to keep building the strength in her muscles. Home health care was replaced by a regular visit to the clinic. Alex slept at his mother's nearly empty home, but he spent every minute when he wasn't sleeping or working at Jane's house, enjoying her progress, and seeing the days being crossed off the calendar as plans for the wedding came together.

Two days before the wedding, both houses became filled as family from everywhere came to town to help with final preparations and to be there for the big event. Alex concluded it was a good thing most of the work was already done, since it was more like a big party than anything, and little seemed to get accomplished. He and Jane shared a deep joy in being surrounded by their families in anticipation of this great day in their lives.

The afternoon before the wedding, the last of their immediate family arrived in town, and among them was Lana. Alex hadn't seen or spoken to her since the day they'd argued in Jane's hospital room. He knew that she'd spoken to Jane on the phone throughout her recovery. Alex had told Jane what had happened, but she'd never mentioned whether or not it had come up in her conversations with Lana. She did tell him that Lana's marriage had come with many difficulties, but she and her husband were finally getting some help, and things were looking up for them.

When Alex turned around in the kitchen and found Lana standing there, he was taken off guard and truly didn't know what to say. He glanced around, realizing that no one else was in the room, and he felt decidedly nervous. He was fully prepared to have her tell him that it was high time he'd done the right thing, or perhaps that he was shallow and selfish to only come around when faced with tragedy. And she might have been right.

Alex saw tears gather in her eyes before she said, "Forgive me, Alex. I was unkind . . . and unfair, and . . . I'm truly sorry."

"It's in the past, Lana."

"It's wonderful to see the two of you so happy; I hope you'll both always be that way."

"I'm sure going to give it my best," he said. "I hope you can forgive me for being so slow and stubborn about getting to this day."

She smiled. "It's in the past." And then she hugged him.

On the morning Alex and Jane were to be married, he walked through the entrance of the Salt Lake Temple with her hand in his. He paused for a moment in the lobby and pondered the years it had taken to build this magnificent edifice, and the joy he felt to be worthy to be within its walls.

Jane sat in the chapel of the temple, surrounded by her family, nervously waiting for Alex to join her. When he entered the room, dressed in white, his father beside him as his escort, she felt as if her heart would burst from the perfect joy she felt. He sat beside her and took her hand, kissing it as he said, "I love you, Jane. And today you will be mine, forever."

Once the endowment session was completed, Alex sat close to Jane in the celestial room, pondering the glory and beauty of this room built by pioneer hands, made to symbolize the heavenly glory they were capable of achieving as they lived for those blessings. Jane looked so beautiful, so healthy, so strong. But he couldn't find the words to tell her his gratitude and all he was feeling. Looking into her eyes, he hoped that she understood. Somehow he knew that she did. From the first time their eyes had met, somehow she had understood.

Alex and Jane were escorted into the sealing room to find it filled with friends and family, all dressed in white, all there to share in the joy of this occasion. After the sealer spoke to them for a few minutes about the incredible miracle of eternal families, he asked Alex and Jane to kneel at the altar, where they were sealed for time and all eternity. Once they had kissed over the altar, and then exchanged rings, they looked one direction into the eternal mirrors while the sealer talked about the generations that had gone before them, preparing the way for this moment. Then they looked in the other direction while the sealer talked of generations to come, of their posterity who would be profoundly influenced by the decision they'd made to start their lives together here, in this way. Alex was too overcome to speak, and then he looked in Jane's eyes and saw the full spectrum of eternity right there, right where it had always been.

Later at the reception, Alex began to accept that he was really married. Jane remained sitting most of the time while they greeted guests in the receiving line, but when it came time to share a bridal waltz, she insisted that she had saved all her energy for this moment.

Alex put a hand to her back while she strategically poised her hand against his shoulder. He took her other hand into his and gracefully waltzed her around the center of the room, looking into her eyes while the years fled behind them. How clearly he recalled the first waltz he'd shared with her and how his life had never been the same. And how could he ever forget how he'd dreamt of waltzing in another time, and the impact it too had had on his life? Lowering Jane into a graceful dip, he couldn't hold back a little laugh, a spontaneous sound of pure joy. Never had he imagined that he could be so completely happy!

Jane realized she had envisioned this moment the very first time they'd danced together. Now, with the train of her wedding gown over her arm, and the satin skirt swirling around her legs, she felt more beautiful, more light and graceful than she ever had. Not only that, but that she was alive and well enough to dance at all. The moment was perfect; absolutely perfect.

"A match made in heaven," Jane said as Alex spun her once more, and they ended gracefully with the conclusion of the music.

Alex recalled hearing those words when they'd first been paired up to do the waltz. He laughed softly and said, "So it would seem."